DATE DUE			
AUG 0 8 '9	MAR 1 6 '95	DEC 1 2 '97	
SEP 1 3 '9	MAR 2 8 '95	NOV 3 '98	
OCT 1 8 '94	APR 2 2 '95	NOV 27 '9	
NOV 0 4 '94			
NOV 19 '9	JAN 1 2 '95	APR 2 8 '99	
DEC 0 1 '9	JUN 0 1 '95	FEB 18 '0	
DEC 1 5 '94	JAN 1 6 '96	JAN 1 8 '0	
DEC 27 '9	MAR 1 1 '96	12-4	
	DEC I 6 '9		
JAN 1 7 '9	JUN 30 '9		
FEB 25 '9	DC 2 2 '97		

BEFORE HONOR

GEO. W. PROCTOR

Before Honor

A DOUBLE D WESTERN
DOUBLEDAY
New York   London   Toronto   Sydney   Auckland

A DOUBLE D WESTERN
PUBLISHED BY DOUBLEDAY
a division of Bantam Doubleday Dell Publishing Group, Inc.
1540 Broadway, New York, New York 10036

DOUBLE D WESTERN, DOUBLEDAY,
and the portrayal of the letters DD
are trademarks of Doubleday, a division of
Bantam Doubleday Dell Publishing Group, Inc.

Library of Congress Cataloging-in-Publication Data

Proctor, George W.
Before honor/Geo. W. Proctor.—1st ed.
p.   cm.—(A Double D western)
I. Title.
PS3566.R588B4   1993
813'.54—dc20   93-15141
CIP

ISBN 0-385-41935-X
Printed in the United States of America
November 1993
First Edition

10   9   8   7   6   5   4   3   2   1

To my uncle, Jack Proctor,
who used to take me rodeoing with him

Before destruction the heart of man is haughty,
and before honor is humility.

—Proverbs 18:12

BEFORE HONOR

ONE

AN INVISIBLE KNIFE carried on the wind slid through the open vee of the unbuttoned fleece-lined coat. The icy blade penetrated Clinton Wayford's chest and drove straight to the rancher's spine, twisting there.

"Damn!" Shock burst forth in a frosty white cloud from Wayford's lips. "Cold enough to freeze the milk in a cow's udder!"

He cupped wrinkle-creviced hands to his mouth and warmed them with another misty puff of breath while his pale blue eyes rolled upward. A blink cut the harsh glare from the kitchen light behind him that flared into the darkness of early morning. Overhead unquavering stars sprinkled the slate gray predawn sky like gems no larger than the points of pins.

Not so much as a high, thin, wispy cloud marred the sky. The situation deserved another curse from the old rancher's lips. Rain in the Trans-Pecos region of Texas always came as a welcomed visitor no matter how short its stay. Here, near the Davis Mountains, rain often was a commodity reserved for those granite peaks rather than the plains sandwiched between the mountain range to the north and the Chihuahuan desert to the south.

A conflicting desire accompanied by a fleeting twinge of guilt kept Wayford's mouth closed to hold back curse and almost whispered a thank-you for the lack of moisture. This morning his sixty-five years weighed heavily on his shoulders. The thought of working in winter sleet or snow doubled the bitter bite of the cold. The below-freezing temperature was enough for any man to contend.

His gaze moved across the cloudless sky again. Without difficulty he picked out the bright blue of the star Spica high in the southeast. Near the western horizon lay white Sirius, the brightest of all stars a man could see from anywhere in Texas.

Wayford felt a momentary swell of pride in his ability to identify the brighter stars and the constellations in which they dwelled. His father had taught him the basics of finding his way in the night when he had been no more than ten years old. The remainder of his knowledge had been gleaned from amateur astronomers who gathered from around the country on the Prude Ranch up in the Davis Mountains for a week every May to attend a conference they dubbed the Texas Star Party.

Although most topics discussed by these night sky enthusiasts soared a mile or two over his head, they were a friendly bunch more than willing to share the views of planets, star clusters, galaxies, and nebulae they located in their telescopes. For ten years Wayford had set aside at least one night during the gathering to spend wandering from telescope to telescope and gazing upon the beauty God placed within the heavens.

Another chill worked its way up and down the rancher's spine as a blast of wind caught him full face and gusted down the collar of the open coat. This morning was not meant for stargazing or woolgathering. In only a few seconds the cold crept into every joint of his body, leaving it aching, especially his fingers. He blew on his hands once again while he leaned down to retrieve the battered pair of boots that stood beside the door stoop. Stepping back, he closed the door to shut out the darkness and the wind.

A halfhearted grunt drew Wayford's attention to a liver-spotted hound curled beside the wood stove. The dog's head lifted a hair, and his brown eyes opened to slits with which to peer at the rancher for a lazy moment. The hound then once more closed his eyes and lowered his head to bury nose beneath tail.

"Anyone ever tell you, you're as useless as tits on a boar hog, Vanberg?" Wayford spoke directly to the dog, but the hound gave no indication he heard or even cared that his master uttered a sound. "Don't know why, but I still hold out hope for your worthless carcass. One of these mornings you're going to fetch in my boots and have them all warm and cozy when I'm ready to put them on."

The dog continued to ignore the man.

Wayford smiled. In spite of his words, he had never owned a smarter dog than Vanberg. The hound knew the morning ritual too well to be stirred until it was time for chores. Then, and only then, Vanberg would be on his feet, eyes open bright and wide, ears perked, and tail a-wagging, ready for the day at his master's side. No man could ask for more than that from a dog, nor did Wayford. Vanberg, however, gave more.

By blood Vanberg was a bird dog, a retriever. He had been given to the rancher as a pup eight years ago by a dry dirt farmer near Lampasas. The hound now bore that man's name. Even as a whelp the dog had been as smart as a whip. While he matured, Vanberg never ceased to amaze his owner. Without a speck of training, the dog proved to be as handy at sniffing out a cougar as any cat dog Wayford had ever encountered during his sixty-five years. Unlike many cat dogs, which cost ranchers thousands of dollars, Vanberg displayed the common sense to stay out of the way of a mountain lion that abruptly turned on its canine pursuers—something that could not be said of dogs specifically trained to hunt cougar.

Vanberg also proved to have more than a bit of shepherd instinct coursing through his veins. With exactly the same amount of training required to learn to track a mountain lion, the dog picked up the ability to herd, whether the animals be sheep, goats, or even cattle or horses.

Wayford proudly studied the sleeping animal. Atop all that, Vanberg could still scare up a jackrabbit or a covey of quail whenever his owner decided to try his hand at hunting.

"But that don't make you near perfect, you worthless flea bag," Wayford said aloud as though afraid the dog might have read his thoughts of praise. "You still ain't got the sense to bring in my boots and warm 'em for me."

Vanberg gave another half grunt when the rancher placed the cold-stiffened boots near the stove's open oven door.

"Yeah, I guess you're right." Wayford took a coffeepot from a cabinet, filled it with water and coffee, and placed it on the stove. "Guess there's no reason for me to leave my boots outside anymore."

No reason, he thought, yet, old habits were hard to break. Lizzie never allowed him to wear his work boots in the house. She contended they made their home smell like a barn. Wayford never argued the point. Sole leather had a way of soaking up various unsavory odors associated with substances a rancher was bound to step square in the middle of at least a dozen times a day. He simply tugged off his boots, left them by the backdoor stoop, and slipped

into the house slippers Elizabeth had always left waiting for him in
the kitchen.

Five years had passed since cancer claimed Lizzie. In that time, he
conscientiously had kept the dirty work boots out of the house. He
liked to think the simple action was a way of honoring the woman
who had shared her life and this house with him. It seemed little
enough to do, and a habit he had no desire to break.

He took a chipped mug with a gaudily colored scene that proclaimed the beauties of Washington D.C. from a cabinet and placed
it on the kitchen table. A lifetime ago when Wayford traveled the
rodeo circuit, he had bought the souvenir. In the early fifties, on the
way to New York's Madison Square Garden, he had rerouted his
drive five hundred miles out of the way just to say he had seen the
nation's capitol.

What seemed like a grand adventure to a young rodeo calf roper
in his twenties now stood as memory a-swirl in foggy haze. Often
the rancher found it difficult to recall the man to whom that memory belonged. The mug, almost forty years old, seemed to be the
only thing real about that distant side trip.

A tilt of his head toward the stove told his ears the coffeepot had
begun to boil. He had time for a cigarette. He lifted a pouch of Bull
Durham from the center of the table and slid a La Ritz paper from
the orange folder attached to the bag. With his left hand he held the
paper slightly curved between his fingers while he sprinkled an even
portion of cut tobacco onto the paper. He used both hands to roll
the cigarette and sealed it with a quick lick of the tongue.

Lifting the coffeepot from the stove, he poked a long splinter of
wood inside the ancient black monster. He waited a moment and
withdrew the sliver, its end dancing with flame. This he used to
light the tip of the cigarette that dangled between his lips. He took
two short puffs to make certain the tobacco was lit, then drew
deeply on the third. He exhaled the smoke in a thin blue stream
while he dropped the splinter into the stove and placed the pot back
on the fire.

The rich flavor of the tobacco in the early-morning hours held a
satisfaction that he had never been able to explain to nonsmokers,
especially his daughter Mary, who constantly nagged him about the
dangers of lung cancer and emphysema whenever she came to visit.
Her mother's death from stomach cancer had tripled Mary's adamant protests against her father's continued tobacco use.

Wayford flicked the ash from the cigarette into a dime store glass ashtray. He had cut back on his smoking, no longer buying packaged cigarettes. He told himself that the flavor of store-bought, ready-rolleds did not compare with that of paper and fixings. The reality of the drastic cutback to those cigarettes he found time to roll himself stemmed from the "sin" tax Congress and the state legislators repeatedly slapped on tobacco products. A carton of smokes cost over eighteen dollars. For a man who found it increasingly hard to pay his feed bill, shelling out almost twenty dollars for a carton of cigarettes was akin to the rancher buying caviar and champagne for his daily meals.

Wayford drew on the cigarette and exhaled again before he switched on the radio sitting atop the refrigerator. The plastic box refused so much as an impolite belch of static. With a sigh the rancher twisted the knob to the off position. The radio had gone on the fritz a week ago and been added to a growing list of items to be replaced when there was money.

A radio sat at the bottom of that roster of needed items. Although Wayford enjoyed listening to music, the selection of channels was limited to one country and western station broadcasting from the nearby town of Alpine. At night that station went off the air by nine o'clock. As for television, there had never been one in the house. The mountains to the north, east, and west prevented any chance of receiving the Midland channels, and the El Paso stations to the west lay too far away. The monthly cost of cable was a luxury beyond his means.

More than the country and western tunes the radio provided, he missed the sports reports. During the fall and winter he kept tabs on the local high school football and basketball teams. When spring arrived, he avidly tracked the progress of both the American and the National Leagues. The New York Yankees remained his long-standing favorite team, but he openly admitted a soft spot for both the Texas Rangers and the Houston Astros. If asked why he supported either, other than both were Texas baseball teams, he would have been hard-pressed for a legitimate answer. Neither team had been more than also-rans season after season after season. The same could be said, he reminded himself, of the Yankees in recent years.

From his spot beside the stove, Vanberg rose and gave a toothy yawn while he stretched his lanky frame. With a glance at the rancher, the spotted dog sauntered to a corner of the kitchen where his food and water bowls sat. He dipped his muzzle to the first and began noisily crunching a mouthful of Purina Dog Chow.

Wayford took the cue from the hound and looked at the stove. The coffeepot percolated strong and loud. Steam rose in a steady column from the spout. The rancher filled the mug with the dark brew and added a spoonful of sugar to cut the bitterness. Five years of making his own morning coffee had done nothing to improve its taste, he realized while he took a tentative scalding sip. Lizzie's coffee he had always taken black. This pot, when he came back inside for breakfast in a few hours, would take at least two heaping spoons of sugar to make it palatable.

"Time to get a move on, Vanberg." Wayford placed the coffee pot atop a potholder on the table for reheating later. "Sun'll be up before we know it."

The dog waited patiently at the back door while the rancher nudged off the house slippers and tugged on the old boots over two pairs of woolen socks. Wayford then buttoned the coat tightly beneath his chin before pulling the fleece collar up snuggly about his neck. A sweat-stained, doe gray Resistol hat that barely retained its steam-rolled brim and crown creases came down from a nail driven into the wall beside the door and was firmly set atop Wayford's head of white hair.

From a coat pocket, he unwadded a pair of thin leather work gloves. When handling stock, whether steer or horse, Wayford usually shunned gloves. A man needed nothing between him and the animal with which he worked. However, frostbitten fingertips did not read the feel of an animal; they only ached.

"Let's get at it," Wayford said to the dog while he lifted the coffee mug from the table, took a sip, then opened the back door.

Vanberg bounded eagerly into the frosty morning and ran straight to a bushy salt cedar that grew at the corner of the adobe ranch house. The hound hiked a rear leg and relieved himself of a nighttime of pressure. Leaving a dark patch of steaming mud behind him, the dog wheeled and trotted to the rancher's side.

Wayford greeted the graying morning with far less enthusiasm. In spite of the coat's thick fleece lining, the freezing cold seeped inward, quickly spreading through the rancher's body until a dull ache throbbed within every joint. He downed two hasty gulps of coffee to ward away the chill and succeeded only in scalding his tongue and the roof of his mouth.

You're getting to be an old man, he lied to himself amid a stream of silent curses deriding the biting temperature. There was no "getting" to it; he already was an old man. *A stubborn old fool!* The addendum brought a ring of harsh truth. Only a fool—a sixty-five-year-old fool—would try to run a two-section ranch on his own. Even in his twenties he had the common sense to know it took ranch hands to work a spread.

Only a bigger fool would consider doin' anything else. Wayford felt a swell of pride edge away the cold in his chest as he surveyed the land that stretched around him. The gray predawn paid no compliment to the winter-browned plains reaching out for miles in all directions. Nor would the rising sun paint a prettier picture, the rancher admitted to himself.

Grassland was grassland; there was no way to escape the monotony of prairie flatness. The only relief offered was the rugged silhouettes of mountains that lay on the horizon no matter what direction Wayford looked. To anyone who had seen the Rockies, the ranges of Texas's Big Bend country appeared more like massive, rocky hills that abruptly pushed out of the flat ground for no rhyme or reason rather than mountains.

The Piney Woods of East Texas and the Gulf Coast were far more eye-appealing than the high plains. But this chunk of prairie contained a hidden beauty for Wayford. It belonged to him. Before him his father, his father's father, his father's father's father, and *his* father had claimed title to the land.

Wayfords were not the first Texans to settle this isolated part of the state, but when they came, they stayed. In the 1850s Amos Wayford journeyed west with a survey team to establish a site for a military fort that would become Fort Davis in the Davis Mountains. Unlike many of his profession who contracted with the U.S. Army, Amos did not buy up large sections of land and then resell them to the government for an exorbitant profit. He bought land and stocked it with cattle and horses. In turn he sold both to the Army and the Butterfield Overland Stage that eventually routed through Fort Davis on its way to the California coast.

Amos Wayford did not get rich, but he found a way to live off the land. So had his descendants. Clint Wayford attempted to do the same—ever since his parents died in the fifties and left the Wide W Ranch—whose brand was a single W stretched to the width of four normal letters—to their only son.

Wayford pursed his lips and shook his head as he walked toward a small corral attached to the left side of a twenty-five-stall red barn a hundred yards behind the ranch house. His youth had not included a vision of an aging man working from sunup to sunset, struggling to milk a living from land that often seemed as dry and ornery as a barren cow.

"I ain't cut out to be no cow*boy*. I'm a horse*man*," he had told his father the day he announced his intention to seek fame and fortune on the professional rodeo circuit.

His father had not condemned the aspirations of a son whose head was filled with dreams of adventure and glory, but said, "This land will be waiting here when you're *man* enough for it."

The Army delayed Wayford's rodeo career for two years—one of those years spent trying to stay alive in Korea while the Red Chinese did their best to see he did not. Another two years of driving from one end of the U.S.A. with a horse trailer hitched behind a pickup truck as he moved from one rodeo to the next had proved he was no Casey Tibbs. He had reached the conclusion he was mediocre, at best, with a rope and pigging string when the telegram arrived that told of the car wreck.

His mother and father had been on a Christmas shopping trip when a young woman more concerned with disciplining a mischievous two-year-old daughter in the backseat than watching the road had run a stop sign and broadsided his parents' car. Neither the mother nor her child received so much as a scratch in the accident. His father lay dead by the time an ambulance arrived at the scene. It took his mother three years to die. Doctors said it was her pancreas that failed; Wayford knew it was her heart—it simply stopped beating, tired of living without the man she had spent a lifetime loving.

Pausing at the corral gate, Wayford drank down another swig of coffee and studied the five gelding two-year-olds standing within. After all these years, he wondered if he had been man enough for the ranch even when youth sided with him. Lately it seemed as though the land would not be satisfied until it broke him and saw his body buried six-foot under it.

If the bill collectors don't take it away first. Downing a final gulp of coffee, he sat the mug atop a cedar post and opened the corral. He latched the gate behind him when he entered. From the fence he lifted a rope halter and shank he had placed there the night before. Without a word from his owner, Vanberg settled on his haunches

on the opposite side of the fence. His eyes followed every movement Wayford made. His ears stood perked, ready for even a mumbled command.

Wayford's knowing gaze moved over the five animals, selecting a
sorrel, shaggy with a winter coat, to begin the day's work. Paul
Moody had assured him the young horses were halter-broke when
he brought them to the Wide W yesterday. Although the fellow
rancher had been Wayford's best friend since grade school, Paul
often exaggerated the handling his ranch hands had given the horses
destined for the Wide W.

Wayford did not like it, but he did not blame the men for stretching the truth. No man in his right mind wanted to break and train a
horse. It was hard, dirty, and often painful work. Wayford had never
made any wild claims about his sanity. It was work he loved.

An amused smile slid across his lips while he opened the halter
and stepped toward the geldings. He still considered himself a *horse*-
man rather than a *cattle*man. Cattle was something he ran on the
ranch. He bred them, fed them, raised them, and sold them for the
best dollar on the pound he could get.

Horses were entirely a different matter. A man and a good horse
were a single entity—two separate creatures that moved, acted, and
became one. Spanish explorers brought the first horses to this country in the late 1500s. More than four centuries had passed and, even
with automobiles and airplanes, a horse often afforded the best
means of transportation in parts of this land.

Wayford approached the sorrel cautiously. He assured the young
animal in a soft crooning voice while he reached out and gently
stroked the horse's broad neck. Even hampered by glove and cold,
the rancher could feel the gelding relax, leery but unafraid of the
strange man's approach.

"You're a handsome-looking young man. Yeah, you are. You just
might be half as good as Paul made you out to be. If that's the case,
you could turn out to be good enough to show your stuff up in
Fort Worth come next fall." Wayford eased closer while he patted
the sorrel's neck. After several reassuring minutes, he slipped an arm
around that neck, working toward the horse's head. "What'd'ya
think, Vanberg? Think this little man's got it in him to be a
prizewinning cuttin' horse?"

From the corner of an eye, Wayford saw the dog stand and wag
his tail at the mention of his name. "If I was to listen to Paul

Moody, I be believin' that this sorrel and that bay next to the fence hung the moon. Which goes to show how much Paul knows. 'Specially since ain't none of these horses ever felt a saddle on their backs."

Like Paul, Wayford hoped. In the past five years, horses he trained for others had given good showings at the annual cutting horse competition in Fort Worth, a show that drew entries from across the country, including a contingency of Hollywood stars who had decided sitting on the back of a working horse was the latest "in" thing. Although the horses he trained had yet to take top honors in competition, their performances kept a small but steady, stream of animals coming to the ranch to be broken and trained. Ten other horses, including one owned by a New York fashion model, were stalled within the barn.

Even greater hopes rode on a quick, firm-ankled bay colt that stood inside. This was Wayford's own three-year-old, carrying the name Frank's Pal because of the shine the rancher's grandson Frank Junior had taken to the colt when he was foaled. Try as he did, Wayford found it hard not to get excited about the bay. Even knowing there were a thousand things that could go wrong with a horse, it was difficult not to consider future possibilities. If Frank's Pal stayed sound, and if the cold . . .

His thoughts shattered in an explosion of pinpointed lights bursting atop a background of spinning gray. He daydreamed, his thoughts wandering months away to ponder might-be's, instead of paying attention to the task at hand. The sorrel's head jerked back and slammed into the bridge of the rancher's nose as he began to slip the rope halter over the animal's muzzle.

"Damn!" Wayford released the horse and backstepped. "Stupid old fool!"

He shook his head and blinked to clear the watery haze of tears blurring his vision—barely in time to see the sorrel rear. The horse's forelegs lashed out. The rancher ducked to the right.

He moved too slowly. The gelding's right hoof struck. Wayford groaned, stumbled back, and dropped to his knees under the force of the glancing blow.

Nostrils a-flare, the sorrel neighed, and was answered by a chorus of snorts from the four other animals in the corral. Together the five geldings broke forward. Like frisky colts feeling their strength with the first hint of autumn chill, they wanted to run. The corral was small, designed to stop penned animals from doing just that. A fact that did not hinder the geldings. Together they surged against the cedar fence. Dry wood creaked, snapped, and splintered. Five geldings, heels kicking high, and teeth nipping at the necks of their companions, raced onto the freedom of the open plain.

Behind the fleeing horses ran a dog with liver-colored spots, barking in full voice as he attempted to retrieve the errant animals.

TWO

CLINTON WAYFORD staggered to his feet and swayed shakily as he stared after the loose geldings and the yapping dog at their heels.

"Vanberg! Come back here, Vanberg!" The rancher yelled in vain. The retriever kept after the horses. "Damned fool dog! You ain't goin' bring 'em back by yourself! Go on and run your feet ragged! See if I give a damn!"

Sometimes Vanberg acted just like a dog. Wayford shook his head in disgust.

That was a mistake. His forehead pounded as though it were intent on splitting open like a ripe melon. His ears rang, and his knees buckled. He caught himself before he fell back to the ground. On quivering legs, he managed to stumble to a fencepost and lean against it, grateful for the support.

He looked back at the disappearing horses and dog. *Damned dog's as crazy as his owner. Better not run off and get himself hurt. Won't be getting much sympathy from me.*

Whether he liked to admit it or not, he did worry about the dog. Since Lizzie's death, Vanberg was the only thing that passed for decent company on the ranch. Although the dog lacked the ability to speak, he did not complain when Wayford dominated their conversations.

Vanberg and the horses were no more than a cloud of dust on the horizon now. Five horses could get one hound, no matter how smart, into trouble. If Vanberg managed to get hurt, it was twenty miles to the nearest veterinarian. Nor was the rancher in any shape to offer aid to an injured animal.

Wayford gingerly probed at his aching head with two fingertips. Blood glistened on glove leather when he eased the fingers away. "Sonofabitch! Damn Paul Moody and his wild stock!"

Keeping a hand on a cedar rail, Wayford moved to the gate and opened it. He released the fence and stood for several seconds to assure himself that his legs could support his weight. He sucked down four steadying breaths and cautiously straightened his spine. He caught himself before he gave a nod of approval. He had made the mistake of sudden movement once and it nearly put him facedown on the ground. *Slow and easy,* he ordered himself.

His gaze lifted back to the horses. He could no longer find a trace of the geldings, not even a hint of dust left in the air. Nor could he hear Vanberg's barking. The rancher drew another heavy breath, one of disgust. This was a damned ridiculous way for a grown man to start a day.

Giving his legs a few more seconds to quiet their trembling, he stood and stared about him. He felt foolish and embarrassed. He had let his mind drift like some wet-behind-the-ears-just-out-of-diapers ranch hand. A man could not do that, not with green stock, and expect to keep himself in one piece. It was more than foolishness, it was damned stupid. He felt—

His lips drew to a thin line before pursing with deepening disgust. He felt old. His mind and body were like worm-eaten wood— brittle and dry. Ten years ago he would have shaken off a bump on the head and gone after the geldings. This morning, there was a taste of accomplishment in being able to stand on two feet.

"Damn!" Wayford's eyes shifted downward.

At the foot of a fence post lay his Washington D.C. coffee mug. The old chipped mug was not worth the fifty cents he originally had paid for it, but the shattered pottery might as well have been one of those rare Chinese vases he had read about displayed in Fort Worth's Kimbal Art Museum.

"Damned silly notion." The sense of attachment he felt for the ancient, brown-stained mug startled him.

That he could buy another mug at a five-and-dime on his next trip into Alpine did not lessen the sense of loss. It was not the mug; it was the memories attached to a cheap, gaudy souvenir he purchased during a crazy moment nearly forty years ago. That was something a dime store did not sell.

"Ain't no reason to go and get all sentimental and soft-headed," he reprimanded himself aloud. "It's nothing but an old mug." He stared at the fragments while he considered gluing them together. Not even one of those adhesives that advertised that a single drop provided sufficient strength to hold the weight of a grown man could salvage the shattered pottery. "Nothing but an old mug—a broken one at that."

He turned his gaze from the mug. No need wasting any more time on something he could do nothing about. He took a tentative step toward the adobe ranch house. Although shaky, his knees held. Another step made it obvious the dizziness remained, but was not enough to rob him of his balance.

Nagging at the rancher like the throbbing of an aching tooth was the repeating thought that he should be sitting astride one of the three range horses he kept in the barn and riding after the escaped geldings. Instead, he felt lucky to be able to make his way into the house on his own.

At the backdoor, he paused, ignoring his pounding head, long enough to tug off his boots and leave them on the stoop. He did not bother with the slippers when he entered the house, shuffled into the bathroom. He dropped the toilet's lid and sat atop it while he leaned over the sink.

Blood felt warm and sticky on his forehead, but none dripped into the water with which he filled the sink. That was a good sign. If the cut had already scabbed, it was not that deep.

Wayford cupped a palm beneath the lukewarm water that trickled from the faucet and lifted it to his forehead. Gingerly he bathed the tender lump on his forehead. The water stung when it reached the open cut. The rancher gritted his teeth against the burning sensation and continued to wash the swelling until pink no longer tinted the water dripping back into the sink. He then lightly patted the bump dry with a clean towel.

He examined the injury in the cabinet mirror above the sink. His earlier disgust returned. He felt as if he had been smacked dead center of his forehead with a sledgehammer, but the lump left by the hoof was no larger than a meadow lark's egg, the cut a minor scratch. The reflection revealed nothing that might put a man out of commission.

His appearance did not decrease the throbbing ache or the queasy dizziness.

Opening the cabinet, he found a bottle of Mercurochrome with an age-faded label. *Monkey blood*—he recalled the all-inclusive name he and his childhood friends had given to any red-colored antiseptic. He also distinctly remembered how much the stuff burned when dabbed on a strawberry knee. He dug deeper and found a tube of clear antiseptic ointment and lightly coated the cut with it. The gel did not sting; for that he was grateful.

Next he took an adhesive bandage from a tin, fumbled with the red thread designed to neatly open the paper package, gave up, ripped it apart with his teeth, and carefully covered the ointment-smeared cut.

"A fine picture of a man you make." He stared at his reflection in the mirror. "If this goes black and blue, you're really going to look dandy."

White hair tousled and sprinkled with dirt and bits of straw and blue eyes still watering, he looked like hell. The bandage and bump did nothing to enhance his appearance. If it were not for the leathery creases that lined his face, someone might have mistaken him for a young rowdy who had come out a loser in a honky-tonk fight. Instead, he looked exactly like what he was—an old man who almost had his head busted wide open by a green two-year-old gelding.

He used a hand to dust the dirt and straw from his hair, then dragged a comb through the strands a few times until it held something that resembled a part. He rinsed his face and dried it. Neither action helped improve the appearance of the old man who stared back at him from the mirror.

Giving up on an apparently useless effort, Wayford glanced around for his hat. It took a moment for the realization to sink in that he had not worn it into the house, but had left it outside on the ground. Although, he never wore a hat in the house—only *women* wear hats indoors, not *men*, was one of the rules of proper conduct Wayford's mother had ingrained in an only child, often emphasizing her words with a mesquite switch—the rancher suddenly felt naked without the hat near at hand. It seemed as though he had been born with a smartly creased and rolled Stetson firmly set atop his head. With so much distance between himself and the hat, he felt a disquiet that was not quelled until he walked outside in stocking feet to retrieve the forgotten hat.

He discarded the thought of going after the missing horses and dog once back in the cold. His boots were back in the house, and he still felt too shaky to ride. Instead, he decided an early breakfast would give him the time needed to regain his strength.

In the house, he hung the hat on its nail by the door, then placed chunks of split mesquite into the black, wood-burning stove. Wayford had retired the gas stove in September, four months ago, when local butane prices took one of those inexplicable rises that seemed to accompany the approach of cold weather each year. Lizzie would have had a conniption fit had she seen the relic in her kitchen, but the stove, which had been gathering dust in the barn's hayloft for more years than Wayford could remember, served its purpose. He could gather mesquite for a pretty penny cheaper than having the butane tank filled.

He gave himself a mental pat on the back for having the good sense to keep the adobe brick ranch house rather than tearing it down and building a new one of fire brick or wood as he had considered in the early sixties. Adobe was a natural building material in this country, used since the earliest settlers migrated to the Bend. It kept a home cool in the hottest of summers and retained heat during the coldest of winters. Wayford stoked the wood stove each night before he went to bed and hardly missed the gas space heaters that once warmed the house.

From the refrigerator, he took a package of homemade venison sausage and worked four balls of the heavily spiced meat into patties. He dropped these into an iron skillet he placed on the stove. Venison, like the mesquite that cooked it, came cheaper than store-bought pork sausage.

Mule deer and pronghorn antelope were numerous in the Trans-Pecos. On a lucky day, there might be a javelino, and wild peccary meant fresh pork. Wayford, in spite of being a cattleman, had a decided taste for pork chops, even with the slightly gamey flavor of javelino. A man with a sharp eye and a rifle easily kept the freezer stocked with meat. If big game did not present itself, there was always an abundance of jackrabbits.

Wayford made a disapproving face without thinking about it. Rabbit sat low on his list of preferred food. Even deep-fried rattlesnake rode a notch or two higher. However, when it came to filling one's belly, a man's taste buds were outvoted by the rumble of his gut.

The rancher never considered slaughtering a calf or steer for meat. When Lizzie was alive, their own beef accounted for most of the meat they ate. Now Wayford's herd was down. Cattle prices had plummeted in the early 1980s and had never climbed back to the heights of the 1970s. The increasing beef importation from Mexico and South America ensured those prices remained down.

Not that a man could judge by the meat prices in supermarkets. Those sky-high tags came from the meat-packers and the stores themselves, not cattle ranchers. During the long drought of the eighties, every day meant the ruin of another rancher who could no longer afford to pay more for feed than he was getting for his stock at auction.

The government's answer to the cattle crisis: import more beef. At times, Wayford was certain the ranchers and farmers of this country meant absolutely nothing to politicians. One day those in Washington and Austin might remember who produces the food for their thousand-dollar-a-plate fund-raising banquets. However, he was afraid that day would not come until there was no food on those thousand-dollar plates.

As he turned the sausage, the rancher considered breaking two eggs into the skillet. He decided against the idea. The hens had been off their laying since mid-November. The eggs in the refrigerator would serve for another breakfast, or even tonight's supper.

Chickens! The thought of eggs reminded him of the red rooster he had promised Juanita Rameriz. He would catch the young cock before he drove into Fort Davis tomorrow. Originally he had marked the rooster for the frying pan, but Mrs. Rameriz had offered pinto beans from her garden for a rooster to replace one taken by a coyote last week.

Beans bartered for a rooster that was more trouble than he was worth was a good trade. A man could make several meals from a pot of beans, and Juanita Rameriz promised enough beans for dozens of pots; a chicken was good for but one supper and maybe a late-night snack.

Besides, Wayford recalled the last trade made with the woman. Juanita Rameriz's pinto beans were hard to beat. The old Mexican woman picked them in her garden during the summer, shelled them, and placed them directly in her freezer. When cooked with a little salt pork or ham hock, they tasted garden fresh. To the rancher a world of difference lay between the flavor of fresh pintos compared to the hard, dried beans bought in a grocery store.

Leaving the sizzling sausage in the skillet, the rancher moved from stove to table and placed the skillet atop a folded kitchen towel. He took two corn tortillas from a plastic bag on top of the refrigerator and poured himself another cup of coffee, heavily laden with sugar, to complete the meal. At the table, he placed two patties of sausage on a tortilla and folded it around them.

Lizzie, who prepared breakfasts consisting of eggs with steak or ham, would have cocked a disapproving eyebrow at such simple fare. Wayford had no complaints. The meal *was* simple, but it was good. He especially liked the sausage. Commercially packaged sausage never contained enough red pepper. Since he had mixed this batch of sausage himself, it contained more than a hint of spicy fire. The one thing time had not changed, he thought with pride, was his cast iron stomach.

Wayford leaned back in his chair as he washed down the first tortilla and sausage with two swallows of coffee. The throbbing in his head subsided, and his stomach was beginning to feel satisfied. Maybe it was not as bad a day as it seemed.

Might be a little short on ready cash, but this house and this land are mine. Food in a man's belly always made thoughts rosier, he realized with a silent chuckle. Like most boys when growing up, he had paid little attention to his father's advice. Except when it came to the ranch.

"This here parcel of land ain't much when put up against what some folks have got in this world," he remembered his father saying. "But it's free and clear. Ain't no man or bank never held a note on it since Amos Wayford bought it from the State of Texas. One of these days, this'll be yours. You keep it away from the banks—and government hands—and it'll stay that way."

His father had spoken with the authority of a man who had survived the Great Depression. That advice had seen a son through recessions and tight times for nearly four decades. Even when his bank account fell to the point of nonexistence, Wayford never considered taking out a loan on the ranch. He watched men who had, like his best friend Paul Moody, prosper into millionaires. On the other side of the scale, he had seen equally capable men lose their land and home when their luck took a sudden downswing.

Hell, half the land in Jeff Davis and Presidio counties is owned by big corporations, he reflected while he wrapped the second tortilla around the remaining pieces of sausage. Once, Wayford knew every rancher and his family members in three counties on a first-name basis.

Today, if those corporations cared enough for their investment, they sent in a foreman to oversee the land. Most foremen did not last long enough for Wayford to learn their first names. The Bend was not a hospitable country, especially for a man who came into Texas from the rich farmlands of the East or the Midwest. Corporation overseers came and went as quickly as the seasons.

As leery as the rancher was of banks, he was twice as suspicious of government—be it county, state, or federal. He shied clear of any government program designated to help ranchers. Another lesson his father taught was that there are no free meals in this life. Sooner or later a man pays for what he receives. With governments, that payment always seemed to come at the whim of some politician who had never worked a plot of land in his life, except maybe for a townhouse flower box filled with petunias.

After Lizzie's death, the economy forced Wayford to let go of the five hands who worked the ranch, which in turn led to the cutback on his cattle herd since he was unable to care for the animals on his own. A smaller herd meant that half the ranch's acreage went unused. Paul Moody had urged him to place that acreage in the government's land bank, a federal program that paid farmers and ranchers for not producing on their land. That the land bank was a government program was enough to make Wayford shy away from it like the plague, but it was the idea that tax money went to people for not working their land that was abhorrent to him.

Not producing was the last thing a government should reward. At least, that was the way he saw it.

He might be wrong, he recognized while he chewed and swallowed another bite of sausage. He seemed to be the only one he knew who viewed such programs as mistakes. Still, he could not help but believe that those who thought they were getting something for nothing would one day have to pay for that something. Who knew what price the government would demand?

He studied the curling column of steam that rose from his coffee to dissipate two inches above the cup's rim. He did not overlook the possibility that he was misguided. Times had changed since his father uttered those unpretentious words of advice. His father came from a time when a man was supposed to stand on his own two feet and make a life for himself and his family. It was more than failure to be relegated to the welfare doles; it was shame, a blight on a man's name.

Lifting the cup, he took a sip. The sugar did not mask the coffee's bitterness. He had been raised to believe the same, that a man's debts were something to be paid no matter how hard or long it took. Although he had never heard it put into words as a boy, his father and friends believed in a simple honor they lived by—a man was only as good as his word. What was borrowed from one man was repaid in full. To do less was to be less than a man.

Today's newspaper headlines echoed new beliefs that left Wayford confused and befuddled. Bankruptcy occurred daily. Corporations and individuals alike sheltered themselves in a legal system that declared their debts invalid with no concern for those they owed.

Pennies on the dollar. Wayford sucked at his teeth with disdain for the judgments bankruptcy courts handed down and declared just. Right or wrong, it no longer mattered. Save your own backside and to hell with everyone else seemed to be the credo for the last years of the twentieth century. As long as a man kept his own head above water, he need not heed the cries of those he drowned in the process.

Maybe that ruthlessness was required to survive today. The rancher examined his own precarious position. Had he taken the bankruptcy route, butane would fill the tank outside and he would not be warming himself with a mesquite fire.

His head moved slowly from side to side. No, he would not have done differently, even knowing where the course he chose led. When Lizzie died, he faced a mountain of medical bills that exceeded the limits of their health insurance policy. To pay them, he had sold two sections of the then four-section ranch. He and Lizzie had worked and saved for years to buy the acreage that had doubled the Wide W's size. It was not something he had wanted to do; it was what had to be done. The debts were his; they had to be paid. To him there were no other options, not if he wanted to retain his self-respect.

Stubborn bastard, Wayford reflected, uncertain whether what he had done was right or just a matter of meaningless pride. *Stubborn* old *bastard,* he amended. Old dogs did not learn new tricks.

He sat straight in the chair. The notion of old dogs returned Vanberg to mind. While he sat by the stove's warmth, the old hound was somewhere out in the cold trying to round up five loose geldings. Time for the man responsible for those horses getting away in the first place to move off his hindquarters and help the dog bring them back to the barn.

Popping the last bite of tortilla and venison in his mouth, Wayford chewed it hastily and washed it down with the three swallows of coffee remaining in the cup. He rose from the table and stopped by the door for hat and boots. Outside the sun rode a hand's width above the distant dark silhouette of the Glass Mountains. The sky was the cloudless deep blue of the high country. A patch of haze hung far to the southwest, which indicated clouds would be rolling up from Mexico by midday. Warm, moisture-laden air colliding with the cold high air of the surrounding mountains might mean rain, or even snow, by evening.

The twinge of guilt Wayford had felt earlier that morning was assuaged. It could rain all it wanted during the night. However, he was not so sure about snow. Nothing was nastier than working in snow; a man never escaped the biting cold.

He reached the red-painted barn, removed the simple snap from the latch, and rolled back the door. In better days, he had built the barn after pictures he had seen of stables on thoroughbred farms in Kentucky. At each end of the one-hundred fifty-foot building stood a large sliding door so that on warm days both could be opened to admit a cool breeze. Riding on rails and rollers, the doors were easily secured to keep out the blast of winter's winds.

A familiar effluvium of odors filled the rancher's nostrils when he stepped inside and slid the door closed behind him. Others might have found the warm scent of horse mingled with straw, hay, manure, and urine offensive. To Wayford it was an earthy, comforting smell.

He reached out in the barn's darkness and found a series of switches on the wall. He flipped them together with the edge of a hand. Light flooded the interior from a line of lamps that hung from the ceiling and bulbs inside each of the twenty-five stalls. A chorus of nickers and snorts greeted the bright flood as fifteen horses stuck their heads from the stalls and turned to the rancher.

"Give me a minute, and you'll have your breakfast," he answered the horses aloud as he crossed a shedrow running down the middle of the barn that was wide and tall enough to accommodate a pickup truck and a two-horse trailer.

Supposedly it was easier to load in a confined space rather than in the open by eliminating the directions in which a stubborn animal could maneuver. The design aided the handling of mechanical horses under a truck's hood rather than those with four legs. Intent and reality were often as different as black and white, Wayford thought as he reached the opposite side and opened the feed room. A horse that balked merely locked its legs and refused to enter a trailer to make a simple task a pain in the backside; a horse did not need maneuvering room, just ground on which to plant its hooves.

The rancher pulled a wheelbarrow filled with a mixture of oats and sweet feed from the open room. He moved down one side of the shedrow and up the other, ladling the grain into the stalls' feed tubs with a quart aluminum can. The horses' impatient nickering faded to the barely discernible sound of oats being ground between teeth.

He replaced the half-empty wheelbarrow in the feed room, then took a rolled garden hose from its place on the barn's wall. Turning on the faucet to which the hose was attached, he retraced his steps down the barn to fill the water buckets inside the occupied stalls.

He reached the door to Frank's Pal's stall and leaned on the webbing to study the young colt. Even with his head half-buried in a feed tub, the animal's confirmation was a thing to behold. The colt looked every bit as quick and strong as he was. Frank's Pal left no doubt that he was every inch a cutting horse.

Wayford's mind wandered to the coming fall in Fort Worth. A win at the competition meant a way out from under the mounting bills that threatened to bury him and steal away the ranch. He had made a good decision not to cut the colt. Not only would a win, or even a place or show, mean more horses for him to train, but he could stand Frank's Pal. Stud fees from a top performance stallion would not make him a millionaire like Paul Moody, but they would get him back in the black and allow him to fill the butane tank again.

Wouldn't hurt to go lookin' for a new pickup either, he mused. The Ford he drove was pushing eight years old. It looked more like a relic ear-tagged for the top of the scrap heap than a vehicle capable of passing yearly state inspections. The rancher feared if he stared at the truck too hard it might fall apart. The interior of the cab looked like hell with its cracked dashboard and threadbare seat. The fenders had more than a few dings and dents, the original maroon color obscured by Bondo and gray primer in a dozen places. *But it still runs,* he said a silent prayer of thanks, *and that's all I need right now.*

A muffled cough wedged into Wayford's thoughts. He pivoted from the colt's stall. His eyes darted from side to side trying to locate the source of the sound. He saw nothing, which gave no reassurance. Though his arms and legs lacked the strength they once contained and his eyes required that printed material be held at arm's length before it focused, his ears were not failing. The cough had not come from a horse. It was human.

Attempting to appear as though all was normal, Wayford recoiled the hose and walked toward the feed room. In spite of his caution, he caught himself cocking his head from side to side, listening; he heard nothing. From inside the feed room, he took down an old double-barreled shotgun pegged on the wall. He thumb-cocked the two hammers of the weapon that had once belonged to his father.

Drawing a deep breath to calm the sudden racing of his heart, he stepped back into the shedrow. Although the Wide W was situated a hundred miles from the Mexican border, the Bend was drug runner country. The border patrol kept a radar balloon aloft forty miles away, close to the town of Valentine, to spot low-flying planes. Immigration now manned inspection stations on all roads coming up from the Rio Grande, something that had not been done three years ago.

The shotgun was Wayford's own form of protection. He had placed it in the feed room after a husband and wife and their five-year-old daughter were killed close to Big Bend National Park by drug runners who wanted their van to transport their narcotic poison.

He had chided himself for overreacting when he had dug the old scattergun out of a closet. Things in this area of Texas were not as bad as they were down in the Valley, where dope smugglers crossing the Rio Grande had killed several people who accidentally stumbled on their illicit operations.

Now he congratulated himself for his foresight. The 12-gauge had a heft to it that bolstered courage. The wide pattern of the buckshot-packed loads eliminated the need for a good aim. All Wayford had to do was point in the general direction of a target and pull one of the two triggers.

Pausing with the scattergun leveled before him, he once more tilted his head from side to side while he strained to hear a sound that did not belong. No noise came except the soft grinding of oats between equine molars. He sucked down a final steadying breath before calling: "You might as well come on out. I heard you, and I know you're in here. I got myself a shotgun with hammers ready to come down on double-ought buckshot, in case you got yourself an idea I'm just an old man you can take down easy. So just come out with your hands up over your head. No need going and getting yourself shot."

He hoped whoever hid within the barn would follow his suggestion and step into the open, but he did not expect it. Nor did it happen. He considered quietly backstepping to the barn door, slipping to the house, and calling the sheriff. This was a matter for the law to handle, not a lone man with only two shells in an old double-barreled shotgun.

He discarded the idea. Jeff Davis County covered a lot of open territory. There was no telling where the sheriff and his deputies might be or how long it would take them to get to the Wide W. Besides, the telephone did not work; he had told the phone company to disconnect it last week. His rationale was that the only one he called regularly was his daughter Mary in Lubbock; it cost a lot less for a weekly letter and postage stamp than a long-distance call. At the moment, he wished he had not been so rational. He was quite prepared to sit and wait for the sheriff or deputy to arrive, even if it took hours.

That was not one of his options, like it or not. He tested the weight of the shotgun in his hands again and realized there was nothing left to do but handle the situation the hard way.

"It really would be easier if you just stepped on out and showed yourself." He started at the head of the barn, peering in the first stall, then crossing the shedrow to the opposite stall. "I don't want no trouble, but if that's what you want, I'm ready to dish some out."

The first two stalls lay empty. He moved on to the next. Cotton filled his mouth and his heart refused to stop hammering. He had not felt like this since Korea when he had drawn the duty of searching Chinese trenches on hills known by map coordinates rather than names. He had not liked the feeling then when he was some forty years younger; he sure as hell did not like it now.

Six of the twenty-five stalls proved empty when he heard a second cough. His gaze darted to the end of the barn. Whoever was hiding had picked the last stall on the right to conceal himself.

"All right,"—Wayford shouldered the shotgun and aimed at the open door to the vacant stall—"I know where you're hiding. Come on out."

He waited, but the cough's owner still declined to present himself.

"If I have to come in that stall after you, I'm coming in shooting," the rancher added as he slowly stepped toward the end of the barn. "I ain't spreading bullshit. I intend to shoot."

He heard three more coughs and the rustle of straw as someone stirred within the stall. His finger tightened on the trigger while he shifted the shotgun's muzzle slightly downward, estimating the height needed to take a charging man full in the chest, if worse came to worst.

The projected trajectory would have been at least three inches too high. A boy—not a man—who appeared several years short of the legal voting age came from the stall. Nor did the boy break forth in a threatening charge. He cautiously crept from the door, dark eyes wide with fear and arms clutching a small cloth bundle bound with twine.

Wayford's trigger finger relaxed as his gaze took in the barn's unexpected occupant. Straw clung to the boy's worn blue jeans and equally worn workshirt as well as a mop of tousled black hair. The rancher released a soft sigh of relief.

"Here I was expecting some bloodletting drug smuggler, and what I got me is a scared little wetback." Wayford lowered the shotgun, watching the boy's fright-filled eyes follow the dipping muzzle. "What in hell are you doing here?"

The boy did not answer, but stood clinging to the bundle while his gaze flitted between the rancher's face and the scattergun.

"*Qu hace usted aqui?*" Wayford repeated in border Spanish. "*Qu hace en mi . . .*" He stumbled, unable to recall the word he needed.

"*Granero,*" the boy spoke softly. "The word you look for is *granero.* You were trying to ask what I was doing here in your barn."

Wayford shook his head in amazement. The Mexican's English was almost perfect. His accent was one of word emphasis rather than pronunciation. Many Anglos in the Big Bend region often picked up the same inflection from living in an area with such a large Mexican population.

"I never was that good with Mex lingo," the rancher answered. "Just picked up what I could from the folks around here. A man can't get very far in this country 'less he can speak a little Mex—and understand a hell of a lot more than he lets on.''

The boy gave a nervous nod. His attention centered on the shotgun. "You seem to speak clearly enough."

"Which ain't got hide nor hair with my question—what are you doing here in my barn?" Wayford pressed.

"Sleeping." The boy tilted his head toward the stall. "The straw was more soft than the ground, and it was much more warm in here than outside."

Wayford's eyes narrowed. Maybe he drew conclusions too quickly. The boy spoke English too well to be from south of the Rio Grande. "You from hereabouts? You in trouble with the law, tryin' to hide out?"

"I am in no trouble." The boy shook his head. "My name is Miguel Santos Joaquin Ramos. I come from across the Rio Bravo— from the village of Santa Maria. I am looking for work as many of the men in my village have done."

The rancher chuckled. "I was right; you are a wetback!" He never liked the term "alien." It made a man, or boy in this case, sound like he was some bug-eyed monster who had stepped out of a Hollywood science fiction movie. "Illegal immigrant," which was popular with politicians afraid of alienating voters of Mexican descent, was totally meaningless, a bureaucratic term that said nothing. It was just about average for politicians.

"Wetback?" The boy's face twisted with befuddlement. "What is this wetback?"

"You." Wayford eased down the shotgun's hammers. "A Mexican that swims across the Rio Grande and is in this country illegally." He watched Miguel Ramos nod in acceptance, then added, "And you'll sure as hell be neck deep in trouble if Immigration catches up with you."

"*Federales?*" The boy's eyes darted about as though he expected to find immigration officers hidden in the barn's shadows.

"The *federales*—the boys from Immigration—they catch you above the border without a green card, and they'll haul your brown ass over to El Paso and dump you in Juarez. Then you'll know what trouble really is. It's a hell of a long way from Juarez to Santa Maria."

Miguel stiffened—whether in fear or pride, Wayford could not tell. Neither would do him much good if Immigration found him.

Times were hard and money tight. Illegal Mexicans were not seen as a source of cheap labor as they once had been. Even native Mexican-Americans in the area did not want them around; they saw their south-of-the-border cousins as competition for the few jobs available.

"I am not afraid of being a long way from my village." The tone of Miguel Ramos's voice said that it was pride, not fear, that straightened his spine. "I have walked a long way since I left my village a week ago . . ."

Wayford edged back his hat and studied the young man. Miguel Ramos walked a fool's path. Yet, the rancher admitted feeling admiration for his courage. Over a hundred miles of hard country, some of the worst God had decided to place on this planet, lay between the Wide W and the Rio Grande. More than half that distance consisted of the rock and sand of the Chihuahuan desert; the other half was simply hot and dry. How a man, let alone a boy, could survive a walk through hell on earth was beyond Wayford. Yet, every day men and boys waded across the Rio Grande in search of wealth above the border.

". . . work is what I look for. I am young, and I am strong. I will work hard."

The boy's voice brought Wayford from his reflections. The rancher drew his lips in a thin line and sucked at his teeth. "Son, if you're lookin' to find work here, you're shit out of luck. Times ain't all that easy right now. Even if I had the spare money to take on a hand, I'd still have to turn you down. The Immigration Service just sends you wetbacks home. They lay a stiff fine on the man who hires you. I can't afford no fine, no matter how big or small, right now."

The rancher paused, looking for some reaction on the boy's face that indicated he understood. There was none. "What I'm sayin' is you got to move on—vamoose. The sooner the better. The immigration boys have taken to droppin' in on ranchers here about to make sure we ain't hidin' nobody like you."

Miguel Ramos did not move. Nor did his expression change. He remained motionless, staring at the old rancher.

Wayford felt a touch of exasperation. A lifetime of dealing and working with Mexicans taught him they all had a common habit—abruptly losing the ability of understanding plain English when they heard something that did not suit their ears.

"Son, don't go and make this hard for either one of us. I can't afford to keep you here. It's not the way you'd like it to be, but that's the way of it. Now, this barn's got two doors. Take your pick, whichever you like, but it was time you was using one of them. *Hasta la vista! Adiós!"* Wayford pointed to the barn's doors with the shotgun.

His grip tightening on the cloth bundle, the young Mexican nodded. He turned, took two steps toward the barn's rear door, and stopped. He looked back at Wayford; his gaze met the rancher's eyes.

"Señor, I understand all that you have said, but it is not easy for me to go." He paused, his eyes rolling downward for an instant. His chest heaved when he looked back up. "It has been a long week since I left my village. The way was farther than I knew. I did not bring enough food with me—only a few tortillas and some water. I ate the last of the tortillas three days ago."

Again Miguel Ramos paused. His voice remained steady, but a plea twisted his brown face. "I do not want to put you in trouble with the *federales,* but I am hungry. If you can find it in your heart, I would like some food." He hastened to add, "I am not a . . . *mendigo* . . . a beggar. I will work for the food. Work hard. The work of a man."

"Dammit to hell, boy." Wayford shook his head. "Didn't you understand what I said about the immigration boys? You're asking me to put myself in a damned uncomfortable position. Don't you understand that?"

"Sí, I understand," the boy answered, "but my belly does not hear as well as my ears."

"Damn!" Wayford could not escape the boy's eyes. It had been a hell of a long time since a man had come to the Wide W looking for handouts. Back in the seventies he and Lizzie had fed more than one confused soul, whether he was a soldier back from Vietnam wondering why his country had turned against him or some shaggy-haired hippie trying to "find himself" or get his head "straight."

Miguel Ramos was not that different from those young men. They all had the same lost looks on their faces, like stray dogs begging for table scraps. He had never refused a dog or a man. Even considering turning the boy away knotted his gut. It was the color of the boy's skin that made him hesitate. That realization tautened the knots.

"Son, I'm goin' against my better judgment, and I guess I'll end up payin' for it if those boys in green decide to pay me a surprise visit. But I reckon I can spare three square meals for a day's work." Wayford wanted the words back the instant he spoke them. Odds were a thousand to one against the Immigration Service checking the Wide W today. But he was in no position to be taking odds, no matter how heavy they were in his favor. A fine for working a Mexican national would be all it took to break him.

"Thank you, *señor.*" A broad smile spread from ear to ear across the boy's face. "You will not be sorry. I am a good worker. I will show you."

Wayford held out a hand to halt the boy. "Now don't go gettin' all excited. You got to understand up front that I ain't offerin' a steady job. We're talkin' about me feedin' you three meals and only that. There ain't no money involved. After today, you'll be on your way and out of my hair. You understand that plain and clear, don't you?"

"I understand. It is clear." Miguel's head bobbed up and down in agreement.

Wayford was less than certain it was all that clear in the boy's mind, but he had to accept him at his word. "Good! Follow me into the house, and I'll see about rustlin' you up some breakfast. After that, we got a long day of work ahead of us."

THREE

CLINT WAYFORD wrapped a potholder around the handle of a cast iron skillet and lifted it from the stove. With a spatula he shoveled three fried eggs beside a pile of six sausage patties on Miguel Santos Joaquin Ramos's plate. While the Mexican boy grabbed another tortilla and dug into his second helping of breakfast, the rancher refilled the two coffee cups on the kitchen table.

"Gracias," Miguel managed to say without pausing while he cut a patty in half with the edge of his fork, speared the meat, and popped it into his mouth. "This is good. It is very good."

Wayford smiled as he sat across the table from the boy and ladled two heaping spoonfuls of sugar into the coffee. "Son, that's your stomach talkin', not your taste buds. I know I'm not much of a hand when it comes to cookin'. Three days without eatin' can make about anything taste good."

"No, *señor,* this is good." Miguel sopped up a pool of egg yoke from the plate with a tortilla and wolfed it down before he went to work on another sausage. "Even my beloved mother has never cooked meat such as this. It is full of . . . *pimienta* . . . pepper."

Wayford smiled again and sampled the coffee. He had forgotten how much food a boy could put away. It had been a long time since a teenaged boy had sat at this table. Miguel's hunger reminded him of—

The rancher swallowed another sip of coffee and retreated from the memories of Tom that welled in his mind. Twenty years did not dull the edge of pain when a man had lost his only son. Tom had been the son most men dream of to carry their name into future generations. At eighteen, Tom had been twice the cowman his father was and displayed an understanding of horseflesh that most men three times his age never grasped.

If only he had stopped Tom from enlisting—

No, Wayford shook his head, refusing to sink into the morass of self-pity and guilt. Blame rested on no one's shoulders, not his, not Tom's, not the Army's, not even a country torn asunder by an unpopular war. A freak accident during basic training left his son crushed beneath the body of an overturned supply truck. The rancher closed his eyes and drew a heavy breath. A freak accident without rhyme or reason—something that just happened.

"Do you live here by yourself alone, *señor?*" Miguel slowed to try the coffee. If he found it bitter, Wayford could not discern it in his expression.

"Clint, my name is Clint Wayford," the rancher said. His gaze wandered around the kitchen. "There used to be a family here, but I'm alone now."

"I am not used to such emptiness in a house." Miguel went to work on another egg. "There are eight children in my family, *Señor* Clint. Four boys and four girls. Two are younger than me. Our house is always crowded."

Wayford nodded. "And that's why you came here, to help your family?"

"*Sí,* I will send them money. It will help," the boy answered. "In my village, I was an apprentice to my uncle. He is a maker of adobe bricks. It is a good profession, but in a poor country there is little money to be made even for one who is a master of his trade such as Uncle Carlos."

"Work ain't that easy to find here in the states. Times aren't as good as they used to be. You might not find what you're looking for here." Wayford tried to explain working conditions north of the Rio Grande.

"Then I will go elsewhere," Miguel said. "I must find work."

Wayford silently wished him luck. Miguel Ramos was small for his eighteen years. He stood no more than five foot six and was built as slight as a quarter-horse jockey. If he made his way to a city like Dallas or San Antonio, he might find a job busing tables in a restaurant, but he was too slight for well-paying construction work. His future in the United States would not be as bright as his hopes. It never was for those who crossed the border illegally.

Miguel took another tortilla from the plastic bag and used it to wipe the remaining sausage grease and egg yoke from his plate.

After downing that, he leaned back in his chair, grinned, and patted his stomach. *"Muy bien!"*

"Son, I know we struck a deal out in the barn, but I ain't gonna hold you to it," Wayford said. "If you're of a mind, you can finish that coffee and be on your way. There's no need for you to stay around here today. You got work to find."

Miguel's eyes widened then narrowed as he shook his head. "No, that would be wrong. I made a promise. I am a man of his word. You have fed me, and I will work for that food. It is what we agreed."

The rancher did not feel up to an argument. He tilted his head in agreement. "Then we'll finish up our coffee and get about our business."

Wayford shifted his weight in the saddle, uncertain whether it was his body or the leather beneath him that creaked in protest. Movement gave no relief to the ache in his lower back. He cursed under his breath. The inescapable pain signaled a pulled or strained muscle. He grimaced with acceptance and tallied another malady resulting from his fall earlier. A throbbing head and a back that felt as though someone had tied a knot in it—what other ailments could he expect to beset him before the day ended, all because of one moment when his mind drifted?

"The horses, they turned here toward those hills." Miguel's voice broke in to the rancher's thoughts.

Halting the bay he sat astride, Wayford turned to the young man, then looked to where Miguel pointed. He saw no sign of the runaway geldings. "What makes you think they're up there?"

"The tracks go that way," Miguel answered. "And the dog followed them. See?"

The boy's pointing finger swung downward to direct the rancher's eyes to the ground. Wayford saw nothing. He squinted, but the tracks refused to reveal themselves. From the corner of an eye, he caught Miguel's questioning expression. He ignored it, stepped from the saddle, and walked to where the boy pointed. The tracks were there, exactly as Miguel had described them. A disgusted "damn" broke from Wayford's lips.

"Is there something wrong, *Señor* Clint?" The Mexican boy eyed the rancher while the older man climbed back onto the bay.

"Nothing 'cept we got to ride a couple more miles before we

catch up with them damned colts. That draw between those rises is the mouth to a box canyon. They won't stop until they reach the end."

A harsh bite cut a sharp edge to Wayford's voice that he had not intended. He could not help it. He had sat less than ten feet away and missed the tracks the boy saw clearly. He told himself the day had been long and he was tired. Self-denial offered no comfort or success in disguising the discouraging chill that seeped through his spine and chest. His body found yet another way to betray him.

He added a drive into Alpine and a visit with an eye doctor to the mental list of matters to attend when there was time—and money. An image of himself walking from the optometrist's office with inch-thick bifocals perched ponderously on his nose popped to mind and lingered there. The portrait left much to be desired. It was bad enough that he now kept a pair of reading glasses on the table beside his easy chair just to read a newspaper.

"*Señor?*" the Mexican boy asked.

Leaving the question unacknowledged, Wayford tapped the bay's flanks with his heels and reined into the draw. Behind him Miguel clucked his own mount forward and moved beside the rancher for a moment before edging slightly ahead.

The young man's action spoke louder than words. He recognized his companion's eyes lacked the sharpness that had once been theirs. For an instant, the rancher contemplated urging the bay forward to retake the lead. He kept the impulse under tight rein. Vanity would not improve his vision; the boy's eyesight was keener than his. Miguel had already proven he could catch signs Wayford overlooked.

Practical though it was, the situation rode on Wayford's shoulders like a loosely cinched saddle on the back of a horse. It rubbed in five different wrong ways all at the same time. He stole a sideways glance at the young Mexican. A hot shame suffused his cheeks, ignited by the commingling of jealousy and contempt he felt for the boy's ability. Miguel carried a passel of problems; he did not need an old man stacking his own shortcomings atop them.

Wayford's gaze and thoughts shifted from the boy to the hump-backed hills rising around him. Time and again since his boyhood, he had ridden over every inch of this land and never failed to be caught up in a sense of wonder. Awe rather than beauty dwelled in its heart. Awe so immense, at times, it seemed as though in the blink of an eye it could swallow a man.

Some of the painters in the art books Lizzie used to buy and pore over in the evenings captured with their oils and canvas a sense of this land's mood. These were not men like the American artist Remington, whose paintings Wayford and Lizzie had seen when they visited that Fort Worth museum. The rancher liked Remington's renditions of range men with their horses and cattle. The paintings brimmed with daring, action, and adventure. Stories of real men living hard times almost jumped from the frames and came to life.

What they were not, were about the land. Not even those who lived here and tried to commit their visions of this country to canvas did more than mechanically render sterile graphics of plains and mountains. In spite of the photographic quality of many such pieces, they fell short of even hinting at the feel of this land.

Lizzie, who had an aversion to hard, vulgar language, cussed a blue streak after any of her countless attempts to breathe life into the landscapes she painted with water colors. Flowers, birds, trees, and people all seemed to live when she painted, but the land—

"It evades me, Clint!" Frustration railed in her voice when she displayed her latest attempt to him. "I don't think anyone can paint this country and show what it really is. No matter what I do, it's no more than a silhouette or a shadow of what's all around us."

The day she found that book in the Midland mall, she came running to him, excited and out of breath. Unaware of the Christmas shoppers who packed the bookstore, she flipped page after page under his nose while she pointed to pictures of clocks melted over the twisted limbs of barren trees and fractured sculptures set amid the desolation of empty landscapes.

The book was about a group of artists called *surrealists.* The rancher was not certain what that meant, although he had looked it up in one of those double-hernia-sized unabridged Webster's dictionaries in Fort Davis's old jail, which now served as the town's library. He did not understand something being so real it was unreal. One of the definitions farther down the page made more sense with its mention of "dreamlike quality."

Lizzie and he had sat on the sofa the night they got back from Midland studying each and every picture contained in the book. The names of those artists meant nothing to him, but the images they created awoke the same feelings that stirred whenever he gazed at the landscape around him.

It struck him as wonderfully strange how those men and women with foreign names found the heart of this country even though they had never seen it. Lizzie laughed at his observation, saying the artists had managed to capture something common in the hearts of all men. To Wayford it still looked as though they knew the same plains he knew.

Dreamlike. The word settled in his mind to find a niche there. The rises through which he and the Mexican boy rode were definitely dreamlike. The way the afternoon sun caught them ignited their western slopes in gold while their opposite sides were cloaked in dark shadows. The sun's passage during the day or the scurrying of clouds across the sky constantly wove an ever-changing tapestry of images.

More than the way the weather played on the country, it was the land itself that held a dreamlike quality for the rancher. The plains were flat, as flat as any of the farmlands in Illinois and Kansas he had driven while traveling the rodeo circuit. Unlike those oceans of grass, here nature punched great upthrusts of granite through the earth's crust. Time and the elements had ground some down to massive mounds like those around him. Others remained mountain ranges with names like Sierra Vieja, Apache, Barrilla, Glass, Bofecillos, Chisos, Del Norte, and Pena Blanca. All of the Texas Big Bend seemed to be either plain or mountain.

Wayford did not forget the third ingredient of the Bend's terrain —desert. With plains of grama grass stretching between the mountains, it was hard to imagine the northern edge of the Chihuahuan desert lay less than fifty miles to the south. All a man had to do was head south on U.S. 67 out of Marfa to dispel any doubts. By the time he reached the old mining town of Shafter, he began to understand the meaning of the term "badlands."

Nineteen miles farther down the highway lay Presidio, sitting on the Rio Grande. It did not take long to learn why the town earned its reputation as one of the hottest towns in the United States. That reputation did not stem from the town's nightlife, but the desert temperature. The heat sucked the moisture from a man's body before he could sweat it.

Scanning the hills, the rancher picked out a variety of desert plants rooted amid the winter brown grass. Prickly pear and cholla stood as the most common cacti, but there were others, smaller and hidden at a distance. Toward the crests of the hills grew yucca and century plants, each surviving where grass struggled merely to take root.

That anything found room to grow was nothing short of a miracle to Wayford. The soil was more rock than dirt, if one could call the fine, dark red-brown sand dirt. But with spring and summer, when moisture-laden clouds pushed across Mexico from the Pacific Ocean to collide with the cool air of the mountains, the rains would return. In a matter of days the crusty dry husks of grass would be supplanted by a green carpet sprinkled with blossoming wild flowers. Nor was the lush green restricted to the plains; it covered the surrounding mountains like deep, rich velvet.

Dreamlike. Wayford rolled the word over and savored its texture. He liked its feel. Whether that dream was an image to strive toward or a nightmare was a matter for each man to decide for himself. In his sixty-five years, the rancher had felt and known both.

"*Señor* Clint, there is something ahead."

The sound of Miguel Ramos's voice pulled the rancher's attention from the hills. He did not need to dismount to see what had caught the Mexican boy's eye this time. "Dammit all to hell."

Wayford's boot heels dug the bay's flanks. The horse broke into an easy gallop to carry its rider a quarter of a mile up the draw before being drawn to a halt. The rancher dismounted and drew a hunting knife from a scabbard tied to the back of his saddle before Miguel joined him.

"*Cabra?*" He stared down at the mauled bodies.

"Two *cabra,*" Wayford corrected as he turned to the bloody animals. "Two rams. From the way they're chewed up, I'd say a cat or coyotes got to 'em."

The rancher knelt beside what was left of the two goats. He had never cared much for goats, except when barbecued. The few he ran were the descendants of a billy and nanny Lizzie's parents had given them shortly after their marriage. He would have given the pair away had they not been a gift from inlaws who came to visit often and were so damned proud of their present to the newlyweds.

Whether he liked the smelly critters or not, he did not like to see any animal chewed up in this fashion. The haunches and shoulders were gone as were the soft innards. That left mostly hair and bits of red muscle clinging to bone. Had the weather been warmer not even that would have remained. Buzzards would have caught the smell of decaying flesh and descended to pick the bones clean.

"A cat did this to goats?" Miguel's voice and expression were incredulous.

Wayford chuckled while he studied both the rams' heads. They appeared untouched. "This weren't a mouser, son. I'm talking a mountain lion, a cougar." He added, *"Cuguar*—that's my bet what did this. The cat population is growing again what with all them environmentalists and animal rights folks worrying about ranchers hunting them to extinction. Those types never stop to think about a goat or a calf's right to live. Guess it's just a matter how a man looks at it, but it seems like those doing all the protesting never set an eye on a mountain lion or a coyote, let alone had to live with them."

He glanced up at the boy and realized Miguel had no idea what he was talking about. When one came from a family of eight children in a desert village, there was only one right way to treat a wild animal—a quick clean kill and then into the cooking pot. Feeding hungry bellies always took top priority. A man did not live in this part of the country without hearing tales of stray cats and dogs ending up on the dinner table south of the border. Wayford had been to Mexico, seen the poverty, and believed those stories.

"On the other hand, it was probably coyotes that did this." He used the blade to sever the first head from the rest of the carcass. "Most cats drag their prey off—take their meal back to wherever they're denned up. Coyotes, a male and female hunting together, are liable to plop down and dine where they make a kill. What I don't understand is why they would kill two rams. One's more than enough for a couple of coyotes."

Brow knitted, the boy watched the rancher take a burlap bag from the back of the saddle and deposit the head within. "You will boil it and make cheese?"

For a moment the question baffled Wayford, then he caught the boy's drift. He shook his head. "Never had much taste for head cheese, though I know a lot of folks who like it. I do intend to boil these skulls and horns clean. Last time I was up in Canton, I saw a fellow sell a ram skull with the horns still attached for onwards up to two hundred dollars. Seems city folk like to stick 'em on their walls for decoration. You know, like a photograph or painting. Reckon I'll try to sell these two at the next First Monday."

The lines on Miguel's forehead deepened with each word the rancher uttered. "Where is this Canton where people would pay so

much money for useless bones to put on their wall? And what is this
First Monday?"

"Canton is a town east of Dallas up north. They hold a big traders' fair every month and call it First Monday." When the boy's
expression remained unchanged, the rancher dug deep into his limited Spanish to come up with, *"Mercado*—where folks come from
all around to sell and trade things. Most of which I think is junk,
but what other folks treasure like gold."

"Ah, un mercado." Miguel nodded.

Wayford was not sure the boy understood or tried to hide his
ignorance of the new country in which he found himself. If he did
not understand, he would learn to do so quickly. A young man in
Miguel Ramos's position either learned or was caught and sent back
across the border to his homeland.

"Sonofabitchin' bastards." The rancher glared at a deformed lead
slug he found on the ground when he removed the second head.
He lifted the flattened piece of metal and held it up for Miguel to
see. "Wasn't cougar or coyotes that killed these rams. It was men.
Coyotes chewed 'em up after they was shot and left here where they
fell."

He tossed the slug over a shoulder and dropped the second head
into the bag. Whether it was hunters who had wandered onto his
property and mistaken the rams for mule deer or kids just out to
shoot something, he would never know. Not that knowing would
change the situation; either way there were two dead rams and all he
could do was save the skulls and horns.

The kink in his back grabbed and crocheted itself into a double
knot when he lifted the bag to tie it about the saddlehorn. He
groaned as the twisting pain left him leaning against the bay's side.
At his feet lay the sack; both heads spilled to the ground.

"Señor Clint!" Miguel leaped from his mount and was at the
rancher's side. "What is wrong?"

"My damned back." Wayford gritted his teeth and stood straight.
He barely restrained another groan when the knots in his lower
back tautened. "I think I must've wrenched it this morning when
them geldings broke away from me. I just need a couple minutes to
get my breath."

The boy nodded, but kept his hands and arms poised to catch the
rancher should the man suddenly collapse.

Wayford drew in several lungsful of air and gradually released them. The grabbing pain subsided. "I think I can get back into the saddle. Can you hand me up them two heads?"

Miguel waited, ready and watching while his employer for the day managed to pull himself astride the bay, before collecting the heads, placing them back into the sack, and tying the bag to the rancher's saddlehorn. "If you wish to wait here, I can go on and find the horses."

Wayford shook his head. "I ain't hurtin' bad enough that I can't do what I rode out here to do."

He clucked the bay forward and immediately regretted his streak of stubbornness. The knots in his back tried to retie themselves with each step the horse took. What he wanted was a long, hot, soaking bath and some horse liniment rubbed deep into his muscles to help work the kinks out. The last thing he needed was to be chasing Paul Moody's green geldings across half of Texas.

The boy did not ride ahead as he had done before. He stuck close to the rancher's side with a watchful eye on the older man. Wayford hid his embarrassment by rolling a cigarette and lighting it. He felt as frail as one of the old men who used to congregate on the benches outside the courthouse up in Fort Davis and spend their days whittling and lying about their past. The young man's obvious concern and attention left him with a rootless disquiet he could not define. At the same time he was grateful for the boy's presence. Had he been alone, he would have forgotten the horses and ridden back to the house.

A half a mile farther up the draw, the rancher heard Vanberg's familiar yap. A smug satisfaction warmed him when he noticed the dog a full minute before Miguel's ears picked up the sound. Two more sharp turns and he rode into the box canyon. Vanberg, who sat at its entrance keeping the five horses within, ran to his side with tail wagging and tongue hanging out of the side of his mouth.

Wayford wanted to dismount and give the hound's ears a good scratch for a job well done, but his back left him in a position where words of praise were the best he could manage. "That's a good boy. You did good. Keep it up and I just might let you stay on the ranch."

The dog responded by wagging his tail double time.

"If you give me the halter and rope, I will catch one of the horses." Miguel held out a hand.

Offering no argument, Wayford untied the rope shank and halter from the saddle and passed it to the boy. He then held Miguel's mount while the youth stepped to the ground and walked slowly toward the grazing horses.

As critical an eye as Wayford cocked, he saw nothing about which to complain. In a soft, gentle voice, the Mexican boy cooed to the five animals in his native tongue as he edged toward them.

With no difficulty Miguel moved beside the very sorrel that had left the rancher in the dirt that morning. While he continued to assure the gelding with his soothing voice, he reached out a hand and stroked the animal's broad neck. The horse stood without flinching. When the sorrel turned its head to study the boy, Miguel deftly slipped the halter over its muzzle and buckled it behind the gelding's ears. The four remaining horses followed as Miguel led the sorrel toward the rancher.

"Mount up and ride to the house. I'll fall in behind to make sure these other four stay in line."

The boy had a way with animals, Wayford admitted to himself. He had watched him work two horses on a line earlier, and Miguel had handled the task without question. Although the job was simple in the scope of training a horse, it did require a feel for the rhythm of an animal to keep him moving in a steady circle.

The rancher also admired the way the boy sat a saddle. He had watched Miguel during their long ride. The way he lightly held the reins of his mount, and the ease with which his body adjusted to the changing gait of a horse, spoke of one accustomed to riding and the feel of a horse beneath him. With his ability, it was unfortunate the horse-racing industry in Texas was still in its infancy after a decades-long ban by the state legislature on pari-mutuel betting. With Miguel's compact body, he might find work as an exercise boy, working horses in the morning, if not a jockey.

Swinging back into the saddle, the boy did as directed. Wayford eased the bay behind the geldings, while Vanberg trotted at his side. He whispered a silent thank-you for the dog's presence. If one of the colts bolted, he doubted that his back would be able to stand the strain of chasing it down. Should one of the animals prove to be stubborn, the hound would handle the situation.

"Crown me!" Wayford settled back in the chair and stared triumphantly across the checkerboard at Miguel. "After you do, sit back and watch me whip your backside for the fifth time in a row. 'Cause that's what's gonna happen in another couple moves."

The boy studied the red and black board and the army of black pieces that faced his five remaining red. He shook his head while he crowned the rancher's piece, adding a king to command that army.

"I do not think that I am good at this game," the boy finally conceded.

Wayford grinned broadly. When it came to checkers, he liked to win. That the young Mexican made it easy did nothing to diminish that pleasure. A win was a win, after all. "You just ate too much for supper, and it's made you sleepy. You ain't thinking at your best."

"I *am* sleepy," Miguel agreed. "And my stomach has never felt so full."

"It wasn't all that bad of a meal I whipped up, was it?" Wayford still savored the taste of the sliced venison back strap and onions and potatoes he had fried for dinner. "I ate a mite too much myself."

"It is getting late." The boy tilted his head to the kitchen window and the darkness outside. "I should be sleeping. I have to be leaving early in the morning. The sooner I start, the sooner I will find work."

"What about our game?" Wayford swept a hand toward the checkerboard.

"It is as you said. You have won already." Miguel pushed from the table and stretched. "I will return to the barn and sleep."

Careful of his back, the rancher also rose. "Wait up a minute, and I'll get you a couple of blankets. I don't want you to go and freeze to death on me tonight."

While the boy stood in the kitchen, Wayford retrieved two quilts and a wool blanket from a hall closet. These he deposited in Miguel's arms. "This ought to stop you from getting frost-bit."

"Thank you." Miguel walked to the back door and opened it to the cold night. "Thank you, *Señor* Clint, for everything."

With that the boy stepped into the darkness and moved toward the barn.

Wayford watched him disappear inside. He felt a twinge of guilt about making the young man spend another night in a straw-filled stall. But then, what did he know about the boy? Miguel Ramos was nothing more than another illegal Mexican drifting through the

Bend in search of imagined wealth. He was like thousands who had come before him and thousands who would follow.

Closing the door and locking it, the rancher threw another mesquite log into the stove. His back needed the hot bath and liniment he had promised it. After that, it was time for his own sleep. Tomorrow was another workday.

FOUR

CLINT WAYFORD opened the back door to collect his boots. Beside them on the stoop lay a neatly folded stack of two quilts and one woolen blanket. He gathered the bedding in one arm and grabbed the boots with his free hand. His gaze lifted to the barn; its door was closed. He saw no movement in the predawn darkness. With a shake of his head, the rancher stepped back into the kitchen and closed the door behind him.

"Looks like the boy's lit out already." Wayford glanced at Vanberg, who lay curled by the wood-burning stove. "I didn't reckon on him leavin' this early. Meant to feed him a good hot breakfast before he hit the road again."

The spotted dog lifted his head, stared at his master, and yawned. His head sank back to crossed paws and his eyes drifted shut again.

"You ain't much help." Wayford's head moved from side to side once more. "That all you got to say on the matter?"

A twinge of pain danced through the rancher's lower back when he turned back to the table and the checker game remaining there from last night. The soaking bath and liniment had done the trick, he thought as he dropped the boots to the floor and rubbed at the back with a palm. The muscles felt stiff, but the soreness was the old sore of healing. Once about the morning's chores, the back would be forgotten—he hoped.

Replacing the quilts and blanket in the hall closet, he returned to the kitchen and the sizzling venison sausage that filled the smoke-blacked skillet. He sucked at his teeth and shrugged. The sausage patties and the biscuits baking in the oven were enough to feed him for half a week. He would not have prepared so large a portion had he known the boy would not be at the table.

"Guess I have to put all this food in the icebox and have it the next couple of mornings," he said to Vanberg, but for the first time since those terrible weeks after Lizzie's death, he realized he spoke aloud to hear the sound of a voice, even if it was his own. "Can't let all this food go to waste."

He felt a tug of regret when he pulled a tray of golden brown biscuits from the oven. Miguel Santos Joaquin Ramos seemed to be a good kid, and he had proved to be a good worker. At least, he had been during his day on the Wide W. The rancher could not say whether or not he liked the boy; there had not been enough time for judgments.

"It would've been nice if there'd been a way for him to stay awhile. You appeared to take a shine to the boy." Wayford watched Vanberg walk to his bowls and take a bite of the dried dog food. "Lord knows I could use another pair of hands to help out around here. He might have been small for his age, but he put in a full day's work."

The rancher sliced open three of the biscuits and used them to make sausage sandwiches. The rest of the meat and biscuits went onto a refrigerator shelf. Taking a bite from the first sandwich, Wayford began to pull on his boots. More than having a hand on the ranch, as much as he was needed, the rancher missed having another soul around. The Wide W did not come close to being the largest spread in the Bend—many considered it small—but it was big enough to make a lone man occasionally desire the company of another human being.

Vanberg sauntered across the room and rested his head on the rancher's knee. His brown eyes rolled up to the man.

Wayford reached down and affectionately rubbed the hound's head. "I ain't saying you aren't good company, but a man needs to hear another voice sometimes. It lets him know he's still alive."

He closed his eyes. The old hollowness welled from deep within, transforming into pain. God, how he missed Lizzie. It was more than growing accustomed to another person over a lifetime. He had truly loved her, more than he had even been able to put into words. There had never been another woman once they had said their marriage vows. He could not remember even being tempted by another woman.

"I told her I loved her every day we spent together, but I'm not sure she realized how much she meant to me. I hope to hell she knew." He continued rubbing the dog's head while he watched the years parade before his mind's eye.

Lizzie and he had been more than husband and wife; they had been the best of friends. In the long haul, that was more important than the passion of youth. Although, he smiled, the loving always had been good between them. Up until he had to place her in the hospital, Lizzie had wanted him in the way a woman wants a man.

They talked, something he often wondered if other married couples ever did. Each day they shared with one another even if it was no more than sighting the first hummingbird of spring or watching the sun break over a grassland covered in heavy frost.

His memories were not selective. He recalled the bad as well as the good. Their marriage had not been a smooth-flowing stream, but a series of white water rapids. What made it all worthwhile was that they rode those rapids together and survived.

He opened his eyes and wiped away the moisture blurring them. "You'd think five years would make missin' her hurt less, wouldn't you, boy?"

Vanberg shifted his head to nuzzle the man's side.

Wayford's fingers directed their attention to the dog's floppy ears, scratching them. Sometimes he had the definite sensation the hound could read his mind, or at least sense what he felt. Then again, he recognized his were the mental meanderings of a lonely old man reading something into a dog's ability that was not there.

"They say a man can tell he's getting old when he dwells on the past more than the future." The rancher reached down and tugged on his remaining boot. "If that's the case, then I must be ancient as Methuselah's ass."

Giving the dog a final stroke, Wayford rose from the table, stuffed one of the biscuit sandwiches into a coat pocket, then grabbed up the coffee cup from the table and his hat from the wall to walk outside into the morning. With Paul Moody's geldings tucked away in stalls, he did not have to concern himself with horses getting away this morning. However, there was still a corral fence to mend.

Inside the barn, he fed and watered the horses before throwing open the barn door and backing his old Ford pickup into the shedrow. From the loft he tossed down five bales of prairie hay and two of alfalfa into the back of the truck—a task accomplished with only minor complaints from his back. With Vanberg sitting in the cab beside him, he pulled from the barn and swung out onto the open plain.

Five miles of teeth-jarring rocks and truck-rattling ruts later, he halted the pickup and stepped outside. By the time he broke open the first bale and spread it on the ground, he heard the distant mooing of a cow. He saw the cattle steadily plodding toward his position while he finished throwing out the last of the alfalfa. He climbed back into the pickup's cab, started the engine, and turned on the heater to cut the morning's chill as he waited for the herd to approach.

He rolled a cigarette and lit it while he studied each cow and steer that came for their morning meal. The winter was not hurting them; they kept their weight. If the spring rains came and brought grass, they would fatten up nicely for market. The money they would bring would give him enough to keep the small herd of six hundred head running for another year.

That's if the bottom doesn't drop out of the market. He stubbed out the cigarette butt in an overflowing ashtray. He tried not to think about that possibility. If beef prices took a sudden downward swing, it would ruin him. He operated on the narrowest margin he could and still stay in business. There was no leeway; he either survived or failed. By spring, he would know which.

He struck the pickup's horn three times in rapid succession to scatter the steers milling around the front of the truck. When they were clear, he shifted into gear and began the drive back to the house while he munched on the last biscuit of breakfast.

When it involved cattle, for Wayford it was work, even the easy task of feeding them. The horses back in the barn were a completely different matter. Each of the animals required at least tenfold the attention of any fifty steers, but that did not tip the scales. Cows were cows, and horses, horses; one labor, the other a labor of love. He did not even mind the less than mentally elevating pursuit of mucking the stalls that waited. It was honest work, although not the cleanest a man might do.

The true pleasure came from the horses themselves. When he worked with them, they were his total focus. The bills, the uncertainty of cattle prices, the rising cost of feed, the lack of butane in the silver tank beside the house, even the loneliness were forgotten.

He had found such consuming completeness in his life in two other places. First as a young man when he entered a rodeo arena and the calf he had drawn for the night trotted into the chute. The instant the barrier went up, his attention drew to needle sharpness. The world collapsed inward until it consisted of a running calf, a lunging horse, a rope, a pigging string, and himself. For a few seconds, until the calf lay tied in the arena's sand, there was nothing else, all was obliterated, even the cheering crowd.

The second was in Lizzie's arms when she drew him to her, their bodies becoming one. The world folded inward until only they existed. With no other woman had he experienced that oneness, and there had been other women before he married Lizzie.

Now, there were the horses. He did not equate them with love, but knew the emotion dwelled somewhere within his actions, in the trust he built between animal and man.

Paul Moody's geldings were where he began his work. He started with curry comb, brush, and rag. He spoke softly while he groomed them, allowing each of the five to learn his scent and the feel of his hands. When they accepted his presence, he placed a saddle blanket on their backs. His soothing voice and palms calmed fears awakened by the strange cloth they carried. Again and again, he slipped the blanket off and replaced it, letting it remain longer each time.

The process was slow, but today—for the next several days to come—he used the blanket to build a foundation for the saddle that would follow. After the saddle came the weight of a man and the taste of bit and rein.

All this would be performed within the confines of a stall. Wayford was not a broncobuster; he was a horse trainer. There would be no bucking, no thrown riders, no horse ridden until his spirit was shattered. The stall's four walls prevented that. A horse was given no room in which to move; the situation and gentle persuasion forced the animal to accept a rider. The process required time and patience; the rancher had both when it came to horses.

From the Moody geldings, he moved to the other horses in the barn. In turn each was saddled and ridden into an arena-sized corral where Wayford honed their feel for the light touch of the reins on their necks and the pressure of a man's legs against their sides. The maneuvering drills were simple, quick spinning turns, lunging sidesteps, sharp, straight retreats.

Like the blanket for the geldings, this was the foundation for the day calves would be released in the pen and each horse would be called upon to cut out one of the animals and keep him separated from the others. That was the moment for which he trained each animal, the moment they became cutting horses. From there, the individual ability and quickness of each animal determined whether he became a work horse or a mount with that special quality needed to enter a show arena and vie for championships.

The key to the latter for a horse was working himself with little or no direction from the man who sat atop his back. For Wayford the horse who could do that best was the last one whose stall he approached with saddle hefted to his right shoulder. Frank's Pal stood calmly while Wayford worked the colt's thick winter coat with curry comb and brush, then slicked him down with rub rag. The colt displayed the same disinterest while the rancher saddled and mounted him. Only when they rode from the barn to the corral and the twenty calves within did the horse's ears prick and his head lift.

Wayford felt the tension build in the colt as they entered the corral and moved toward the calves clustered at the opposite end. Like steel compression springs, the horse's muscles tautened. Yet, Frank's Pal kept his gait to a steady walk, waiting until his rider selected the calf they would work this day.

The rancher's choice was a Brahma. The calf had not been castrated and was beginning to feel the hormones coursing through his body that would transform him into a bull to be reckoned with. That developing streak of meanness is what Wayford intended to use. The calf would repeatedly challenge the colt's ability to cut him out from the others.

A horse must be told which calf is to be worked. A rider cannot do that with words or pointing to the desired animal. Wayford spoke to Frank's Pal with the pressure of his knees and the light movement of his left wrist as he eased the reins from side to side. This was the man's portion of the task, to weave his mount through the herd to the chosen animal. He worked his mount until the horse was certain of his target. If trained correctly, the horse took over at that point, and the man was along for the ride.

Frank's Pal took over the instant Wayford singled out the Brahma. As the rancher wanted, the calf refused to give in easily and allow himself to be cut from the others. He darted to one side and then in the opposite direction. He spun about and broke in an all-out run. The colt's movements anticipated rather than reacted to the calf.

Only once did the Brahma pull a number that appeared to have outwitted the relentless horse. The calf ran directly toward the other animals that scurried away from horse and rider. When Frank's Pal lunged to block his intended escape route, the feisty calf spun about. The colt reacted by lunging to the opposite side in an attempt to check a break in that direction. The Brahma did not stop the turn at a hundred and eighty degrees, but did a full three hundred and sixty degrees to continue on his original path. In midstride Frank's Pal reversed himself. He took two lunging steps and placed himself between the Brahma and the other calves in a maneuver that left the rancher grasping the saddlehorn with both hands to retain his seat atop the magnificent colt.

After that it was almost routine as Frank's Pal worked the calf into a corner of the corral and kept him there until Wayford eased back on the reins to signal that the colt had completed his task. The instant the horse's head turned away, the Brahma bawled loudly and trotted across the corral to rejoin the other calves.

With Vanberg trotting beside them, horse and rider returned to the barn, where Wayford unsaddled the colt, bathed him, threw a blanket over his back, and cooled him out by walking him up and down the shedrow and allowing him an occasional drink from a bucket hung outside his stall. Thirty minutes passed before the horse was dry and watered out. Returning the colt to his stall, the rancher once again applied curry comb and brush. He finished off the daily routine with a rubbing alcohol brace and bandage for each of the colt's ankles and shins. None of Frank's Pal's legs held heat that forewarned weakness, but Wayford wanted to keep them that way; the brace and bandages were preventive care rather than corrective.

After raking loose straw and hay from the barn's shedrow, the rancher applied a fine spray of water from a hose to the sandy loam to help keep the dust down. He gave the barn a survey to make certain all was as it should be, then turned to Vanberg.

"Boy, we got us a rooster to catch before we can clean ourselves up and drive into town." He reached down and patted the dog's side when Vanberg moved to him. "After all, it's Saturday, and a man's got to find out what's happening in the world!"

Vanberg offered no protest, but followed eagerly after his master as Wayford left the barn to chase down the rooster to trade for pinto beans.

FIVE

CUPPING HIS HANDS beneath the faucet, Wayford filled them with water, then bent over the sink to rinse the traces of shaving cream from his face. He toweled dry and ran a palm over cheek, chin, and throat to make certain the razor had left no stubble. Since his whiskers had turned white, he found them more difficult to see in a steamy bathroom mirror.

He opened the medicine cabinet and took down a bottle of bay rum. Sprinkling several drops on a palm, he patted the after-shave on his face. The man who stared back at him from the mirror winced when the biting astringent began to sting. He could think of no reason why he continued to use the after-shave, except that Lizzie had liked the scent. Like keeping his work boots outside, it was a habit he could not break.

In the bedroom Vanberg waited at the foot of the bed. He sat on his haunches and watched his master pull a crisply starched and pressed white shirt and an equally sharply creased pair of khaki pants from a closet and lay them on the bed. Both were Western cut, minus fancy design work. Gaudy designs and colors, the rancher believed, were better worn by country and western singers and drugstore cowboys than a working man. His one concession to style was imitation mother-of-pearl snap buttons. Anything flashier than that and a man looked like some strutting peacock.

At the same time, he frowned on men who wore their work clothes, often soiled, into town. A man was supposed to be presentable when he decided to show himself to his neighbors. Worn blue jeans, a stained shirt, and a dirty give-me cap did not fit his image of presentable.

He pulled on the shirt, buttoned it, then stepped into the trousers. The belt he chose was plain brown leather with a large oval silver buckle. Adorning the buckle, in gold, was the image of a roper putting his loop over the head of a calf. Wayford had won the buckle when he took first place at a rodeo in the old Cow Palace in San Francisco.

He returned to the closet to retrieve his good hat and boots, and a Western cut camel-colored corduroy jacket. This completed what Lizzie had dubbed his "business uniform." Each Saturday as they dressed for their weekly trip into Fort Davis, she would tease him about his set ways of dressing and suggest that he try a change of fashion. He met each of those comments with a disapproving scowl that was as much a part of the playful ritual as were her comments.

When he finished dressing and stood waiting for her to put the finishing touches on her hair, she would walk to him and say, "Well, all I can say is that you certainly clean up good, Clinton Wayford." She would punctuate the remark with a kiss on the lips.

She had said those very words the last day he visited her in the hospital. He entered her room in his "business uniform," and she looked up from her bed and whispered, "You certainly clean up good, Clinton Wayford." She had long before lost the strength to walk to him, so he moved beside her bed and leaned down to kiss her lips. Two hours later, as she slept, her hand clasped in his, she gave a soft sigh, a sound he had heard a thousand times over when she settled into his arms in their bed, and she passed away.

Slipping into the coat, Wayford eyed himself in a full-length mirror attached to the closet door. His fingertips lightly brushed over his forehead. A slight hint of red marked what had been a bump yesterday. However, the dark scab which covered the cut left by the sorrel's hoof drew his eyes to it like a magnet. He considered hiding the cut under another bandage, but decided that would only emphasize the embarrassing injury.

He stepped back and let his gaze run up and down the reflection. The shirt, pants, and coat appeared clean and pressed; the boots gleamed with a glossy spit-shine. The hat held in hand was without spot or flake of dust.

So much for clothes making the man. He looked presentable, but he could not say he cleaned up all that well anymore. To his own eyes, he looked like an old man in khaki pants, white shirt, and coat. Except for less stoop in the shoulders, the image in the looking glass might have belonged to his father. Johnny Lee Wayford had appeared much the same the last time the rancher had seen him. Were the passing decades merely a slowly turning wheel that transformed a son into his father? Had Tom lived, would he have found himself gazing into a mirror one day wondering the same thing?

Turning his back on the reflection, he walked to a small roll-top desk pushed into the corner of the bedroom beside one of the two windows. He lifted a stack of bills from a drawer and removed the rubber band that held them together. A hasty perusal of amounts to be remitted and due dates while he sifted through the pile produced three bills which he placed into the inside pocket of his coat. The remainder he rewrapped with the rubber band and dropped back into the drawer. He picked up a checkbook from the desktop and added it to the pocket.

"Let's go." He snapped his fingers.

Vanberg heeled, walking beside his owner through the house. Outside, the dog leaped into the pickup and took his place on the passenger side of the worn bench seat when his owner opened the door.

Wayford pumped the gas pedal once then twisted the key. The old Ford started without so much as a sputtered cough. In spite of the mounting mileage on the odometer, the engine purred as smoothly as the day the rancher had purchased the truck. He switched on the radio and shifted into gear.

Rather than the sports report he wanted, the Alpine station blared the sounds of something the disc jockey called "new country." If the rock and roll guitars and drums filling the background were "new country," the rancher concluded that he preferred old country. He was no great admirer of popular Cajun music—he feared that any band that employed an accordion, no matter that they called it a "zydeco," would suddenly break out in a rendition of "Lady of Spain"—but it was far more ear-pleasing than this caterwauling.

He wondered whatever happened to the *western* in country and western music. Except for a few singers like Waylon Jennings and Willie Nelson—both good Texas boys—western was ignored by singers and musicians today.

The strains of an old Marty Robbins melody drifted to mind. Ignoring the singer on the radio, who proudly proclaimed his friendship with people in low places, Wayford whistled aloud while he imagined Marty once more singing about that cantina in the West Texas town of El Paso.

The sports came on by the time he covered the ten miles of dusty, washboard-rough, dirt road that led to Highway 166. While the announcer rattled off the Friday night losses by the local high school football teams, the rancher stopped at his mailbox and opened it. Nothing of interest caught his attention as he thumbed through an assortment of more bills and advertising flyers.

He placed the stack of mail on the seat beside him, checked for traffic, then pulled onto the two-lane highway, heading toward an imposing mass of rock to the east called Blue Mountain, which jutted over seven thousand feet into the air. On the radio, a sports-caster updated the latest Texas Rangers player negotiations. Last summer he had checked out a book on modern baseball from the Fort Davis library. The fortunes the major league teams made off television telecasts boggled the mind. Once he had sided with man-agement when it came to player contracts. Now he hoped the play-ers would stick it to the owners every chance they got. Any group of men who even considered replacing the solid crack of a wooden bat against a hardball with the ping of an aluminum bat deserved any and all misfortune that passed their way—and then some.

Fifteen miles later Wayford pulled to a complete stop to allow a small caravan of vans and recreation vehicles to pass before he pulled onto Highway 17. Although several of the drivers lifted a single finger from their steering wheels in a wave of acknowledgment, the rancher did not recognize a face or vehicle among the only traffic he had seen that day.

The drivers and their passengers were part of the steady trickle of nameless tourists who traveled through the region to see Big Bend National Park, which lay over a hundred miles to the south. These probably were fresh from a visit to Lajitas and Presidio down on the Rio Grande. Before moving on, they would stop to see the old military fort in town and drive out to take a look at the white domes and the massive telescopes they held at McDonald Observatory atop Mount Locke.

Wayford had heard many of his neighbors complain about the tourists. He brushed aside their complaints. The local paper once reported McDonald Observatory's top year for visitors was one hundred thousand people. In a world filled with billions, that was no one. Besides, tourists brought tourist dollars into an area that had nothing to offer the average person except unusual scenery. Although a rancher's pocketbook did not grow fatter off the tourist trade, many of the area businesses would dry up and blow away without that money.

He entered the town of Fort Davis from the south, passing the high school with its gymnasium and football field. He stopped at the triangular intersection with Highway 118 by the courthouse to let a pickup with at least five Mexican children in the back turn toward Alpine. In a town with a population of about six hundred people, Highway 17 formed Fort Davis's main street. Businesses had sprouted on each side of the road. Most of the buildings appeared as old as he. As far as he could remember, they were.

Near the Limpia Hotel, he halted outside a white-painted cinder block building which housed the local electric company. He ordered Vanberg to wait in the pickup and entered the office to exit a few moments later with two bills remaining in his coat pocket. His next stop came a quarter of a mile down the highway at Ivan Sierra's. Dogs were welcome in the cobbler's shop. Vanberg hastened past his owner and went straight back to greet an old friend.

"How you doin', boy?" Ivan, ten years Wayford's junior, stopped his sewing machine and scratched the bird dog's ears with both hands. When he looked up, he greeted the rancher with a wide grin. "And you, Clint? How are you doing?"

"Well as to be expected." Wayford shook the man's hand when he extended it.

"Reckon you heard about ol' Elrod Hornsby by now?" Anticipation lit the bootmaker's face.

The rancher shook his head. He knew that even if he had heard, Ivan would tell the story, embellishing it with every detail gleaned from the townfolk.

Ivan's grin widened. For the next thirty minutes he relished retelling how their mutual friend had returned late Tuesday night from a honky-tonk up in Pecos. In spite of his inebriated condition, the carpenter managed to safely execute the serpentine twists and turns of the mountain roads and pull into his own driveway. "Then it hit the fan. He slipped and fell flat on his face when he got out of his car—flopped down smack dab atop a fire ant mound. You could hear him hollering all the way down Marfa!"

The picture Ivan painted did not strike the rancher as humorous as it did the cobbler, who laughed until tears rolled down his cheeks. Wayford once misstepped into a fire ant bed three years ago. By the time he noticed the mistake, the ants were in his left boot.

They bit him a dozen times; his foot swelled so that he could not get the boot back on for three days after removing it to brush away the pesky critters.

Nor did Wayford find it funny that Elrod Hornsby was hospitalized in Alpine and that his wife threatened to divorce him as soon as he recovered. Ivan did; the shoemaker held his sides as he concluded the story. He was still chuckling to himself while he rummaged through a tin filing box to find the rancher's bill.

"Repairs on six halters and that old saddle of yours. Comes to forty-two sixty-seven, including the tax." Ivan passed the bill to Wayford, who, in turn, pulled out the checkbook and paid the full amount.

Ivan placed the check in a drawer, then glanced down at the rancher's boots. "What about your footwear? It's been a few years since I fitted you for those. They need new soles or heels? Maybe I could interest you in a new pair? I got some mighty fine silver-gray ostrich in the back that's just hurtin' to be stitched into boots."

"When you make a man a pair of boots, you make 'em too good, Ivan," Wayford answered. "I'll still be wearing these the day they lay me in the ground. And they'll look just as good as they do today."

The boot smith grinned. "You're a lying old bastard, Clint Wayford, but you say the right kind of lies."

Bidding Ivan goodbye, Wayford waited for Vanberg to receive a parting pat then returned to the pickup. A block to the north, he wheeled from the highway onto the dusty dirt streets of residential Fort Davis. He stopped in front of a yellow frame house with the door to a single-car garage open. A man lay across the fender of an '85 Chevy half-hidden beneath the car's hood. While the rancher extracted another bill from his coat and wrote a check for a hundred and fifty dollars, the heavyset man in a hunter's camouflaged jumpsuit abandoned his repairs and walked to the pickup.

The rancher rolled down his window, shook the man's hand, and handed him the check. "Sorry it took so long getting this to you, Manuel, especially since you dropped everything you were doing to come out and fix my pump."

"There was no worry, Clint. I knew you were good for it." The man tilted his head to the garage. "Besides, the winter's been cold, and everyone in town is having car trouble. Haven't stopped working since the first day of December. That Caprice belongs to one of Paul Moody's hands. He hauled it in this morning."

"Glad they're keeping you busy," Wayford said. Manuel Clancy, whose dark skin and black hair were inherited from his Mexican mother rather than his flaming-haired Irish father, was one of fifty all-around handymen who kept alive by taking on any job that came his way, whether it be filling in at one of the town's service stations when an employee became ill or handling any construction or plumbing task that presented itself. "A lot of folks are havin' a hard time findin' work."

"And you? How you getting along, my friend?"

Wayford shrugged. "About as good as my git-along will let me git. I guess a man can't ask for more than that."

"He can ask, but he ain't likely to get it," Manuel said as the rancher started the pickup. "You take care, Clint. Thanks again for bringing this out. It's appreciated."

"Your help was appreciated. A man can't water his stock if his pump isn't working." Wayford tilted his head in a gesture of farewell. "Remember to bring those kids of yours out to the Wide W when the weather warms up. I promised them they could go riding."

"I'll do that." Manuel waved goodbye. "The boys won't let me forget you said they could take out a couple of horses."

The rancher smiled and tilted his hat again as he cut a sharp U-turn and headed back toward the highway. He liked Manuel almost as much as he had the man's father. Wayford especially liked the three young Clancys. The boys, all under ten, were spirited and ready to try any adventure a ranch might offer. The day Manuel spent working on the pump, the brothers thoroughly explored the barn's loft and found the calf pen. Wayford chuckled aloud as he recalled the three's repeated attempts to ride whatever calf they could chase down. Given another day or two, they would have succeeded.

He missed having children around. The hardest thing about Mary living all the way up to Lubbock was that he never saw his two grandchildren except during Christmas holidays and for a week in the summer. He could not count the hours he had spent trying to figure out some way of being closer to those kids. Lubbock sat at the bottom of the Panhandle, and the Wide W was closer to Mexico than it was to the rest of Texas. There simply was no way to be around Frank Junior and little Elizabeth. That left the feeling that a portion of his life had passed him by, a portion he could never recover.

A block south of the Anderson School, he made a left into Sid Stilwell's service station and stopped beside the regular pump. A young man, whose name always escaped the rancher, ran out and asked, "Same as usual, Mr. Wayford?"

"I need 'er filled up," Wayford answered while he stepped from the cab and snapped his fingers for Vanberg to follow. "If I left her here a couple of hours, you think you'd have time to change the oil and filters?"

"Shouldn't take more than an hour." The boy gave a nod as he lifted the hood. "I ain't got nothing on the rack. I can get to it right away."

"Clint!"

Wayford turned to find Sid Stilwell standing in the door of the service station. Sid had been three years behind Wayford in school, which made him sixty-two years old. He looked forty-two. He was one of those damnable men who appeared to age no more than a single year for every decade they lived.

The slender, handsome man had made the most of his good looks and charm. For most of his life, Sid had considered every female in five counties fair game. Rumor had it he was an accurate marksman, especially when it came to divorcees and newly widowed women.

That was until fifteen years ago when he ran headlong into Lucille Washburn, who was still wearing the black of mourning for her recently departed Edgar. One day whispers abounded about Sid's car being parked outside Lucille's house all of one night. The next day the whole county buzzed with the announcement of Sid and Lucille's marriage before a justice of the peace over in Brewster County.

Since then, Sid had acted like a bird with a pound or three of salt poured on his tail. Not that the rancher blamed him. Lucille was a big woman—outweighed Sid by at least a hundred pounds—and had the temper of a demon belched straight from the bowels of hell. If it ever came to fisticuffs between the husband and wife, Wayford knew who he would put his money on, and it would not be Sid.

"Clint, if you've got a minute, I'd like to talk with you." Sid signaled him into the station's office. When Wayford and Vanberg entered, Sid cleared his throat and began awkwardly, "Clint, I don't like to press you or have to ask this, but . . ."

"But you were wondering if I'm ever going to get around to settling up my bill?" the rancher finished for him.

Sid released an overheld breath and nodded.

Wayford pulled the last bill and checkbook from his pocket. "I thought I'd settle this today."

An embarrassed smile moved across the service station owner's thin lips. "You want me to add in your fillup?"

"And an oil and filter change," the rancher amended. "The boy said he could get right to it."

Sid located a pocket calculator on the counter beside the cash register and did a tap dance on its keys with his fingertips. "That'll total out at two hundred twelve dollars and forty-six cents."

Taking a pen from a battered coffee can on the counter, Wayford wrote a check for the exact amount and handed it to the man. While Sid punched the cash register, the rancher tallied the money left in his checking account. Two hundred dollars remained for some unforeseen emergency—a small emergency. Two hundred dollars was not enough to buy a man a decent pair of boots today.

Wayford closed the checkbook and slid it back into his coat pocket. He would forgo the luxury of his usual Saturday night meal —chiles rellenos at one of the two Mexican restaurants in town. The five dollars the meal would cost could be better used elsewhere.

"Clint, you're looking a little thin on those back tires." Sid pointed to the old Ford. "You should think about replacing them."

"Have any retreads?" The rancher could not call the tires bald, but it would not be long until he was riding on the steel belts.

"Not today. I've got some that are supposed to come in from Midland next week or so."

"Save me a good-looking pair. I'll stop in and have the boy put them on in the next couple of weeks." Wayford moved toward the door. "I'll be back before you close to get my truck."

"Clint," Sid said as the rancher opened the door, "I hope you don't think I was being pushy—I mean about your bill. I would have let you ride longer, but what with the Republicans in office and all, times are hard."

"It was your money, and you had a right to it," Wayford answered. "Like you said, times are hard."

"Damned hard," Sid replied while the rancher stepped outside and started toward the old drugstore.

Wayford also wished Sid had let the tab slide for another month or two. Having another two hundred dollars in the bank would have eased the pressure. But a man had to feed the horses under the hood of his pickup as surely as he had to grain flesh and blood horses. Ranching without a truck to haul feed and grain would be akin to a cowboy trying to work a herd without a string of horses back when Amos Wayford first settled in the Bend.

A stray dog sniffing around two trash cans outside a motel caught Vanberg's eye. A bitch in heat if the attention the hound gave her was any indication, Wayford realized. Although Vanberg kept her in sight, nearly twisting his neck a full one hundred eighty degrees to accomplish the task, the dog never broke his stride and stayed at his master's side.

Wayford looked down at his canine companion. "Sorry, boy, I guess I haven't been thinkin' straight lately. Reckon I've thought that my needs and yours are the same. From the eye you were givin' that young lady, it appears I'm way off base."

Vanberg lifted his head to the rancher and wagged his tail. He then glanced back at the bitch busying the trash cans.

Wayford knew the hound was just a dog, but it *did* seem like there were times he understood every word a man uttered. "The weather's a mite too cold for you to be out sowing wild oats. Come the first warm spell, I'll let you have a free run for a few nights. That should improve your love life."

Vanberg nuzzled his owner's hand until the rancher stroked his head.

A line of vehicles stood outside the old drugstore. They were the usual assortment Wayford was accustomed to seeing, a mixture of local cars and pickups sandwiched between tourists' vans and RVs. The drugstore and the hotel rooms on the second floor of the building had changed ownership at least a dozen times during the rancher's lifetime. The patronage remained the same: folks from throughout the county gathered to sort out the events of their lives with friends while tourists sought a brief respite from their sightseeing to enjoy the tempting offerings of the old-fashioned soda fountain.

Without a word from his master, Vanberg took his usual position beside the drugstore's double doors. The dog settled to his haunches and did his best to look lost and forlorn.

Another trait flowing in the hound's blood was that of beggar. It had taken Vanberg only a couple of trips to the drugstore to realize that tourists and townfolk alike had handouts aplenty for "that poor, pitiful-looking puppy." Broken-off portions of hamburgers, sandwiches, and candy bars were tossed his way. On a good day his reward could be a double-dip ice cream cone dropped to the sidewalk by a child who stumbled when he exited the store.

Wayford would never accuse the bird dog of running up and accosting someone for a handout. However, the rancher would not put it past Vanberg to give an unwary toddler a friendly nudge to help loosen an ice cream cone from an uncertain grip. Children with chocolate scoops were his favorite target.

"Clint Wayford," George Scheppler hailed the rancher as he entered the store, "come on in out of the cold." The drugstore's owner waved to one of the four high school girls working for him. "Get Mr. Wayford his usual, coffee and a piece of lemon meringue pie. Take it to the table in the back."

Wayford stepped to a counter piled with boxes of candy bars surrounding an ancient manual cash register. He grasped George's extended hand and shook it firmly. "How's the world treatin' you?"

"Could be better. The weather's too damned cold for the tourists. It's keeping them away in droves," the drugstore owner replied. "I'm making the bills, but that's about it. Spring can't come too fast this year. This whole season's made me wonder why the hell I ever left Dallas."

A former jingle writer for radio advertising, George Scheppler and his family had traveled to the Bend on vacation eight years ago and ended up staying. He had searched for the "quiet, good life" away from the day-to-day struggles of the city. Since buying the drugstore, he had learned that the Big Bend was often too quiet and it was a day-after-day struggle to keep the doors to his business open.

"You heard anything from Tomas Juárez lately?" the rancher inquired.

Twelve years ago Tomas had worked part-time as a hand on the Wide W while attending Sul Ross in Alpine. After obtaining a degree, the young man moved to Dallas, where he went to work for the same advertising firm that had employed George. Tomas made a good living writing ad copy, but it was his poetry the rancher admired. Although he had never been published by one of the big houses up in New York City, two volumes of Tomas's verses were now circulated by a regional publisher out of Austin.

"Talked with him this week. He sounded all right, but his wife told me it wasn't good. The doctors say it's lupus. It's got at his heart. They don't think he'll make it another year. None of the medicines they're giving him are doing any good," George said.

"I don't like hearin' that." Wayford pursed his lips. Tomas had been a good boy, full of life. It flowed in his poems. He wrote about the land of his birth and the people who populated it. His poetry was not the clever and cute rhymes of the so-called cowboy poets who had sprung up in the past decade. Tomas's words were real reflections of life in the Big Bend; a view that was neither overly harsh nor sticky with sentimentality.

"He asked after you, Clint," George continued. "Said he'd like to see you again. He reminisced about working on the Wide W. From listening to him, he looks at it as the best time in his life."

Wayford nodded. "Reckon I should drop by his house one of these times I drive up to First Monday."

"I think he'd appreciate that. He thinks the world of you, Clint. You're like a second fath—"

Six tourists, three bald men with three purple-haired women, approached the counter with bills in hand, cutting George's sentence short. Wayford stepped aside and let his gaze survey the drugstore.

It was hard for him to remember when the business had actually been a pharmacy. For more years than countable on fingers and toes, the sole remnant of the drugstore was a rack of headache remedies and antacids hung on the wall near the cash register. The store was now a restaurant specializing in several homecooked lunches each day and one of the best hamburgers to be found in Texas. Filling the old drugstore were three lines of tables covered with red and white checkered tablecloths. Most of the tables were occupied by customers engrossed in their meals. A soda fountain, complete with swivel seat stools, ran along one wall for the length of the store.

From a double-length table at the back of the room three arms lifted and waved to catch the rancher's attention. Wayford returned the waves and wove his way toward the table and the five old men sitting around it.

"Looks like every old codger in the county's dropped by today," a gravelly voice said when Wayford reached his friends. "Paul Moody and Jimmy Solar were here about an hour back. They were too busy stuffin' their faces with chicken fried steak and cream gravy to have much to say."

The voice and a face that looked like weathered granite belonged to eighty-year-old Sam Norwood. Norwood, who had turned the management of his ranch over to his son fifteen years ago, was responsible for dubbing the weekly gathering of aging cattlemen the Greater Fort Davis Old Codger Society.

"Sam." Wayford acknowledged the society's unofficial grand poobah's presence with a tilt of his head.

"That damned panhandling pooch of yours is at it again." Bill Sallis, who foremanned the Black Diamond P, threw a thumb over a shoulder toward the drugstore window.

Outside Vanberg wolfed half a hamburger one of the purple-haired women fed him when she stepped outside.

Sallis shook his head. "It's taken me a few years to figure it out, but I think I know why you let that mutt trail with you to town every week. You don't feed him. The poor bastard survives on what he can beg here on Saturday."

Wayford shrugged and grinned as he pulled a chair to the table. "You found me out. No man in his right mind would waste good money buying food for a flea bag like Vanberg."

Sam Norwood cleared his throat. "If that dog's so useless, why don't you sell him to me? I'll give you fifteen hundred for him right on this spot."

"Double the price, and you might have you a deal." The hint of sobriety in the retired rancher's voice caught Wayford off guard. He set the price high to make certain Sam knew Vanberg was *not* for sale.

More surprising were the moments that passed while Sam studied the hound through the drugstore's front windows. He finally shook his head. "Not today, Clinton Wayford, but I'd be mighty careful about your askin' price in the future. I got me a bitch back home damn near as smart as Vanberg there. The pups they'd have would be more intelligent than most men that I know."

"Maybe we could work out a stud service deal?" Wayford suggested.

"Let me take him home with me tonight and keep him a day or

so, and we'll each take the pick of the litter and split it down the middle on what we make off the rest of the pups," the older man countered without blinking an eye.

"Have him back at the house tomorrow afternoon and you've got yourself a done deal." Wayford realized he had found a solution to the hound's nonexistent love life.

"Deal." Sam stuck out a ham-sized hand that felt as rough and leathery as it looked when Wayford shook it. Grinning, he pushed from the table and said his farewells. "Got to be getting home. My bitch is in heat and she'll welcome Vanberg's company."

Wayford rose with his friend to make certain Vanberg understood it was all right for him to go with Sam.

Bill Sallis called after them, "Let me know when your bitch whelps. If the price ain't too high, I'd be interested in one of the pups."

Outside Vanberg followed Sam to his truck and climbed in while Wayford watched, nagged by an uneasiness at loaning out the dog. Sam's offer was too good to pass by. Most men in the county had admired Vanberg and offered to buy him at one time or another. His pups would bring top dollar. Meanwhile, Vanberg would have no complaints about his scheduled evening activities.

"Now that you and ol' Sam have gone and cornered the market on dog breeding in Jeff Davis County, why don't you sit back down and say hello?" Martin Thon said when Wayford returned to the table to find his coffee and pie waiting.

"*Qué pasa?*" the rancher asked while he settled back to his chair.

Martin held out an extended hand with palm down and wiggled it from side to side. "*Así, así.*"

"Cut out the Mex lingo." This came from Henry Buckner, the final rancher at the table. "This is America, and it ain't no place for pepper-belly talk."

Wayford saw no trace of anger on Martin's face, nor had he ever in all the years he had known the Mexican to endure Henry's racial slurs. He assumed Martin, like the rest of the gathered friends, took Henry for what he was—an ill-mannered, ignorant bastard who did not have the sense God gave a pissant. Still, the comments about Martin's heritage Henry always slipped into the conversation made Wayford uncomfortable.

"Last time I looked on a map, Mexico was still part of the North American continent." Wayford took a sip from his cup, delighted by the taste of coffee that did not need sugar to make it go down the throat.

"Yeah, but it ain't part of the United States," Henry replied. "We talk American north of the border."

Wayford prepared to continue, but caught Martin shaking his head. The Mexican rancher silently mouthed the word *pendejo,* a Spanish pejorive that compared the size of a man's penis to a shriveled pubic hair.

Wayford let the matter drop. Martin was right; Henry was a *pendejo.* And he was too old to change his ways. However, had Wayford worn Henry's boots, he would be damned careful about where he opened his mouth. At least half the people living in the Bend were of Mexican descent, and the majority would not be as tolerant as Martin. It would not surprise Wayford to one day learn Henry had been found dead beside some out-of-the-way dirt road with a knife in his gut.

"You got any rain out your way?" Bill Norward said, looking at Wayford.

"Heavy dew and frost is about it," the rancher replied. Rainfall was a favorite topic in the Bend. Spring grass depended on it. "Haven't seen a cloud for nigh on a week."

"We picked up a sprinkle for about an hour last Tuesday," Martin added. "Didn't do much except keep the dust down for the rest of the day."

"I was watching one of those weathermen on cable last night," Bill said. "He was showin' some of them satellite pictures they take from up in space. He pointed out what he said was a big storm brewin' in the Pacific. From what he had to say, we could be in for some wet weather when it starts to move in. Not just rain, but maybe ice and snow. Somethin' to do with the storm runnin' into an Arctic cold front comin' down from the North Pole."

"Damn." Henry spat the curse with disgust. "Ain't it cold enough as it is without throwin' in ice and snow?"

Wayford worked through half the piece of pie and a cup of coffee while the table of cronies discussed the first of their standard topics, the weather. The rancher put little store in the predictions of weathermen. They never seemed to be able to put a finger on exactly what a man could expect from nature. Like meteorologists, ranchers studied and dissected the weather, and all to the same end. When it came to the bottom line, the old adage proved true; the weather was something everybody talked about, but could do nothing to change.

Stock ailments, feed prices, the current shape of the beef market, taxes, and bankers all fell into an unspoken agenda formalized over the years. The young waitress filled Wayford's cup a fourth time when family and acquaintances rolled around. This subject was divided into two subcategories. The first was sickness and injuries, wherein each man recounted the various aches, pains, and illnesses that had beset themselves, wives, and mutual friends during the preceding week.

The second part was the most relished. Snapshots were pulled from pockets and passed around the table while each man proudly recounted the latest achievements of his children and grandchildren. Wayford dutifully examined each of the overexposed photographs and politely voiced the obligatory praises whether the grandchild pictured was dressed for a piano recital or football game, or held forth his most recent scouting merit badge.

For all the pride each man felt for his sons and daughters and the children they had brought into the world to continue the bloodlines, Wayford always sensed a bittersweetness in these moments. Their families were not the families in which they had been raised. Except in cases like old Sam's, where a son took over the ranch, each man's family members spread across the state and country as they sought jobs to provide for their own families. The rancher often felt the families they proudly bragged on were not families at all, but relatives strewn from coast to coast. Offspring they might be, but it was damned hard to call such a family.

Holding a hand over his cup when the waitress brought the pot for another round, Wayford wished each man at the table well and bid them goodbye until next Saturday. Outside he snapped his fingers for Vanberg to heel. He jerked around, searching for the dog when the hound was not immediately at his side. Then he remembered Sam and his bitch and Vanberg's scheduled evening of romance.

The rancher climbed into his pickup, backed away from the drugstore, then U-turned northward on Highway 17. An hour later he had placed an order for feed, traded the young rooster for fifteen plastic sacks of frozen pinto beans, which sat in the back of the truck to keep cold, and bought a pound of coffee, a bag of flour, and three pounds of salt pork at Baeza's General Store. Rather than following his usual routine of stopping for a Mexican dinner, the lightness of the thirty dollars in his billfold and the skimpy balance of his checkbook kept him driving tonight. After all, he had already paid for the gas in his tank.

Proceeding through town, he passed the site of old Fort Davis and the rugged ridge of granite called the Sleeping Lion that ran behind it. Several tourist vans and cars sat in the parking lot of a reconstructed military fort from a bygone age while their owners listened to guides spiel out a thumbnail history of the black buffalo soldiers who had once manned the fort on the frontier of a growing young nation.

Before the ranchers, before the buffalo soldiers, before the Butterfield Stage running west to California, the site of the fort had been a camping ground of Apache and Comanche Indians. Game on the plains and in the mountains was plentiful—mule deer, pronghorn antelope, javelina, wild turkey, and rabbit. Limpia Creek, which meandered through the mountains, provided a source of clean, sweet water. The name "Limpia" meant exactly that.

Close to the old fort, Wayford's gaze ran up a dirt road that still marked part of the route taken by the Butterfield stagecoaches. Fourteen miles of that rocky and dusty road still existed, more than anywhere else in the country. South of town, at the base of Blue Mountain, a roadside park sat in the shadow of a towering, jagged chunk of granite called Pointed Rock. This had been the stage line's first westward stop on the route to El Paso.

Instead of making another U-turn at the edge of town and heading south to the Wide W, the rancher swung left onto 118, a narrow road that the Texas Highway Department proclaimed to be the highest thoroughfare in the state. To Wayford the road was the long way home. It intersected Highway 166 about twenty-five miles to the northwest and with 166 made a scenic loop around and through the mountains. He took the route at least a half-dozen times a year, when he needed time to think or just wanted to soak in the mountains' beauty. He was not sure of his reason this late afternoon, but the drive offered an undefined comfort.

He glanced at the elongated form of Scobee Mountain to his right. The rocky mount was named after the writer Barry Scobee, who some claimed was the first man to call this region the Big Bend. Scobee supposedly used the term in an article he had written for an

El Paso newspaper right after the turn of the century. The rancher could not verify the story; he was old, but not that old.

Wayford kept the speedometer needle at a steady forty to negotiate a series of sharp turns that followed the meandering bed of Limpia Creek. A trickle of water ran down the center of a wide swath of gray, water-rounded river rock, testimony to the season's lack of rain. When the spring storms arrived, Limpia would swell her banks and cascade with white water.

Moving past the entrance to the Davis Mountains State Park, the rancher wheeled through another series of snaking turns until the road straightened as it ran by the Prude Ranch. Several RVs and campers were parked beyond the ranch's fence. The Prude was what most people called a dude ranch. A constant stream of tourists made use of its facilities, which included a swimming pool, one of the few in the county. Besides the annual convening of amateur astronomers, bicyclists, backpackers, and motorcyclists used the ranch as a gathering point each year for their exploration of the mountains.

Wayford mentally checked off the names of the peaks and canyons he passed. He understood the lure that brought tourists back to these mountains year after year to discover some heretofore unseen splendor. As boys, he and his friends had explored every inch of the mountains on horseback and foot. A curse of adulthood was the lack of time to continue such pursuits. He missed that sense of adventure which surrounded those boyhood expeditions. Back in the mountains, away from the highways and roads, it had been easy to imagine he was the first man to ride into this country. War-painted Comanches waited behind each boulder ready to take his scalp should he stumble upon their secret gold mine.

A smile spread across his lips. Fifty-fifty would be the cut Jesus Batista and he had sworn when they finally found the cache of Spanish treasure they were certain was cleverly concealed in the mountains. They were wrong, of course. The history books told that. The closest Spanish explorers had come to the Davis Mountains was in the 1530s when a remnant of Cabeza de Vaca's party passed through the Fort Stockton area to the east on their way to the Rio Grande.

Wayford's head moved heavily from side to side. He had not thought of Jesus in years. The young Mexican had also been among those sent to Korea to stop the advancing tide of Chinese. When he came home, it had been in a sealed coffin. A direct mortar hit left little to be viewed during a funeral.

The road demanded Wayford's full attention as he began to wind up the side of Mount Locke. The rancher leaned forward and glanced up at the peak. The white domes of the observatory glared in the afternoon sun.

If funds were found, another telescope was planned for the mountain—the largest ever to be built in the world. He hoped it would be realized in his lifetime; it was something he'd like to see. The construction of the facility was still up in the air. The last time McDonald Observatory vied for a new major project, the funding had gone to some place in Hawaii.

To others, the white domes appeared incongruent, out of place, set atop a lofty peak once viewed by passengers in a stagecoach. Wayford did not agree. The observatory was but an extension of a long history of frontier life. McDonald with its giant telescopes and lasers that bounced off the moon opened man's newest frontier. There was no inconsistency, but a flowing from one age to another. It was appropriate that the Davis Mountains had been chosen for the observatory's site.

The west side of Mount Locke brought the intersection with Highway 166. Wayford stopped to let three tourist cars turn toward McDonald's visitor center, then steered home.

The western side of the mountains was as different as night and day compared to the eastern slopes. Vegetation, fed by more frequent rains, flourished. The mountainsides were covered with forests of stunted piñon pines and junipers. For those who knew where to look, there were even ponderosa pines for the viewing. The rancher imagined the cactus blooms and the bright swaths of Indian paintbrushes and bluebonnets that colored the mountainsides in spring.

Not far from there, highway engineers discovered a rock in the early 1940s. Carved on it was the name of Kit Carson and the date December 25, 1839. Wayford wondered what had driven the famous Indian scout to take out a blade and whittle his name into the rock. Was it simply to mark his passage, to tell future men that he had trod this land before them? Or was it the date that was significant? Had Carson felt the tug of loneliness being so far from the warmth of human companionship on Christmas Day?

Eventually, 166 gave way to rolling humpback hills and then the flatness of the plain. The rancher reached the dirt turnoff and moved toward the Wide W. At home, he returned to his bedroom and quickly changed back into work clothes, hanging khaki pants, white shirt, and corduroy coat carefully in the closet. As he moved through the house, he was struck by how immense and empty the rooms felt without Vanberg by his side. In turn that thought left him feeling old and foolish. A man should not depend so heavily on the company of a dog.

Work hat and fleece-lined coat collected in the kitchen, the rancher pulled on his boots and stepped outside. He still had to feed and water before the sun went down. After that, he would sleep and ready himself for another day of work.

SIX

CLINT WAYFORD'S RIGHT HAND tingled with the pressure
and warmth of the handshaking while he neatly arranged his Sun-
day-go-to-meeting suit on a wooden hanger, carefully pressed it
with a palm, and hung it in the closet. Usually he savored the sensation. Part of the ritual of going to church each Sunday was the
shaking of hands, and the exchange of pleasantries and well-wishing
with friends. Pastors had a word for it: "fellowship." It was a good
word and summed up the feelings awakened in a man who gathered
with friends to worship his God.

Today the residual feel of so many hands clasping and shaking his
left the rancher uncomfortable as he left the house and walked to
the barn to saddle Frank's Pal for an afternoon workout. The hon-
ing of his focus, the exclusion of the world from his thoughts as he
worked with the colt, failed him this Sunday. His mind kept turning
back like a slowly moving wheel to the preacher's sermon. The
adamant fury that had spewed from the pulpit refused to lessen its
strength as it echoed in his mind over and over.

That only increased the uneasiness while he stepped into the saddle and reined the colt out onto the open plain. Bootheels un-
adorned by spurs tapped the animal's sides. Frank's Pal came alive;
in an easy gallop he moved over the ground. The sound of hooves
striking the winter-hardened earth, the creak of saddle leather, and
the rush of the wind filled the rancher's ears in a song that swelled
to envelope him.

Wayford gave the colt his head, allowing the horse to pick his
own course. This afternoon there would be no calves to cut, no
repetition of drills to sharpen animal mind and movement. Exercise
was the only goal of the ride, to give Frank's Pal the opportunity to

stretch his legs and use the muscles with which God had endowed him.

God—the smooth rhythm of the colt broke to a rough bounce beneath Wayford. He jostled from side to side, balance lost.

The rancher caught the saddlehorn with his right hand and held tight. A second passed before he realized that it was himself and not the horse who had lost the rolling flow. Feeling like some young child attempting to keep his seat during his first time on horseback, he held tight to the horn while he trod the saddle until his body once again matched the cadenced strides of the colt.

Wayford sucked at his teeth in disgust; a saddlehorn was meant to anchor a rope, not a man. Time was when he would not have had to use it. His legs and back would have been strong enough to maintain his balance until his body readjusted to a horse's gait. Only a child used a saddlehorn to keep in the saddle.

Frank's Pal slowed to a trot and then to an easy jog before moving into a leisurely walk. Wayford glanced over a shoulder, estimating the horse had covered two miles, a good workout. He reined the horse about, letting the animal cool out himself during the walk back to the barn.

The preacher's sermon stirred anew while the rancher groomed the colt and began to brace the animal's legs with alcohol. Wayford had heard the radio preachers rant and rave on the subject, and seen front-page newspaper headlines emblazoned with the matter, but he had never listened to it while sitting in a pew. Maybe that was why it bothered him; it had invaded his own church.

He did not like what he had heard this morning; it went against the grain of all his Christian upbringing. The preacher had called for an all-out war against Satanic cults. He urged those gathered before him to take up figurative arms in the name of the Lord and wage a battle against those who worshiped the prince of darkness. "It is time for all men, women, and children to do as the hymn says," he cried out to the congregation, "and become Christian soldiers and go marching as to war!"

The young preacher, with all the zeal and fervor of a man six months out of seminary school, held up magazines, newspapers— some the tabloid variety usually found by grocery store checkout counters—and rock and roll album covers to illustrate how he saw Satan and his worshipers infiltrating every phase of today's society. He focused on the Matamoros mass killings of a few years back as proof that the Devil and his followers warred against those who believed in the Lamb.

"Time has come for Christians to recognize the peril that surrounds us," he demanded from the pulpit. "If it's war Satan wants, it's war he'll get. Today we declare war on Satan and his unholy minions!"

Wayford watched the heads in the congregation nod in approval and acceptance. Even now, hours after the service, he found it hard to believe what his eyes had seen. Fire had flashed across the faces of those he had known for years as the young preacher called them to arms. At that moment they appeared ready to do battle whenever and wherever.

The rancher shook his head as he wrapped Frank's Pal's right foreleg in cotton and bandage before pinning it with three safety pins. He did not doubt that there were crazy men and women in the world who killed people, some who believed they did so in the name of the Devil. All those bodies they had dug up in Mexico outside of Matamoros were proof enough of that. He was certain some folks saw themselves as witches. He had met more than one old Mexican fortune-teller who claimed to commune with spirits, both good and evil. What he did not believe was that armies of Satanic cults marched on Christian nations.

Something in the preacher's words rang hollow. It was like listening to a politician rallying voters around some nonexistent issue as a subterfuge to evade facing the real troubles of the country.

He tried to recall the last time he had heard a preacher speak on the Golden Rule and how one man was supposed to help another. No specific sermon came to mind while he moved to the colt's hind legs. He did remember a lot of hellfire, damnation, and brimstone. Sometimes it seemed like men in search of their God had enough religion to learn to hate that which appeared to go against their beliefs, but not enough to love the teachings by which they were supposed to live.

An all-out war against the Devil, he guessed, was easier to understand than turning the other cheek and loving those who sinned. It was not that Wayford doubted the Devil's existence. The Bible said he was real, and the rancher believed the Bible. However, he had never seen Satan, just bad men. And in the scope of things, he had met far more good men than bad.

He had just finished the colt's last leg when he put his finger on what had bothered him about the sermon. With so much suffering in the world—in this country alone—to him the church's efforts would be better directed relieving that suffering rather than warring against imagined armies of men transformed into demons.

The crunch of tire on rock and dirt pushed into his reflections. He leaned toward the stall door and listened. Someone was driving to the house. *Ol' Sam finally bringing Vanberg back.* He rose, brushed off the seat of his pants, and walked outside.

"I'll be!" His face broke out in an ear-to-ear grin of unbridled delight.

Not Sam Norwood and Vanberg, but his daughter, Mary, and her brood drove beside the ranch house. His son-in-law, Frank Senior, braked, shifted the maroon and white Ford van into park, and killed the engine. Mary waved to him from behind the expansive windshield, while Frank Junior and little Elizabeth shoved open a side door and bolted out in a dead run for the rancher, shouting, "Grandpa! Grandpa!"

Wayford squatted and threw open his arms. He enfolded the two children when they reached him, hugging them tightly and kissing the tops of their heads. They showered his cheeks with moist kisses in return.

"You two still have the sweetest sugar around." He hugged and kissed his grandchildren again, attempting to squeeze the love he felt into their small bodies. "The bigger you get, the more honey you put in your kisses."

"Seems like I remember you used to say that to someone else, Daddy."

"You've gotten big enough to get a touch of vinegar in you." Wayford stood and hugged his daughter to him. "God, but it's good to see you." He warmly kissed her. "I don't know why I'm getting this unexpected visit, but I'm not complaining." He kept an arm around his daughter's waist as he reached out and shook his son-in-law's hand. "Frank, you're lookin' fit as a town dog. Life must be treatin' you good."

"Better than to be expected." Frank answered. "That's one of the reasons we drove down today."

Wayford sensed his son-in-law wanted to say more, but a half-formed frown on Mary's brow cut him short. A tickling sensation worked up the rancher's spine. There was more to this visit than the desire to see him.

"Grandpa, will you take me riding like you did last summer?" Elizabeth tugged at a pant leg and smiled up at her grandfather. A missing front tooth tripled the charm of that smile.

"I'll saddle up a horse for you and me and we'll ride all the way to sundown and into the night if you want, little lady." He ruffed the soft, silky strands of her hair, then looked at Frank Junior. "And I've got a bay filly that's just waiting for a boy like you to ride her. That is, if you want to go for a ride?"

Frank's smile grew as wide as the one Elizabeth wore. "Why are we standing here wasting time?" He repeated the words he had heard his grandfather say a thousand times.

Wayford chuckled. "Well, young man, just give me a—"

"I thought you two were talking about catching lizards on the way down," Mary interrupted. "Why don't you run along and do that, or play in the loft awhile? Let me and your grandpa have a chance to say hello."

The rancher detected a hint of distress on his daughter's face and in her voice.

"But Momma," Elizabeth started, and Frank finished, "who wants to hunt lizards when Grandpa said we could go riding with him?"

"Don't give your mother a rough time"—this from Frank Senior. "Go and do like she said. If there's time, we'll talk about horseback riding later."

Both children looked to their grandfather. Wayford shrugged. "Guess we're outvoted for the time being. I got a fresh load of straw in the loft. You're welcome to play in it until we get done with the grown-up talk. Think you can handle that?"

The boy and girl nodded, then turned on their heels and darted toward the open barn.

The rancher gave his daughter's waist another squeeze. "Why don't you two come on in the house? I'll put on a fresh pot of coffee. It'll help take the chill off the day."

"Coffee sounds good," Frank said with a tilt of his head. "It's a long way down from Lubbock, and there's not a lot open along the way, except for some Dairy Queens."

"Nothing wrong with a Dairy Queen. They still make a good hamburger," the rancher said as he escorted his daughter and son-in-law into the house. The Dairy Queen was the national restaurant of Texas. Any town in the state big enough to claim to be a real town had one, even in the era of Ronald McDonald.

After exchanging boots for house slippers, Wayford took the coffeepot from the stove, emptied out the stale brew and grounds, then filled it with fresh water and coffee. He placed it back atop the stove and began to take down clean mugs from the cabinet.

"Daddy, what is that?"

He glanced over a shoulder to find Mary pointing at the stove. "It's what it looks like—a stove."

"That's not the stove that was in this kitchen last summer." Her eyes narrowed as her head turned to her father. "That's the old wood burner that used to live up in the loft. You said it belonged to Grandma and Grandpa Wayford."

The rancher nodded. "It does the job for me just as good as it did for them."

Mary's mouth drew into a tight line. Her expression reminded Wayford of the look Lizzie used to give him whenever he did something to anger her.

"What about the butane stove? Did it break down on you?" his daughter pressed.

Wayford shook his head while he placed the mugs on the table. "Didn't see much need for butane when I had this, and it works. With me here alone, it's all I need."

Mary rubbed at her arms. "I thought it seemed chilly in here. You're using this stove to heat the house, too, aren't you?"

"Spend most of my time here in the kitchen. There's quilts to pile on the bed when I sleep and plenty of hot water for bathin'," Wayford answered. "I don't use the other rooms that much, so there's no need for heatin' them."

"Frank, he's stopped the butane." Mary sank into a chair and rested her elbows on the table.

"The phone's dead." Frank placed the wall phone's receiver back into its cradle. "It's been turned off."

"Of course, it's been turned off." Wayford's spine went straight. "I had it turned off last month. I wrote you about it. Seemed like a waste. I've got nobody to call, and nobody's got want to call me."

The rancher watched his daughter's head move wearily from side to side without her eyes leaving him.

"You didn't mention the phone in your letters," Mary said. "And what to you mean '*nobody*'? Is that what I am—*nobody*?"

"I know I wrote you about—"

"Nobody!" she cut off his reply. "Daddy, we're the only family you have. Don't you realize that? Don't you know that we love you? Care about you?"

Wayford tried again to waylay his daughter's worries. "Mary, there's no reason for this fuss. Everything is—"

"Fuss!" Her voice jumped two octaves. "We got up and left Lubbock at three this morning to drive here, because last night I tried to call and the phone wasn't working . . ."

"I know I wrote you about having the phone cut off," the rancher said.

Mary did not hear him, or chose not to hear him. ". . . I was worried sick that something had happened to you, that you had an accident or a heart attack and were lying dead out in the barn or here on the kitchen floor."

With patience, Wayford tried again. "Mary, as you can see, I'm fit as a fiddle. If something had happened to me, you know Paul Moody would have gotten—"

"Neither Frank nor I slept a wink last night, we were worrying so about you. It's not right the way you've treated us. You can't cut yourself off from your family. You—"

"Mary, hush!" He employed a stern parental tone in his voice that he had not used since his daughter was in her teens. "Hush, take a deep breath, and listen for a minute."

The rancher pulled a chair beside her and reached out to gently enclose one of her hands in his. "Mary, I'm not dead on the floor, sick in the hospital, or stoved up in some canyon after an accident. You've let your mind run wild and worked yourself into a tizzy. I'm sorry you went and worried yourself over me, but it's not my doing. I know I wrote you and Frank about having the phone disconnected."

"I got your letters," Mary answered with accusation glaring in her dark eyes. "You never mentioned the phone being turned off. Or the butane. Why were you trying to hide them from me?"

Wayford sucked down a breath and gradually released it. Mary made this difficult. He had not seen her so fit to be tied since he had grounded her a month for staying out late with Howie Bass her junior year in high school.

"If I did forget, and I ain't sayin' I did, it wasn't because I was trying to hide something. It's because the phone and the stove just ain't that important to me. I can't even say it's an inconvenience not having them." His voice grew softer as he attempted to quell her concern the way he had once soothed away the pain when she skinned a knee.

"Daddy, you didn't turn off the phone and start using that old museum piece of a stove because you wanted to." She calmed, but the undercurrent of accusation ran in her tone. "You've got money problems. And they have to be bad for you to start turning off your utilities. Are you going to turn off the electricity next and start burning candles for light?"

Wayford leaned back in the chair and studied his daughter for a few moments. When he'd seen the van pulling up, this had been the farthest thing from his mind. Now he saw there was no way of getting around it.

"Mary, Frank, I've never tried to keep it from you that these aren't the best of times for me." He waved his son-in-law to the table. "You know Lizzie's medical bills took about everything we had."

"We offered to help with that, Clint," Frank said as he settled beside his wife. "We knew how hard Elizabeth's death hit you."

Wayford could only hope neither Frank nor Mary ever discovered the pain of losing the other. The hard had nothing to do with medical bills.

"I know. I thank you for the offer," the rancher said. "But the bills were my concern. You and Mary have two concerns of your own playing out there in the hayloft. You take care of them. That's the way it's supposed to be."

Frank pursed his lips and nodded as though he understood what Wayford had said.

Mary was another matter. "But the phone and the stove, Daddy."

Wayford squeezed his daughter's hand and smiled. "Your momma and me saw some pretty hard times when we were first trying to make a go of it. About the time you came into this world, we had to have the telephone company cut off the phone so we could make ends meet. That's all I'm doing now."

He tilted his head to the wood-burning monster across the room. "As for the stove, it served my grandma and grandpa well, and it's doing the same for me. It cooks my food and keeps the house warm enough. Hell, I haven't had a sniffle all winter. You can't ask for better than that."

He noticed the column of steam that poured from the coffeepot's spout. He rose and walked to the stove, used a dish cloth to lift the hot pot, and filled the waiting mugs.

"The one thing that ol' stove can't do is make my cookin' better." He smiled while he sank back to the chair. "Milk's in the icebox, if you need something to cut the taste."

Neither Frank nor Mary spoke while they sipped at the hot brew. Frank got the milk and added a dollop to their mugs, as well as a teaspoon of sugar from the bowl at the center of the table.

"Daddy," Mary finally said, "I want you to sit there and listen to me without trying to break in until I've had my say."

Wayford did not like the sudden somberness of her tone, but he nodded. "I'm listening."

Mary glanced at her husband, whose expression signaled her to continue. "Frank and I have been talking about something for about a year now. This morning as we drove down, we decided it was time to stop talking and let you know what we think." She paused for a deep breath and abruptly said, "We want you to come and live with us in Lubbock."

"What?" Wayford sat straight, his mind reeling. "You want what?"

"You said you would listen to me," Mary demanded as though she had carefully prepared a presentation that could not tolerate interruption. "That's what we want, and we think it's time for you to listen to us."

"Mary, you're talkin' silly." Wayford found it difficult to believe that he heard his daughter correctly. "I can't up and go to live in Lubbock. I've got the ranch."

Mary released her husband's hand and laid a palm across her father's forearm. "Daddy, now it's your turn to hush and listen. Be honest with yourself. There isn't anything left for you here. This ranch hasn't been anything but a millstone around your neck since Momma died. You're about to go down for the third time, and you're too blind to see it."

The rancher eased his arm away from her fingers. This was his daughter speaking; yet she could not be saying the words he heard. Didn't she know what the Wide W meant, had meant to generation after generation of Wayfords?

"Daddy, don't go and close off your mind," Mary pleaded. "Listen to what I have to say. It'll make sense, if you'll listen. You'll see this is the right thing to do."

The rancher gazed across the room, staring at the wall, but seeing nothing. He listened, unable to accept that his own daughter could even suggest what she proposed.

"Frank's got a surprise, Daddy," Mary continued. "Listen to what he's got to say."

Frank cleared his throat. "This has taken six months to come about, but Saturday they made it official. It's the reason Mary tried to call last night. She wanted to share the good news with you."

The wall did not dissolve and offer Wayford an easy exit from the room no matter how hard he stared at it.

"I'm no longer working for TI," Frank said. "I'm the manager of Matsumoki-Lubbock. They've just opened a new facility for research and development on the Levelland Highway. They intend to produce a new generation computer that will cut into the Cray market. This is a major opportunity for me, Clint. It means a relatively secure future. But immediately, it means twenty thousand dollars more a year."

Wayford wished himself elsewhere. It was Sunday, a day of rest. A man did not need his own family plaguing his mind with matters they should have more sense than to bring up in the first place. He strained to hear Frank's and Elizabeth's laughter as they romped in the barn's hay. His imagination failed him.

"Daddy, there will be no money problems if you move in with us." Mary's voice brought Wayford back to the situation at hand. "We're your family, Daddy. You took care of me. Now, it's my turn to—"

"Take care of me?" The rancher barely held his mounting anger in check. "Young lady, I don't need anyone to take care of me. I've managed to do that since I was old enough to climb atop a horse, thank you very much!"

Mary sighed and gazed at her father. Wayford saw the love and concern in her eyes. Couldn't she see the hurt in his?

"This place hasn't made a dime since Momma died, and you know that, Daddy." She refused to let the matter drop. "Maybe if you were just old enough to get on a horse, you might have a chance of making the Wide W work, but you're not that young anymore. Daddy, you're sixty-five years old. Most men these days retire at sixty-five."

"I'm not most men. I'm Clinton Wayford," he replied with a disgusted snort.

"You've got two grandchildren who are going to be grown with families of their own before you know it. And you'll never have gotten to know them."

The rancher winced inwardly. His daughter had found the vulnerable spot and struck below the belt. Spending time with his grandchildren, watching them grow, was something he wanted with all his heart and soul.

Frank cleared his throat again. "If you think living with us would be too much like charity, it won't be. We'll invest what you get for selling this place, or put it in the bank. You'll have money of your own. We just want you to move in with us so we'll be there to care for you."

"Listen to Frank, Daddy," Mary picked up when her husband stopped. "We're your family. We want what's best for you. We love you."

"You love me so damn much you want to kill me." They had the chance to say their piece. Now it was his turn. "Why don't you go in there and get my old forty-five out of the bedroom stand, put it up to the side of my head, and pull the trigger? That would be a mite kinder than what you want."

Mary shook her head in exasperation. "Daddy, you're exaggerating. Nobody's talking about killing you."

"You're not? What the hell do you think taking me away from this ranch would be? I'll tell what it would be—a poison and none too slow a poison either. Each day I would grow a little weaker until I dropped and died. Then you wouldn't have to worry about me anymore. I'd be neatly put away in the ground."

"You didn't listen to a word we said," Mary protested.

Wayford pointed a finger at his daughter. "I heard every sound you uttered. What's wrong here is that you and Frank are blind. Baby, this ranch is my life. Working it is the only thing that kept me going after Lizzie died. Keeping it going is all I have now. Take it away and you take away the only life I've ever known. This is where I was born and raised. This is where your mother and I managed to raise a family of our own. And it's here I plan to stay until the day the good Lord calls me to join Lizzie. There's nothing left to say on the subject."

"Stubborn." Mary's lips drew into a tight thin line again. "You're just being stubborn."

The rancher shoved from the table. "I said there's nothing left to discuss. We've talked it out, and I've settled it."

"Nothing's settled," Mary went on like a dog chewing an old bone. "There's more we need to talk about."

"Not with me there's not," Wayford answered curtly. "I've listened to all the foolishness I'm going to listen to. Now, I'm going to take my coffee into the living room yonder and sit myself in an easy chair. If you and Frank would like to join me and talk about something else, then I'll be happy for the company. If not, then you're wasting my time and yours."

Without waiting for a reply, he did exactly as he said. He walked from the kitchen, down the narrow hall, and into the living room. There he settled into a reclining lounger. The coffee he sipped seemed twice as bitter as usual. He had forgotten the sugar.

"It's not over. I don't care what he says, Frank." He heard Mary talking with her husband. "This ranch will kill him. We have to convince him to come live with us."

You'll have an easier time teaching pigs to fly, he thought. How could she have thought he would yank up the stakes of a lifetime and go traipsing off to Lubbock!

"Mary, Clint's a good man." Frank's voice floated in from the kitchen. "But he can be stubborn as an old jackass. We aren't going to accomplish anything here today. Let it be for now. We'll talk with him later. Things will get worse. He'll listen to reason then."

Jackass, Wayford snorted into the coffeecup. What in hell did Frank know about a jackass? He was Dallas bred and raised. He'd never seen a jackass in his life until Mary brought him home to meet her parents.

The rancher turned off Mary and Frank and their whispered voices. Lubbock? No man in his right mind would pick Lubbock to live in, not if he had a choice. The winters were twice as cold there, and the flat land made the plains of the Bend look like a roller coaster. Lubbock? He snorted again.

And Matsumoki-Lubbock? Wayford had held his tongue when Frank mentioned his new employer. The rancher's father had fought and helped win a war against Japan. He would turn over in his grave if he knew his granddaughter's husband was working for a Japanese company.

Wayford tried to keep an open mind about Japanese interests in this country. However, he could not shake the feeling that Japan's government attempted to conquer in the economic arena a nation it could not bring to its knees with guns and bombs. He had read about the ranches Japanese companies bought in the Western states; they wanted to raise their own beef to circumvent paying the high price of beef imported from the United States. Tariffs were jacked up artificially high by a Japanese government that sought to block foreign products from reaching their country's markets.

Automobile trade with Japan made headlines, but the same thing was happening—had happened for years—with agricultural products. And agriculture remained America's largest business. That fact appeared destined to be overlooked by the news media until there was no food for American tables.

The start of an engine drew him from his thoughts. He cocked his head. It was the van. He discerned his grandchildren's voices over the rumble of the motor, but could not make out what they said.

He gripped the arms of the chair to stand, then sank deeply back into the cushions. Stubborn, he might be, but he was also right. It was Mary's place to send the children in to say their goodbyes. She should—

The van's engine gunned for an instant then dropped to a steady purr. Rubber crunched over rock and dirt as he listened to the van back up, turn, and pull away. A minute passed and the engine's sound was but a memory.

Wayford closed his eyes, shutting out the sudden vast immensity of the empty ranch house. His mind skirted back and forth to avoid the welling sensation of abandonment that ached in his chest—and failed. In her own way, he was certain that Mary meant to do right. Yet, he felt betrayed by his only living flesh and blood.

Did his own daughter know so little of her father? Did she really believe he would walk away from all that was his, from his life?

He did not like the answers that wedged into his mind. The ranch had never held Mary. It was merely a place to come for a visit. Her life lay north in Lubbock, mingled with the computer industry.

Still, she should know him better than she did. This land was more than a spread to which he had given his life; it was a legacy handed down to him by generations of Wayfords. Once he had hoped to pass that legacy to a son; now he held it in trust for his grandchildren.

He leaned his head back to ease the tension cording his neck. Maybe he nursed an old man's delusion. What did young Frank and little Elizabeth know of ranch life? Urbanized Lubbock, except for their visits with their grandfather, was what they knew. If they ever did get out into the countryside, what they saw was farms growing cotton and sorghum, not cattle and horses.

He held close to the dream of passing the ranch into his grandchildren's hands; after all, both Frank and Elizabeth were just children. Time might draw one of them, perhaps both, close to this land.

Opening his eyes, he stared about him. Through the windows, he saw the long shadows of late afternoon. Pushing from the chair, the rancher walked back into the kitchen. Self-pity did not get the chores done. It would be well after dark before he finished the day's work.

Hat and coat taken from where they hung on the wall, he pulled on his boots outside. He stopped abruptly after three strides. A young Mexican, short for his eighteen years, stood in the open barn door.

"*Señor* Clint," Miguel Ramos greeted the rancher.

Wayford eased back the brim of his hat, stared at the boy, and finally shook his head. "Son, you're the last person in the world I ever expected to see again."

"I did not know where else to go," the young man said. "I could not find work." Miguel's gaze rolled to the ground with shame. "Or even a ride north."

"I told you before that this was the wrong place to come looking for work." Wayford guessed at what churned in the Mexican's mind. "I ain't got a thin dime to spare."

The young man nervously licked at his lips. "But you need someone strong and willing to work."

A humorless chuckle pushed from Wayford's throat. "I ain't denying that. But the straight of the matter is that I'm broke, son. I ain't got spit to pay. There's no job for you here."

"You have this barn for me to sleep in." Miguel waved an arm to the open structure. "And you have food. I would work for that until I find a job."

The mention of food caught the rancher's attention. He realized why the Mexican returned. Miguel had not eaten since he'd left the Wide W two days ago. Wayford rubbed a hand over his chin. The idea skirting the edge of his thoughts had trouble written all over it, if Immigration got wind of his keeping the boy. The federal boys would accuse him of exploiting a poor downtrodden illegal alien since he paid the boy no wages. Hell, if the newspapers ever found out, they would probably tag it slavery.

On the other hand, he could not run the Mexican off. It was obvious the boy had no idea what he was doing in this country. In five days, the only food his stomach had known had come from Wayford's table. Left to his own means, Miguel Ramos was likely to starve to death or get himself shot while trying to steal some food from a grocery store. That was if he did not freeze to death first sleeping out in the open.

"All right," Wayford finally acquiesced, against all common sense. "You can stay. I'll give you a place to sleep and three squares a day until you can find a job or a way to get yourself north—or decide to head back home. But get this straight in your mind, you *don't* work for me. I ain't goin' to complain if you want to help out with the chores, but I'm not hirin' you on as a hand. You understand that?"

Miguel tilted his head and smiled with relief. "I understand."

"Good," Wayford said. "And there's something else. The immigration boys drive dark green cars and pickups. You see one of them coming up the road, then you make yourself scarce. I don't give a damn where you hide, just make sure you hide good enough that you can't be found. I can't afford trouble, let alone a fine for having a wetback on my place. Got that straight?"

"Got it." Miguel gave another nod.

"Then you can find yourself a pot of beans and some corn bread in the icebox in the house. Heat 'em up and eat your fill. I've got work to get to." Wayford pointed the boy toward the house. "Go on get yourself something to eat."

As Miguel followed directions and hastened to the kitchen door, the rancher called after him. "Miguel, remember this ain't no job, and you don't work for me."

"I know, *Señor* Clint," the boy answered as he opened the door. "I know."

The rancher shook his head and turned back to the barn. It was not enough to be perched on the edge of being penniless or having his daughter trying to drag him off to Lubbock like some senile old bastard; he had to go and get himself involved with this kid. *Looks like you've the makings of even a bigger fool than you thought you were,* he chided himself.

SEVEN

THE BUCK stood across the highway from the mailbox. His head lifted when the pickup approached, but he did not turn toward the vehicle or twitch his ears. It was as though the deer was oblivious to the world around him.

Wayford pulled beside the mailbox and killed the engine. He quietly opened the door and stepped to the ground. From behind the seat, he edged a rifle kept there for just such an opportunity. Vanberg sat motionless in the cab, his brown eyes trained on the buck in anticipation.

The distant rumble of approaching cars drew the rancher's gaze to the south. At least three vehicles trundled toward him. In all likelihood more tourists driving up from Big Bend National Park, Wayford thought. He cursed under his breath and held himself in check. He would have to risk the cars scaring off the mule deer. Although he could get off a quick clean shot, he did not want some gray-haired woman from somewhere in Ohio or New York complaining to the law about a crazy old man taking potshots at passing cars.

He found himself silently counting the seconds in a one-Mississippi-two-Mississippi cadence while he waited. Two hundred forty Mississippi slipped by as the final blue and white van rushed by him. A woman on the passenger side, gray hair tied in a bun atop her hair, waved when the vehicle passed. Wayford tipped his hat, then turned his attention to more important matters—that of tonight's supper.

Though it defied reason, the buck remained exactly where he had stood when the rancher sighted him.

With a hasty glance up and down the highway to make certain it was empty, Wayford eased toward the pickup's fender and hiked the rifle snugly to his right shoulder. He took a bead on the deer, curled a trigger around the trigger, and squeezed.

The deer never heard the rifle's crack before the slug tore into a spot behind his left shoulder, driving straight to the heart. The animal dropped to the ground, dead.

Wayford slid the weapon behind the seat and restarted the pickup. Three minutes later he had the animal's carcass loaded and the tailgate closed. He said a silent prayer of thank you for deer season. Venison kept the freezer stocked. With a brief stop at the mailbox, he turned back toward the ranch house.

An hour later, with Miguel's help, the buck hung cleaned and dressed from a mesquite tree at the side of the house. While the two admired their handiwork, Vanberg feasted on the pile of entrails cast to the side.

"We'll let it hang for another hour to make certain all the blood drains," Wayford announced. "Then we'll go about the butchering and get the meat in the freezer."

"Tonight, we'll eat like kings!" Miguel grinned and winked at the older man.

"Maybe not like kings, but we'll eat, and that's what's important." Wayford opened and closed his hands. Blood crusted on them, leaving his fingers stiff. "We'd better clean ourselves up. We both look like we got the short end of a fight in a Fort Worth honky-tonk."

"I'll get the hose in the barn," Miguel suggested.

"There's warm water in the house," the rancher answered. "It's too cold to be washing in water straight from the well."

The Mexican's head turned to the ranch house. Uncertainty clouded his cinnamon-hued face.

"It's all right," Wayford assured him. "I ain't some Mexican *patrón,* just an old rancher with deer blood and guts up to his elbows that needs washin' off. From the looks of it, you're in the same shape."

Miguel examined himself and grinned again. "It appears that way to me, *Señor* Clint."

"Then let's wash it off." He waved the Mexican youth toward the house and began walking toward the kitchen door.

Miguel froze at the sound of the approaching vehicle. His dark eyes went round as saucers.

Wayford released the gelding's ankle and slipped the foot pick into a back pocket. "Put him back in the stall, and I'll see who's coming."

While the boy led the chestnut gelding toward a fresh stall at the end of the barn, the rancher stepped to the front of the structure with the fingers of his left hand massaging his lower back. Outside he saw a familiar red pickup barreling up the dirt road with a cloud of dust billowing behind it.

"It's all right, Miguel. It's only Paul Moody come to visit. Probably wants to check on how I'm treating these geldings of his." Wayford turned back when the boy did not answer.

The chestnut stood in his stall and Miguel was nowhere to be found. The rancher shrugged. The boy was taking no chances. He had found himself a place to hide and stayed out of sight. Wayford could not blame him for being cautious. In fact, he preferred it that way.

His attention returned to the approaching pickup. For the lifetime they had known each other and called one another friends, Paul Moody had driven a red pickup. It was always the latest model with the biggest engine and longest bed available. And it was always a GMC.

On at least a million or five occasions, Paul had ribbed Wayford for his devotion to Fords, saying that Ford was short for "Found on the Road Dead." The rancher always countered with the fact that Paul found it necessary to purchase a new truck every year, while his own Fords lasted well beyond a hundred thousand hard-driven miles.

Dirt and stone flew from behind the red pickup as Paul Moody swerved around the ranch house and slammed on his brakes to bring the truck to a skidding halt ten feet from Wayford. Like the color and make of his pickup, Paul's driving habits had not changed since the first day he had climbed behind a wheel. A car or a truck had one gear—high—and the gas pedal but one position—pressed flat to the floor.

The door on the driver's side flew open and a man in pressed gray slacks with boots, coat, and hat to match stepped out of the dust cloud. "Hell, you look healthy enough to me!"

Wayford's brow furrowed. "I didn't know I was supposed to be otherwise."

"After listening to that daughter of yours yesterday, I was expecting to find you riding a wheelchair with hoses up your nose and tubes jabbed in your arm." Paul dusted off his coat with one hand and then the other. The action was futile; more dust from the cloud settled to his clothing before he rid himself of the first layer.

"Mary stopped by your place?" Wayford felt the heat of embarrassed red flush his cheeks. Mercifully, the dust kept Paul's eyes blinking and hid Clint's discomfort.

"Yeah, the way she went on, I thought you were standing with one foot in the grave, and the other in a slippery pile of goose shit. But from what I can see, you're still your mud-ugly self. Can't for the life of me figure out why I wasted my time drivin' all the way over here to check on you."

Wayford's embarrassment transformed to the steam of anger. Mary had overstepped the boundaries of common decency by a mile or two. The next time the rancher saw his daughter, she was assured of the worst dressing-down she had received since the time he caught her and Tommy Ray Janson about to go skinny-dipping in the west tank.

A choked cough came from the passenger side of the pickup's cab as the door swung open and the lanky form of Bryan Owens unfolded. Bryan, looking more like a down-on-his-luck ranch hand in tattered coat, faded blue jeans, and weather-beaten hat than one of the more prosperous ranchers in the area, batted a gloved hand back and forth in front of his face to clear the dust.

"Don't listen to the bull Paul's spreadin', Clint." Bryan hacked on the dust a couple more times before continuing, "He's been frettin' about those horses of his for the last thirty-five miles. You could be laid out in a mortuary amid a bed of petunias for all he cared—as long as his horses were fine."

Wayford took Bryan's hand and shook it. "Since you boys took all the time to drive out this way, you could've brought some warmer weather with you."

Bryan grinned. "Hell, I heard it was balmy as South Padre Island over here. That you've had enough rain to open one of them water parks and had sweet young things runnin' around in skimpy bikinis all over the place."

Paul snorted while he stepped toward the pickup's bed. "Lot a good it would do him. It's been so long since he's laid eyes on a half-naked girl, he's forgotten what to do with one. That is even if his equipment still worked."

Usually Wayford would have countered with the properly derogatory comment about his old friend's flagging sexual prowess. Mary's audacity to burden Paul with her imagined worries ate at him. His daughter appeared determined to suddenly reverse their parent-child roles. Apparently all he had said yesterday ran off her like water on a duck's back.

"The reason we drove over was to bring you these." Paul lifted the cleaned skulls of a ram and a steer, complete with horns, from the pickup. "Thought they might do you some good up in Canton."

Bryan nudged Wayford in the ribs. "And to eye his horses."

Wayford took the two skulls. "I thank you. They look in good shape. Bound to catch somebody's eye." He placed the skulls on the ground, leaning them against the barn. "Paul, your geldings are toward the back, if you want to go in and take a look."

"The thought never crossed my mind." Paul winked at his companions and double-timed it into the barn.

Bryan eyed the skulls. "You can thank a cougar for those. Damned cat's been comin' out of the mountains at night for the past two months and hittin' my stock."

Wayford pursed his lips and nodded. "The cats are breedin' again. Their numbers are growing each year. The park rangers down in Big Bend have been puttin' out lion warnings for three years now to keep the tourists out of trouble."

"Yeah, I read in an Austin paper the other day that the Sierra Club is considering asking the legislature for a season on cougars. You know the situation's got to be gettin' bad for that group to take notice and suggest a mountain lion hunting season." Bryan pulled a half-crumpled pack of Lucky Strikes from a coat pocket and lit one with a match.

While Wayford took out a bag of fixings and rolled his own, Bryan puffed on his smoke for several seconds before saying, "My granddaddy and pa used to hunt wolves here about. Hunted so good my grandkids have never set eye on a wolf 'cept in a zoo. I don't want to see that happen to the mountain lions. This was their land long before a rancher ever stepped foot on it."

Bryan took a final drag from the half-smoked cigarette, flipped it to the ground, and crushed it underfoot. "Hell, I don't mind losin' a few steers or goats to the cats. Always felt like that was the way I sort of paid rent to Mother Nature. But this son-of-a-bitch has gotten greedy. Last night he took a filly foaled three days ago."

"You're going after him?" Wayford lit his cigarette and inhaled. He knew the answer to the question, and why Bryan visited the Wide W.

Bryan nodded. "Reckon I can't wait for the legislature to pass a season and make it legal, not with this one. The cat's costin' me too much. I've asked Paul, Tom Voss, and Warren Alexander to come over to my place in the morning. I'd like you and your dog to be there, if you can make it."

"Vanberg and I'll be there," Wayford answered without hesitation. The rancher trusted Bryan's judgment as to whether a mountain lion was a danger more than he would ever trust the state legislature or the Sierra Club. "Should I bring a horse and saddle?"

Bryan shook his head. "I'll have mounts for everyone. No need for everybody hauling a trailer over to my place. I've got a rifle, if you need one."

"I'll bring my own," Wayford replied. "And a pistol."

"Thanks. I appreciate it, Clint."

"I'd expect the same from you."

"And I reckon you'd get it." Bryan grinned as he dug another cigarette from his pocket and lit it. "Don't look like you've been gettin' a lot of rain out this way."

"Dew and frost is about all the moisture I've seen for a month now." Wayford felt Bryan opening the way for a question his friend asked each time they met.

"Don't reckon you've changed your mind about sellin' out to me?" Bryan blew a thin stream of smoke into the air. "From what Paul was sayin' on the way over, your daughter's got it in her mind that you should move up to Lubbock and live with her and her family."

"My daughter's apt to get a lot of strange notions in her mind from the looks of it." *Damn Mary! She has no right to go meddlin' in affairs that are none of her business!* Wayford felt the steam rising again.

Bryan studied his friend for a moment and smiled. "Don't let her get under your skin, Clint. All children, at least them that gives a damn, get strange notions about their parents soon as they're old enough to fill their breeches. Ken, my oldest, has been tryin' to get me to move down to Houston ever since he started readin' about how bad the cattle market is. Crap, the ranch still brings in five times what he makes as a college chemistry teacher."

"I always thought Kenny got all the brains in your family." Wayford chuckled.

"So did his momma and me." Bryan laughed. "I guess I'd rather have him worryin' about me than bein' like Tom Voss's son Michael. Tom ain't heard a word from Mike since he up and ran off to join the Army five years back. Tom's frettin' Mike might have got himself killed over in Desert Storm."

Wayford did not mention that no matter how the government ignored the needs of people, it always found time to tell a man that his son had been killed while in the service. The rancher knew that fact too well.

"But it ain't Mary that got me askin' about your spread," Bryan went on. "I'm not out to run off a good friend. I'm just proposin' a way we can both make some money off this stretch of bone-dry land."

Since Wayford had sold Bryan those two sections to help pay Lizzie's medical bills, the man had been like a hound on a fresh scent. Friend or not, he wanted the Wide W's two remaining sections.

"I got a new twist today, something that occurred to me while I was riding over with Paul," Bryan said. "Let me buy you out, but you stay on and ramrod this land and four more sections for me. I'll even let you run the cattle of your own you've got now. No need for you to move. You'll stay right here in your own home. I could use a man that knows horses like you do. I've been thinkin' about pickin' up some racing stock—quarter horses, not thoroughbreds."

Wayford took the last puff from his cigarette before he dropped it to the dirt and ground it beneath the heel of his boot. "I'm not in the mind to sell today, Bryan. Nor can I see a day in the near future that I'm likely to change my mind. Times aren't all that good, but I've seen worse. If it gets to the point I can't handle the Wide W, I'd come to you before talkin' with the corporations that seem set on buyin' up this country."

Bryan nodded. "Reckon that's what I expected to hear."

"On the other hand, if you've got a mind to start a string of race horses, I know just the man who can saddle-break 'em for you. And my price is reasonable." Wayford's tone was light and joking, but his proposal was dead serious. He needed more horses to break; he could spend the money they would bring in ten times over.

"I might do that," Bryan replied, then amended, "if I decided to pick up those horses."

"Horses? If you want to see horses, you ought to take a gander at those five geldings of mine in there." Paul Moody came striding from the barn. "Especially that chestnut. Only thing would make him look better is to have a silver-inlaid saddle sitting on his back."

Wayford winced inwardly. In their long years of friendship, Paul and he had never competed—except for one spring night during their senior year in high school. Actually, the rancher admitted to himself, it was the only night he had felt the competition. In truth he and Paul had gone head-to-head in roping events at local rodeos throughout their high school days. Paul, while handy with a rope, never had the speed needed to take the prizes.

That was until that spring night. The prize, rather than money, was a brand new saddle all the way from Fort Worth. Shining silver rimmed the horn and seat of that sleek black leather throne. Although Paul and he had seen fancier saddles, they had never considered owning one with even a touch of silver. Both openly admitted the saddle was a worthier prize than any amount of money that might have been offered.

Maybe it was visions of sitting astride that saddle that set Wayford's mind wandering as his calf broke from the chute that warm spring night. Not that it mattered to anyone after all these years later, except for Paul and himself, but he missed his mark. His loop flew over the calf's head and landed uselessly in the dirt. In spite of absolutely no chance of winning the event, he drew another loop, caught, and tied the calf.

Paul, however, performed the best in his life. He left the crowds in the stand on their feet whistling and cheering. Paul, not Wayford, walked away with the black saddle and its shining silver, a fact Paul had never let his lifelong friend forget. Paul managed to mention the saddle whenever the opportunity presented itself, and when an opportunity did not present itself, he could divert the course of a conversation and seed an opportunity.

"Hell, I've heard so much about these horses, I'd better go in an' take a look at 'em myself." Bryan turned toward the barn.

Paul looked at his friend. "When will you put a saddle on them?"

"Couple of days," Wayford replied. "They're accepting the blankets without much fuss, except that little bay. He'd like to put a hoof through my chest if I gave him the chance."

"Means you'll be ridin' 'em by the end of next week. I'll drop by then."

Wayford hiked an eyebrow. "To check on the horses . . . or me?"

"Kill two birds with one stone," Paul answered.

"Don't you go and let Mary get to you," Wayford warned. "I ain't as old as I look."

"You're older, Clint. Remember, you've only got a month on me when it comes to age. It wouldn't hurt for me to drop by more often. After all, you're out here by yourself now. A man too much on his own is liable to go wild."

Wayford jerked a thumb toward the feed room. "I keep a double-barreled shotgun filled with double ought to handle critters who make a pest of themselves. You might keep that in mind, rather than Mary's rantings."

Paul laughed and shook his head. Abruptly he changed subjects. "Oh, by the way, after the hunt tomorrow, everybody's invited over to the house. I'm slaughtering a couple of goats today. We'll put them on the spit tomorrow morning. Some potato salad, a little cole slaw, a dab of beans, and few bottles of beer will make mighty fine eatin'. If you're not too busy changin' into a wild man, why don't you plan on droppin' by?"

Wayford stuck an arm behind his back and hiked it as high as he could. "You've twisted my arm. But I plan to drink more than a couple bottles of your beer."

"Get commode-huggin' drunk if you're a mind. I'll get one of my men to drive you home. Hell, it might improve your sour attitude to get piss-faced."

Before Wayford answered, Bryan walked from the barn, shaking his head sadly. "It's like I always suspected. Paul wouldn't know good horseflesh if it came up and kicked him in the ass. It's a damned good thing he knows something about cattle or he'd be diggin' ditches for the county to stay alive."

"And if I keep you here any longer, Clint will be shovelin' all the way to summer to clear away the bullshit." Paul pointed to the red pickup. "Put your scrawny butt inside, and let me get you out of here. This man's got work to do."

"Thanks again for thinkin' of me." Wayford nodded to the skulls.

"And don't stay away so long. I'd almost forgotten what you two looked like."

Bryan paused beside the truck's open door. "Speakin' of bein' a stranger, Betty Lou sent along an invite for you to drop by for supper whenever you get a mind. She said it wasn't healthy for you to be holin' up like some hermit. You can add my invitation to hers. It's been too long since you and me shared a bottle of Jack black and howled at the moon."

"Tell Betty to keep an eye open for me." Wayford waved as Paul gunned the engine alive.

Dirt and stone spewed from beneath the rear tires while Paul wrenched the steering wheel around. The red pickup did a 180-degree turn and disappeared in a billowing cloud of red-brown dust to equal the one that accompanied its arrival.

Wayford did not follow the truck's departure. He retreated into the barn before his nostrils and lungs clogged with the heavy dust. A quick glance revealed that Miguel kept to his hidey-hole.

"You can come on out, son," the rancher called. "They've gone, and the coast is clear."

A rustle of hay turned Wayford's head. The Mexican's head poked out of the loft. Straw clung to his thick black hair. Miguel smiled sheepishly and shrugged as he found the ladder nailed to the wall and began to climb down.

"You ever work cattle down in Mexico?" the rancher asked, remembering the way Miguel had sat a saddle.

The eighteen-year-old gave a hesitant nod. "But only a few times for *Señor* Vasquez. He hired boys from the village to help when it was time to"—he stumbled for the correct English word, but was unable to find it—"*marca* the young calves."

"Brand," Wayford corrected, "brand the calves."

"The others from the village always worked with the fire and iron," Miguel continued, "but *Señor* Vasquez let me use a horse and rope. He said that I was born to be a *vaquero.*"

"Let's see what kind of eye that Mr. Vasquez had for cowboys." The rancher jerked a thumb toward the tack room. "Get yourself a saddle, bridle, and blanket. Put 'em on that blaze-faced bay and take him out to the calf pen."

The rancher watched while the boy did as ordered. Miguel handled himself well enough around a horse, and he knew how to place a saddle on a mount's withers rather than directly on the back. The boy even popped the bay's belly with a cupped palm to make certain the animal expelled the air in its lungs when he tightened the cinch. In spite of his height, or lack of it, he did not ask for a leg up. With both hands he gripped the saddlehorn, took a half step backward, gave a springing step forward, and swung upward. His feet slipped into the stirrups just as his backside touched the saddle.

Wayford walked at his side as Miguel reined from the stall to the open door of the barn. Outside, the rancher opened the pen's gate and let the boy ride into the makeshift arena.

"See that Hereford?" The rancher watched the acknowledging tilt of the boy's head. "What I want you to do is cut him out from the others and bring him up here to me."

Miguel glanced at the saddlehorn. "I have no rope."

"We're trying to shape this bay into a cuttin' horse," Wayford explained. "The idea is to let the horse, not a rope, do the work."

Miguel's forehead lined with questioning wrinkles.

"Now this horse ain't the brightest animal God ever created. He's got a good neck on him, so don't overwork the reins. And he understands the feel of a man's legs. That means you don't have to go kickin' him. But his attention wanders. What you have to do is see that he keeps his mind on business. Do that, and he'll get the job done."

The boy's expression betrayed no hint of confidence in either himself or the horse, but he did not question what the rancher wanted. His sneaker-clad heels lightly tapped the horse's sides as he clucked the bay toward the calves drawn together at the opposite end of the pen.

What happened next was exactly what Wayford expected. The Hereford took only a second or two to realize he was the Mexican's target. He quickly trotted to the right, pushing to the center of the other calves. Overreacting, the boy yanked the reins. The bay responded in kind and spun totally around, nearly dumping his rider amid the cowpaddies littering the pen.

Holding tight to the saddlehorn, Miguel managed to right himself. His head jerked from side to side as though uncertain of exactly where he was. When he located the Hereford, he reined the bay toward the calf with a lighter hand.

The calf cut to the left, leaving Miguel staring at a fence post. He reined the bay after the calf again.

Wayford lightly bit the inside of his cheek to stop from calling out to the boy. Like the horse he rode, Miguel needed time to learn. If he picked up the basics on his own, then the pointers the older man gave would mean something and help to hone his skills. If he failed to grasp what was needed, then he had no business sitting atop a cutting horse.

For fifteen minutes, the calf darted from one side of the pen to the other with horse and rider moving helplessly after him. As the Hereford did another lazy turn to evade his pursuers, he found the bay blocking his path. The calf lunged in the opposite direction; Miguel was ready. He gently eased the reins to the right, and the bay responded.

Another half hour passed before the Hereford gave in and trotted up the pen to where Wayford sat on the fence. Behind him came Miguel with an ear-to-ear grin on his face, obviously delighted at his accomplishment.

"Not half bad for your first time." The rancher did not lie, but his words were less than the truth. During the past five minutes, he noticed the boy begin to sense the rhythm of horse and calf. "Put the bay back in his stall, saddle up the sorrel filly across the shedrow, and ride her out here. I want you to do the same thing with that black-spotted calf."

Miguel glanced over a shoulder to locate the calf while the rancher opened the gate. "I will try to do better this time."

"That's what I expect from you." Wayford pulled out a bag of Bull Durham and rolled a cigarette while the boy returned to the barn.

Placing the cigarette in his mouth, he lit it, then reached down to scratch Vanberg's ears. "What'd'ya think?"

The dog looked up at him with his tongue hanging out of the side of his mouth.

"Yeah," the rancher agreed, "it's too soon to be making a decision."

By the time Miguel worked the sorrel filly and sent the spotted calf running toward the rancher, Wayford reached his decision. Mr. Vasquez had been right; Miguel Ramos had the looks of a natural-born cowboy. The rancher did not withhold his praise as the boy drew beside the fence.

"Now I want you to sit here and watch me put a couple of horses through their paces. You're still working the reins with a heavy hand," Wayford said. "I think you'll *see* it better than I can *explain* it. Now give me the filly and get up on this fence."

The boy did as told. Wayford walked the sorrel back toward the barn with Vanberg at his side. The man glanced down at the hound and said, "I reckon that ride proved you wrong. The boy will be riding better'n me in a couple of days."

EIGHT

WAYFORD unlooped a canteen from the saddlehorn, unscrewed its top, took a sip, then passed the water to Paul Moody, who leaned against a lichen-splotched boulder.

"Thanks." Paul swallowed a mouthful and handed the canteen back. He scanned the sloping walls of the canyon they rode. "I didn't reckon on this hunt takin' all day. Hell, I might've told Bryan to find another man if I'd known it was going to be this much work."

"Yeah, hell would have to be froze over in ten feet of ice before you missed a chance at a cougar." Wayford smiled at his friend as he took another swig of water.

"You could've spiked that canteen with a little bourbon." Paul rubbed his gloved hands along the sleeves of his gray leather coat. "It might have taken the bite out of this weather."

"Isn't it enough I've got to ride with a man who brought a silver-inlaid saddle on a cat hunt?" Wayford inclined his head toward the black saddle sitting atop Paul's mount. "I don't need to be watching out for a drunk."

Paul's eyes shifted to the saddle; a wide grin spread across his face. "Still irks you, doesn't it? Me walkin' off with that grand prize saddle. Sort of rubs at you like a burr under a blanket?"

"Paul, I accepted you takin' that saddle when I was eighteen years old." Wayford squatted on his heels to fill a cupped hand with water and let Vanberg lap it. "What does rub me is the way you act sometimes. Hell, a lot of water's run down the creek in forty-seven years."

An amused laugh came in reply. "And that saddle's given me forty-seven years of pleasure."

Wayford considered mentioning that the saddle could not be that pleasurable since he had seen Paul use it only a dozen times in all those years, but he let it pass. Instead he refilled his hand to give Vanberg another drink.

"Seems to me that's a waste of water, Clint."

The rancher glanced up to see Jeff Milton, Bryan Owens's nephew, and his friend Wayne Goggins eying him. Both men, in their early twenties, were college students in El Paso. They had visited Bryan over the weekend to gather material for a project needed to complete an agronomy class. Mention of a possible cougar hunt had been motivation enough for them to cut classes and stay with Bryan a few extra days.

"I don't seem to recall that skinny old hound pickin' up a scent once the whole day, do you, Jeff?" Goggins winked at his companion.

"That's the way I remember it." Jeff spat a stream of tobacco juice to the ground. "Four times the other dogs picked up a scent and went howlin' after a cat. That mutt never lifted his head, just kept ploddin' along beside Clint's horse."

"You smart asses might also recall," Paul spoke up, "that the only thing the other dogs, including mine, which cost me a cool three thousand, managed to scare up is three jackrabbits."

Wayford smiled to himself. With rifles cocked and ready, the other men had spurred their mounts after the yapping dogs, hot for a quick kill. The rancher, although he reined after his companions, trusted Vanberg's nose and kept his rifle snug in its saddle holster. Four times the eight-year-old dog had proven correct.

"That worthless hound hasn't even managed that. He hasn't done anything except stick close to Clint's side like some scared pup," Jeff answered. "I can't see that he's worth the water Clint's givin' him."

Wayne chuckled. "Hellfire, how old is that dog anyway? Were you and him pups together, Clint?"

Jeff's laughter chorused his friend's. "Damn, that would make old Vanberg at least a hundred and five."

"And that would make you two still wet behind your ears." Bryan walked up and pointed to the young men's mounts while Wayford still sought an appropriate answer. "Why don't both of you get your butts back in the saddle instead of shooting off your mouths? We've rested the horses long enough."

"Uncle Bryan, we ain't doing—" Jeff started.

"You ain't doing nothing, and that's the problem." Bryan edged the men toward their mounts. He then turned to Wayford. "Clint, they didn't mean nothing. They're just young and full of piss and vinegar, lookin' for something to get into."

"No offense taken, Bryan." Wayford gave his friend a smile and a shrug. As Bryan walked away, the rancher looked down at Vanberg. "It wasn't me they were badmouthin'. I expect you to teach those young peckerwoods a thing or two today."

The hound pranced from side to side in a four-footed dance. He thrust his head against the rancher's hand in anticipation of an ear scratch. Wayford complied, vigorously massaging one ear and then the other. Vanberg's tail double-timed its wag.

An off-key whistle floated over the rancher's shoulder. It took a second for the rancher to catch the tune. Paul butchered a rendition of the old song "Whenever I Come to Town, the Boys Keep Kicking My Dog Around" as he shoved from the boulder to remount. Wayford rose and answered the tune with a disapproving scowl, which brought a laugh and a shake of the head from his friend.

"You know, those kids might be right, Clint," Paul suggested, glancing at the spotted dog. "Vanberg there is getting along in years. He might have lost the edge. What is he now? Nine? Ten?"

"Eight," Wayford replied while he stepped into the saddle. "And the only one that's gone and lost an edge is you, Paul Moody. You don't notice Vanberg carrying a spare tire around his gut."

"Spare tire?" Paul's laughter increased as he patted the slight, rounded protuberance of his belly, barely visible under his leather coat. "I always looked at this little extra weight as a badge of prosperity. Seems I remember you carrying around some excess flesh when Lizzie was feedin' you regular. Hell, the only reason you're skinny as a bean pole is that you can't tolerate your own cookin'."

"Fat's fat." Wayford clucked his mount forward, following the other hunters. "It's got to do with a man gettin' lazy. You need to put your butt in that fancy saddle more often and work off some of that fat."

Wayford's comment brought another laugh from his friend, who moved his horse after the rancher. Both men fell to silence as the riders moved into a wide canyon that ran between two hogback-like mountains.

Wayford's eyes surveyed the pillars of granite that pushed from the earth on his right in search of a small cave hidden among the rock. His gaze slid across the canyon to climb the sharp slope of the opposite mountain. He watched for the shift of shadows amid the stunted junipers and piñon pines or the movement of grass. The dull yellow-brown of the dry winter grass offered a perfect camouflage for a cougar. A man could ride within ten feet of a cat and never notice him, if he did not keep an eye peeled for sign.

The mountain lion they tracked was old; of that, Wayford was certain. Mule deer were plentiful in the mountains, but the cougar they sought preyed on cattle and goats. That indicated two possibilities: the cat was too old to run down wild game or was crippled. The rancher discarded the latter. The tracks they crossed displayed no indication of injury. The puma's strides were smooth and even. Old remained—a cat with the spring and power gone from his legs.

This puma kept his wits about him, Wayford reflected. A big cat did not live long enough to grow old without being wily. The lion they tracked was definitely that. The way he crossed his own tracks, leaving confusing scents to throw off the dogs, bespoke a cat wise to the ways of hunters.

A sharp yap broke the air. Ahead five dogs answered in a chorus of barks. Six dogs broke into a run.

"Looks like they've got the scent again." Paul tilted his head toward a branching in the canyon that split to the left. "The smell must be strong. They're more excited than they've been all day."

Wayford checked Vanberg out of the corner of an eye. The hound ignored the other dogs. His head lifted, snout testing the air. Vanberg gave a high-pitched whine that concluded in a throaty growl. He shifted his weight from one side to the other anxiously. Something held his attention, and it came from the canyon's right branch.

"The other dogs are chasing another false lead." Wayford pointed to Vanberg. "We should take a look in the other direction."

"It's six dogs to one, Clint." Paul yanked his rifle free from its holster and examined the load in the chamber. "I'll go with the majority."

In the next instant Wayford and Vanberg found themselves alone as Paul spurred his mount after the other hunters a quarter of a mile ahead.

Vanberg yipped. The dog danced about impatiently. His focus remained transfixed on the canyon's right branch.

Wayford watched Paul for a moment, then turned to the hound. "All right, I'm listenin'. Let's take a look at what you think is up yonder."

The rancher snapped his fingers and pointed to the right. Without a bark or a yap, the dog bounded forward. Wayford unholstered his own rifle, loaded the chamber, and flipped off the safety. Balancing the weapon in the crook of his left arm, he nudged the bay with his heels and followed the hound in an easy lope.

A half mile into the canyon's branch, Vanberg came to a dead stop. His head lifted high, nose stabbing the air in one direction and then the other. Next his muzzle dropped to the ground; he circled as though trying to pick up a lost scent.

Wayford scanned the sloping sides of the mountains. Vegetation grew thick among the shafts of naked granite that pushed above the topsoil like jumbled piles of boulders. Live oak and mesquite mingled with piñon and cedar. Thick-padded prickly pear grew to half the height of the trees.

Another whine-growl rose in Vanberg's throat. He no longer pranced and circled. In the classic pose of a pointer, he stood with tail extended behind him and nose directed toward the rocky upthrusts on the right.

Wayford shouldered the rifle. Sighting down the barrel, he systematically shifted the muzzle across the face of the rocks. Nothing, not so much as the flutter of a dried leaf revealed itself. Vanberg held his position.

Rifle ready, the rancher tapped the bay with his boot heels. The horse stepped forward, uncertainty in its stride. The alert pitch of his ears and wide flare of his nostrils confirmed the cougar's proximity.

Where? Twice more the rancher cautiously probed the granite's crevasses with gaze trained down the rifle's barrel. He saw nothing. Scrutinizing the high grass tufted around the base of the rock, he watched for the slightest movement of the dried stalks. Nothing.

The scream, as expected as it was, took the rancher unprepared. Not from the rock, but out from a dense copse of junipers the cougar leaped. In three lunging strides that betrayed no hint of infirmity, the cat covered the ground and leaped atop a granite upthrust. A dozen feet above horse and rider, it crouched, muscles corded to spring, and screamed again.

Wayford swung the rifle upward. At that instant, the bay broke, spurred by fear rather than rider. The horse reared high, forelegs striking out in answer to the mountain lion's challenge.

The rancher moved too slowly. He grasped for the saddlehorn and missed. Feet losing the stirrups, he tumbled from the saddle. Arms and legs flayed the air as he fell, unable to hold on to the rifle. The ground came up fast and hard. Pain lanced through Wayford's right ankle as he tried to get his feet under him and failed. Rock bit at rib when he toppled to his right and slammed back to the dirt.

Another scream rent the air. The cougar inched toward the edge of the granite uptrust. Yellowed fangs exposed in a feral snarl, the mountain lion crouched once more as it glared down at the vulnerable man.

Wayford's gaze darted about, unable to locate the lost rifle. Pain flared anew in the ankle when he twisted to his back, right hand fumbling to open the snapped holster on his belt.

The cougar sprang. In midair the cat twisted, turned, its tawny body wrenching violently. Recurved claws slashed out to rake the emptiness for an invisible foe. Then it struck the ground three feet from the sprawled rancher, body a-twitch with the last spasms of fleeting life.

Even with the echoing crack of a rifle report and the blood that oozed from the mountain lion's side, it took the clop of approaching hooves for Wayford's mind to accept what had happened. His head turned. Paul Moody rode toward him, rifle in hand.

"Common sense got the better of me," Paul said while he eased his mount to a halt a few feet from Wayford. "I decided to listen to Vanberg rather than dogs who had been wrong four times today."

Wayford gave a weak smile when he pushed to his elbows. "Damn lucky thing you did. The cat spooked the bay, and he threw me."

"I saw from back there." Paul threw a leg over his horse's neck and dropped to the ground. He offered his friend a hand to help him to his feet. "You all right? You took an ugly spill."

"I'm still alive. I guess I'll be all right."

Wayford accepted the proffered hand and pulled upward. The instant he placed weight on the right leg fire flamed through his ankle. He floundered back to the dirt nearly yanking Paul down with him.

"Son-of-a-bitch!" the rancher reached out and tested the ankle with fingertips and palms. "I've gone and sprung the bastard!"

"Then you sit there while I go and get your horse. No need for you to hurt yourself more. We'll get you to a doctor and have him take a look at it." Paul started to remount.

"I said it's sprained, not broke. I don't need a doctor." The adrenaline that flowed in Wayford's veins played out. Fully aware of his present situation, he felt a total fool. He had let a horse throw him and nearly turned himself into cougar bait. "What I need is for you to help me up so I can lean against that rock over there. That shot will have the others here in a few minutes. I don't want to be sprawled on my ass when they ride up. Now give me that hand again."

"Clinton Wayford, I don't know how me and you have kept being friends for as long as we have. Sometimes you're as stubborn as a jackass—an old jackass." In spite of his words, Paul offered the hand again.

This time with a maximum of gritted teeth, Wayford got to his feet, or at least his left foot. Leaning heavily on Paul, he hopped to the boulder and leaned against it.

"Now you can go get my horse." He made no attempt to curb the sharpness of his tongue. Twice in almost as many days he had been called a jackass; he did not like it, not one bit.

His mood blacked three shades when the others rode up and Paul returned with the bay. Unable to stand on the ankle, it took both Jeff Milton and Wayne Goggins to help him back into the saddle. Both college students kept their comments to themselves, but he could see their eyes shooting at each other, expressions questioning why they were burdened with an incompetent old man.

Wayford edged the remaining bites of barbecued goat around on the paper plate, studying them for several minutes before shoving the plate away. He lifted a Lone Star Beer from the table and drank the two remaining swallows from the long-neck bottle. Like the meal, the beer was tasteless.

"Your ankle hurting? You barely touched your potato salad or cole slaw."

The rancher looked across the wooden picnic table at Rachel Moody, smiled, and lied with a shake of his head. "My eyes were bigger than my stomach. What I did eat was awfully good."

"And you, Clint Wayford, are a bald-faced liar, but thank you for trying." The woman hugged a mink-collared coat closer to her. "I tried to tell Paul that midwinter was no time for a barbecue, but he wouldn't listen. He said everybody could keep warm by the fire." She glanced at the men huddled beside the flame-flickering pit. "Guess he was right. That's all anyone's done tonight. First they toast one side then turn to toast the other."

She paused and looked back at Wayford. "That and let Paul retell how he shot the cougar three or four hundred times."

The rancher smiled. "You don't hear me complaining. If Paul hadn't got off a clean shot, I'd be that cat's supper right now."

"For all anybody's eaten tonight, ya'll should have let the cougar live and given him this goat for dinner."

Wayford watched the woman stand and begin to clean off the table. How similar she and Lizzie had been. He could almost see his wife in her movements, the way she held herself. He told himself that something was bound to rub off after a lifetime of friendship the two women had shared. That wasn't it. Even back when the two had been schoolgirls two classes behind Paul and him, they had been more like sisters than mere friends. Had Lizzie not been there, Wayford realized, Paul and he would have had more than a silver-inlaid saddle to compete over.

"You certain you won't let me take you to a doctor so he can look at that ankle?" Rachel asked while she stuffed a stack of soiled paper plates into a plastic bag. "I wouldn't mind."

"This ankle's fine. The bandage helps some, and with the cane Paul loaned me, I can hobble around as good as an old man can expect."

Rachel used an arm to rake a line of empty beer bottles into the sack. "Personally I think you're being stubborn."

"If you say as a jackass, I'll show you this cane has other uses than helpin' a man get around." The rancher wrenched the cane high above his head in a mock threat.

The twist of disgust on Rachel's face transformed into a grin when she laughed. "I'd be more frightened if you were able to get up and use that cane."

He shrugged and let the cane dip back to the ground. "When you're right, you're right."

"Want me to fix up a doggie bag for Vanberg out of some of these scraps?"

"That dog can fend for himself," Wayford answered. "Fix me up a people bag. I hate to see good groceries go to waste."

"I've already got a plate made up for you to take home," she said. "What about Vanberg?"

The rancher shrugged again. "It's all right by me."

"I'll be back. I've got to go into the house and get some tin foil." Dragging the garbage bag behind her, she turned and walked across the wide flagstone patio toward a pair of sliding glass doors at the rear of the house.

The black mood that had settled over him while he lay in the dirt this afternoon returned. He glanced at his friends joking by the open barbecue pit. Usually good company would have been the medicine required to shake a case of the low-downs. Not tonight. His mind kept turning over the events of the hunt.

The bay was not to blame for what had happened today. The fault lay with the horse's rider. No matter how many times he retraced the afternoon, Wayford found no justification for why he chose to remain on horseback rather than dismount to search out the puma. He had noticed the horse's reaction to the cat, the pricked ears and flared nostrils. Those were signs of fear, and he damn well knew it. Why had he stayed in the saddle?

He did not lay the blame on Jeff and Wayne. The younger men's cockiness had galled him, stopped him from riding into the left fork of the canyon with the rest of the hunters. But they had not crossed his mind once he had been certain Vanberg had the mountain lion's scent.

I wasn't thinking. He grimaced at the conclusion he reached. *I just wasn't thinking.*

His gaze dipped. Two pairs of socks failed to hide the swollen thickness of his bandage-wrapped ankle. It was bad enough that his brain had shut down on him today, but his body had to provide him with a reminder of his mistake. If the ankle's constant throbbing were any indication, he would pay for the lapse of reason for at least a week.

Old fool. That was the worst of it. He felt like an old fool. One whose mind and body were slipping away from him, and he was too stubborn to face reality. Maybe Frank and those college boys had hit the nail on the head. He was a stubborn jackass. Lord knows, he'd acted like one this afternoon.

"Here you go, Clint." Rachel stood at his side. In one arm she held a paper grocery bag and in the other balanced a heavy plastic, covered cake tray. "This is for your dog and this is for you." Her head tilted to the bag and then the tray.

Through the translucent plastic Wayford saw a mound of smoke-darkened barbecued goat, and mountains of potato salad and cole slaw, each separated by aluminum foil. "You've overdone it a bit, haven't you, Rachel?"

"It'll spoil around here. If you can't eat all of it, give it to the dog. I've seen him eat scraps and know he can handle all this." She started to place the food on the table.

Wayford managed to stand and take the bag from her hand. "I might as well take this on out to the pickup. I should be headin' back to the house."

Rachel shot a knowing glance at his ankle. "I knew that was hurting you. You and Paul are usually up hours after all the other guests have gone, talkin' about anything and everything."

He let a shake of the head lie for him a second time. "I'm tuckered out. It's been a long time since I've sat on a horse from sunup to sundown."

"If that's the way you want it, I won't say you're acting stubborn again." A disapproving frown moved across Rachel's forehead. "But I'm going to carry this out to your truck for you."

"I'd appreciate that. Don't think I could manage both, not with this cane." With Rachel beside him, he hobbled to the house's glass doors.

"The reason I put the food in this container is because it's a favorite of mine," she said while they moved through the house and out the front door. "That means you have to bring it back, Clinton Wayford. When you do, I expect you to stay for dinner. You and Paul can catch up on all your talking then."

"Never knew I needed a reason to drop by." The rancher opened the pickup's door and placed the bag of scraps on the floorboard near the passenger door. Vanberg, who lay curled asleep on the seat, awoke. His nose eagerly poked at the sack.

"You don't, and you know it. Trouble is, you don't just drop by anymore. Paul's even noticed it. This way I make sure you have to come back." She handed him the cake tray when he slid behind the wheel. "The last names might be different, but you're family, Clint. You know that, don't you?"

"I know, Rachel." Her words sent a warmth radiating through his aching body. They were the only good thing to happen to him this day. If he had been able to stand on his two feet, he would have climbed out of the pickup and given her a tight, squeezing hug.

Perhaps she sensed his thoughts. She leaned down and lightly kissed his cheek. "You're a special man, Clint. I want you to take care of yourself, understand? With Lizzie gone, I've got to keep an eye on you for her."

"I do the best I can, Rachel. That's all I know how to do." He closed the door when she backed away from the truck.

Starting the engine, he turned onto the long dirt road that led to the highway. He kept his eyes straight ahead, never glancing at the side or rearview mirrors. If he did, he was afraid he would see Rachel standing there watching him depart. For some reason he did not understand, he knew if she were he would break down in tears.

NINE

MELODY AND CISSY HARPE sat beneath the canvas awning that covered the small wooden deck outside the mobile home, which the two widowed sisters consistently called "trailer house." They lived fifteen miles back in the southern side mountains in a conglomeration of small plots of land called the Davis Mountain Resort. Although there were many permanent residents within the resort, the majority of the five- to seven-acre tracts were weekend getaway spots belonging to people from across the state.

Wayford never understood that. The Davis Mountains were so far from any major Texas city that most folks spent a weekend driving to and returning from the area.

Both sisters stood and waved as he turned onto the strip of sand that served as a driveway to their home. He tipped his hat in return, unsure whether the two elderly women saw the gesture through the thick dust coating the pickup's windshield. By the time he pulled to a stop, the sisters, each carrying bundles in their arms, carefully picked their way down the three steps that led from the deck.

"Howdy, ladies," the rancher called out when he stepped from the truck to lean lightly on his borrowed cane. "Sorry I'm late today. Snuffy Vardeman dug up about twice his usual amount of 'antiques' he wants me to peddle for him. Took about three times as long to get him all loaded up."

"That old man never moved fast even when he was young," the rotund Melody Harpe said. " 'Cept when Juanita Ramon was tryin' to get him to stand up before a priest."

"Even then, she moved faster than he did," Cissy, the younger of the two sisters, added. "Roped and hog-tied him, she did."

"And kept him that way 'til she died," Melody, who was eighty-five, concluded. "Never saw a woman go after a man the way

Juanita lit out to get Snuffy. Not that I ever understood what she saw in him."

Cissy, eighty-three, glanced at her sister with an expression of mingled surprise and smugness as though she knew more about her older sibling than she was willing to say—in Melody's presence.

With a slight limp, Wayford stepped to the horse trailer hitched behind the pickup. He had misjudged the damage to the ankle the day of the cougar hunt. Two weeks had passed, and he still was careful not to place his full weight on the injury.

He opened a small door at the front of the trailer to reveal a compartment meant to store tack during a haul. The compartment was immaculately clean; he knew how particular the Harpe sisters were when it came to their quilts. A year ago he left several straws on the compartment's floor. Melody had crawled inside on her hands and knees to remove them. The width of the woman's hips almost left her a permanent addition to the trailer.

"This has three quilt covers in it." Melody tapped the cardboard box she carried. "A Texas Star, a Dutch Doll, and a Wedding Ring pattern. Get whatever you can for them."

"Yes, ma'am." Wayford accepted the box and carefully placed it in the trailer.

The sisters managed to survive on their Social Security checks. The quilts he sold at First Monday provided the extras they needed to do more than survive, like the flower and vegetable garden they began behind their home each spring. Each month the two turned out one to three quilt covers. When the rancher found a buyer, they paid up front. Wayford returned the cover to the sisters, who finished the quilting and mailed the finished item to the buyer. Most buyers were willing to pay four to five hundred for one of the handmade quilts. Three months ago the sisters had sent a down-filled, wine red comforter with him. He had brought back a check for a thousand dollars from a middle-aged Dallas couple.

"And these boxes are the quilts we finished up." Melody took the two brown paper–wrapped packages from Cissy's arms. "If you wouldn't mind mailin' these for us, we'd appreciate it. That nice Mr. Weaver who comes down each month to spend a few days up at his place on High Lonesome was going to do it for us. But he had to drive back to San Angelo before we had them ready."

"Two completed quilts and three covers!" Wayford added the

packages to the trailer and securely closed the compartment's door. "You two ladies have the quickest fingers in the West!"

Melody smiled, obviously pleased at the compliment. "Quick fingers wouldn't be much use without you takin' these things off to sell for us."

"Glad to be of help. I'm headin' that way anyway, so I might as well take whatever else I can."

Cissy's voice came from behind the horse trailer. "You most certainly do have a full load this time." She peered into the trailer. "Is all this Snuffy's stuff?"

" 'Bout half of it." Wayford walked beside the woman and studied the load he had gathered from around the county today.

"I'd bet all those rusty things are Snuffy's." Cissy pointed at two wooden apple crates overflowing with everything from old irons to horse bits.

"Reckon you'd be right," the rancher replied with a nod.

"Antiques? Snuffy's got some nerve calling them that. How do you ever find anyone to buy that worthless junk?" Melody's head moved from side to side in disapproval.

The rancher shrugged. "I guess one person's junk is another's antique. Sort of like one person preferring an electric blanket over a good, warm quilt. Doesn't make much sense, but that's the way of it."

Snuffy Vardeman, a retired groceryman, had an eye for what the public wanted. He spent most of his time rummaging through old barns and houses about to be torn down in a five-county radius. He collected anything that might bring a price, whether it be pieces of old barbed wire or ancient farm tools. Wayford rarely brought back any of the items Snuffy sent with him.

Actually, his trailer was usually empty on the return drive from Canton. Even the wagon wheels Luis Estaban nailed together and weathered to make them appear antique and the hand-whittled geegaws Jorge Teodoro carved all sold well.

Like the ram and steer skulls Wayford carried for himself, each of the boxes represented an effort to scrape together extra money. For the most part the items came from the elderly like the Harpe sisters. However, five boxes were packed with wooden toys made by Jesse Huggins, whose world was limited to the places a wheelchair could carry him. Jesse had been born without legs. His hands, however, worked magic with wood, producing marvelous pull toys that danced and spun when yanked along by some toddler.

Twenty people in all loaded their hopes for a few dollars of pocket cash into the horse trailer. Wayford took from them the money required to pay for the gasoline needed to make the twelve-hour—there and back—drive. He did that only after months of protest on his part. Those whose goods he carried and sold demanded he take at least that. Jesse Huggins explained that demand best to him when the young man first began to sell his toys.

"I'm not looking for pity or charity, Mr. Wayford." Jesse stuffed twenty dollars into the rancher's hands. "I've had that for the twenty-two years of my life. I'm looking for a way of putting together a life on my own. You and that horse trailer of yours give me that. So I'd like you to take that money and let that be the last of it."

Afterward Wayford carried a pocket calculator and a receipt book on each trip. He carefully figured each person's percentage of the gasoline cost and gave them a receipt, even if it amounted to only a few dollars, for their share of the cost. He understood a man or a woman wanting to pay their own way; it was the opposite that eluded him.

"Mr. Wayford, do you have time to come inside for a few moments," Cissy asked. "Melody and me just baked up a German chocolate cake. Coffee's always in the maker."

"Not today, ladies." The rancher was truly disappointed to decline the invitation. He liked the smell of the sisters' home. The aroma of freshly baked breads, cakes, and pies always wafted in the air. That was something he had not smelled in his own home since Lizzie's death.

"I'm runnin' late today. Got to get home to feed." Noting the disappointment on the sisters' faces, he added, "However, if I could talk you into a piece of that German chocolate cake to take with me, I'd be obliged."

Cissy grinned and hastened into the trailer house, leaving her older sister to discuss the weather with Wayford. Two minutes later the younger Harpe reappeared with a three-piece-thick chunk of cake wrapped in a paper napkin and steaming coffee in a paper cup. Thanking the two for their hospitality, the rancher climbed into the pickup's cab, swung around the circular drive, and moved onto the twisting and turning dirt roads that wound through the resort.

The warm sweetness of German chocolate cake filled Wayford's nostrils with every breath he inhaled. He smiled. The treats the Harpe sisters always had waiting for his visits were one of the fringe benefits of collection day. He resisted the urge to pinch off a sampling of the sweet goody. The portion Cissy had sliced was enough for desert that evening for both Miguel and himself.

Pride rose in the rancher's chest at the thought of the young Mexican boy. During the past two weeks, Miguel proved to be quite a rider, as well as a worker. He still had a few things to learn about handling a horse, but that would come. It was a simple matter of experience; the more horses he rode, the better he would be prepared for that unexpected moment any horse was capable of giving his rider.

The rancher slowed to a halt as the wide dirt road leading from the resort intersected Highway 166. He glanced to the left and right before pulling onto the pavement. It was too late in the afternoon for traffic. Working folks were about their evening chores, and the tourists had found roosts for the night.

He resisted the temptation to let his foot depress the accelerator a little more than usual. A trailer carrying a full load might hit a bump, twist wildly, and overturn a pickup before a man knew what had happened. A medium speed and steady hands on the wheel were the best way to keep everything under control. Besides, it did not matter if he was late today. Miguel could handle feeding on his own.

A pleased smile slipped across the rancher's lips as his thoughts returned to the young man. As uneasy as he had first been about having Miguel on the ranch, he now recognized the boy had been a lifesaver. With the bummed-up ankle after the cougar hunt, Wayford would have been helpless without Miguel. For a week the rancher had found it difficult to walk, let alone ride. Miguel had taken on that task all on his own. Even Paul Moody's geldings appeared to be none the worse for having a green rider as the first to sit on their backs.

Only Frank's Pal presented a problem to the young man. At least the first time Miguel saddled him, Wayford reflected. The problem stemmed more from the boy being leery of the rancher than the horse. Miguel recognized the importance of the colt to the older man. After his first workout with Frank's Pal, Miguel relaxed and accepted the colt as just another horse. The boy looked almost as good astride Frank's Pal as Wayford did.

Hell, the rancher admitted to himself, *Miguel probably looks better.* The seed of an idea had been rooting in Wayford's mind for the past week. He was afraid to put too much store in it, since he still was not certain that one morning he would awake and find Miguel gone. The good Lord knew three meals a day and a place to sleep, even if the rancher had moved the boy from the barn into a spare bedroom, Mary's old room, was nothing in exchange for the work Miguel did.

But, if Miguel did stick around, come time for the Fort Worth competition, Wayford toyed with the possibility of letting the young man take Frank's Pal into the arena. He had no doubt that Miguel would be able to handle the colt. Whether Miguel could take the pressure of competition was another thing.

There was a way to test the boy's mettle. Several lesser competitions around the state offered a proving ground for rider and horse. That meant Wayford would have to find a way to bring Miguel out in the open. It would not do to have the boys in green snatch up his rider and send him back to Mexico minutes before he was to enter the arena, whether it be in Fort Worth, Houston, or San Angelo.

Drying off Miguel's back and making him legal was a stumbling block Wayford had to overcome. He had not come up with anything that might convince Immigration the young man had a legitimate reason to cross the border, but he was thinking on it.

Those thoughts dissipated in a rifle-like crack and the abrupt jerk of the pickup's steering wheel.

Blowout! Wayford reacted immediately. His foot came off the gas pedal. Without hitting the brakes, he applied gentle pressure to the steering wheel to counter the sudden pull of truck and trailer. Gradually he slowed and edged onto the two-lane road's grassy shoulder.

Outside, he stared at a shredded right rear tire and remembered Sid Stilwell's warnings to replace the tires during his last three visits to the service station. The rancher held back a string of curses that sizzled on the tip of his tongue. Instead, he whistled while he pulled jack and spare from the back of the truck. It was not that he felt like whistling, but something Lizzie had said when a nail had flattened a tire on one of their very first dates brought a forced tune to his lips.

"You can tell a lot about a man's character in the way he handles himself with a flat tire. There's something about a flat that brings out the worst in a man," she had said. "I can't tolerate someone who dregs up every cuss word he knows and spews them out while he changes a tire."

That night Wayford had contained his anger over the flat by whistling. He had done so with every flat encountered thereafter. This afternoon, continuing to whistle threatened the limits of endurance. He popped the hubcap and slid the lug wrench into place. Pain shot through his healing ankle as he attempted to break the first of the rusted nuts. Shifting his weight to the left leg, he tried again.

The unbalanced position left him sprawled facedown in the grass. He shoved to his feet and attacked another lug, only to find it solidly locked in place by rust. Nor were the others in better shape; none would budge so much as a fraction of an inch. If he maneuvered to put his whole weight into the lug wrench, his right ankle gave way under him. Any other position lacked the leverage to break the locking rust.

A half hour passed before he accepted the futility of his efforts. Hell would freeze over with six feet of ice before any of the lugs broke this afternoon, no matter how much he banged on them with a hammer he took from a toolbox in the back of the truck. He climbed into the cab, turned on the engine, and let the heater ease the cold from his feet and hands.

The two young cowboys worked together. One tugged the blowout off and the other swung the spare into place. The lug wrench spun deftly under their hands, and the jack was released.

Wayford watched, doing his best to disguise the humiliation of finding himself in such a helpless situation. For an hour he had sat in the cab until he saw a pair of approaching headlights. He switched his own lights on and off several times to signal for help.

The two young men, with horse trailer hitched behind their pickup, were on their way from El Paso to a rodeo in Alpine. Both were construction workers, jobs needed to feed new families. Their dream, one once shared by the rancher, was to find fame and fortune with horse and rope.

"There you go, old timer," one of the young cowboys said to Wayford while the other moved to their trailer and checked on the two horses inside. "You're lucky we came along. There aren't many people out at night in this part of the country."

The rancher nodded. "If I didn't know it before, I know it now. I'd just about decided I was going to have to spend the night in my pickup."

The cowboy edged back his hat and nodded. "That wouldn't have been wise on a night like this."

Wayford held out a hand. "Thank you for your help. It *is* appreciated."

"You take care now." The young man nodded and walked to his truck.

Wayford opened the door to his own pickup and sat behind the wheel. One of the young men's voices carried on the wind as they climbed into the truck ahead:

"An old man in that sort of shape shouldn't be allowed on the highway alone. What if we hadn't come along to help him? Hell, the old coot might have been stuck here all night. He could have froze to death!"

If the other man answered, the pickup's slamming door spared the rancher his reply. Closing his own door, he turned the key in the ignition and watched the two young men pull away before moving back on the road.

Old coot. He could not work up even a little angry steam. The cowboy was right. Not about him freezing to death; the pickup's tank had plenty of gas to keep the heater running through the night. But about not being allowed on the highway. A man who could not change a flat had no business behind a wheel.

Mary's face pushed into his mind. He heard her pleading for him to return to Lubbock with her. She insisted they were family and that's the way things should be.

Would living with his daughter and her family be that bad? Like Frank said, it would not be charity. He could support himself. He would have money from the sale of the ranch. Bryan Owens would snatch up the Wide W in a New York minute; he had made that more than clear these past years.

And he would be close to Frank Junior and little Elizabeth. God knew he wanted that. Being someone they visited once or twice a year on holidays was not his idea of being a grandfather. There was a lot he could teach those two about the world and life. He could show them . . .

His thoughts skidded to a halt. What could he show or teach them in Lubbock? He would be no more than an old man who stayed in a spare bedroom in their house, someone who sat around reminiscing about once-upon-used-to-be times that had nothing to do with his grandchildren's life in the city.

Damn Mary! Damn Lubbock! His spine grew as stiff as a rail. Take him way from the land, and he was nothing. What he had to teach his grandchildren was rooted here deep in the dry West Texas earth. He knew nothing else.

And damn me! If that's what it took to survive, then that's what he would do. He might be a stubborn old jackass. Hell, enough folks seemed to think so lately, but he was not giving up the only life he had ever known to let his daughter care for him. He would rather freeze to death like some homeless vagrant, along the side of the road, unable to change his own truck tire, than suffer the fate Mary planned for him.

He threw back his head and brayed at the top of his lungs in the best jackass imitating voice he could manage. He then slammed the accelerator to the floorboard. There was no need to waste more time. If Miguel had not finished the chores yet, he needed to lend a hand. He had worked the Wide W for most of his adult life, and there was always work to be done on a ranch. That was the life he had chosen for himself, the life he intended to live until the land drew him six feet under.

TEN

WAYFORD'S EYES carefully worked down the figures that filled the yellow sheet of paper while his finger stabbed the tiny plastic keys of the calculator. Reaching the end of the second column, he checked the total. A satisfied smile touched his lips. Three times straight he added the figures, and they totaled the same.

Vanberg's bark reached his ears, as though the dog congratulated his owner on the mathematical achievement.

"Not a bad take for three days, is it, you ol' flea bag?" The rancher looked up from the ciphering that had occupied the last half hour. Vanberg was not at his side.

A glance found the hound cavorting with a shaggy white Heinz variety dog with whom he had made friends during the three days in Canton. From the pickup's cab, the rancher watched the two for several moments as they played like puppies. He enjoyed their romp as much as they seemed to delight in chasing each other in circles. It was a good day for play, for dog or man.

Wayford slowly inhaled, savoring the taste of the air. The flavor was spring, in spite of the fact that the calendar date read late January. Texas weather was as unpredictable as a young girl's mind. For the long weekend of First Monday, temperatures stayed in the low seventies during the days and only dipped to the fifties at night. For the first time since fall descended on the state, the rancher had not minded spending the nights sleeping in the pickup.

The word "invigorating" wiggled to mind and hung there. It was not a word he often used, but it fit the day. He felt invigorated. The warm promise of spring was like a shot of bourbon coursing through his veins. Here, more than half a state away from the Wide W, the mounting bills and the daily problems of keeping the ranch afloat appeared more manageable. If he kept things on an even keel until spring's breath brought grass, his calves would fatten. When he sold them, the money they brought would give him a little room to stretch, at least through the summer and into early fall.

And with fall came the Fort Worth cutting horse competition. Frank's Pal would be there among the finalists when the judges handed out the prizes. All the colt had to do was remain sound until then.

Although the rancher could not call the future rosy, he definitely viewed it with a pink tint this afternoon. He smiled, his attention returning to Vanberg and the dog's shaggy friend. It had been a long time since he had seen the hound play. The Wide W provided little time for play even for a dog.

Shifting around in the pickup's seat, Wayford gathered the calculator and the papers on which he kept his totals and stuffed them inside a metal box brimming with money. He snapped the lid and slid the weekend's profits far back under the seat.

The box and its contents stood at the center of his improved outlook. The warm weather had brought out the bargain hunters in droves from nearby Dallas and Fort Worth. The only items left in the trailer were the Harpe sisters' quilt tops; each of those had the name and address of their buyer pinned to it.

When it came to profits, Snuffy Vardeman topped the list. A Texana collector from the Gulf Coast had rummaged through two of Snuffy's boxes with ever-widening eyes for ten minutes before digging out a checkbook and hastily scribbling the asking price of two thousand dollars. The man had been so excited about the "treasures" discovered in the boxes, he had forgotten to haggle over the price. Snuffy would not mind.

Nor did Wayford. A thousand of the dollars within the box came from his skulls and assortment of worn old saddles, bridles, and other tack items. While by no means a fortune, the money would eliminate many of the small bills he had let slip for months. There would be enough left to add a couple hundred to his slim bank account. With luck and if the creek didn't rise, he could scrape by until spring and the sale of his fattened calves.

Yes, he relished another breath he sucked into his lungs. A different light brightened this day. He slid from the seat and gazed around. Acre upon acre of traders busily packed the items they had not been able to sell into the cars and trucks which had been their business offices for the tradefest. Straggling bargain hunters scurried from one location to another, hopeful of finding a last-moment good buy.

The enticing aroma of hickory smoke wafted in the air. The rancher turned toward the exit to the First Monday grounds. A minor traffic jam clogged the streets as traders tried to maneuver from the grounds with their cars and trailers while buyers exited the parking lot across the street, pushing toward Interstate 20.

The smoke, not the traffic, demanded Wayford's attention. The smell of barbecue rising from an oil-drum pit Harley Cowens ran by the exit had tempted him throughout the First Monday meeting as it always did. He had lived on cheese and crackers during the three days. Stuffing his belly with two of Harley's sliced brisket sandwiches, a-drip with spicy sauce, onions, and sweet pickle relish, had developed into a ritualized conclusion to the three-day flea market over the past years. The time beside the smoke-billowing oil drum gave Wayford the opportunity to stretch his legs and say goodbyes to those traders who had become friends during the monthly meetings. Besides, next to Raul's Barbecue in Fort Davis, Harley pre pared the best brisket in Texas. The rancher could think of nothing better with which to fill his stomach before the long drive home.

"Clint!" a woman's voice called.

He turned to see Thelma Ranson standing by an old, paint-flaking Chevy station wagon. The red-headed woman waved and shouted. "Take care of yourself, Wayford. We'll see you next month."

Returning the wave, the rancher watched the shorts-attired forty-year-old walk around her station wagon and climb behind the wheel. He caught himself grinning when he realized his gaze homed in on the sway of Thelma's tight backside. Feelings he thought dead within him for years stirred with that alluring rhythm.

Appears someone other than Vanberg has cavortin' on his mind today! The awakening of desire surprised him; it was a most pleasant surprise. Had he been a few years younger, he realized that he would have been tempted to apply a large portion of his weekend profits in an attempt to romance Thelma into a nearby motel for the night. If nothing else, age brought a semblance of wisdom. He locked the metal box in the pickup, walked to Harley's, and ordered two sandwiches and a bottled Barq's Root Beer.

A three-day regimen of rattrap cheese and saltines combined with the incredibly delicious aroma of the hickory-smoked meat had

Wayford's mouth watering as he folded back the unwaxed paper wrapped around the first sandwich. With unashamed relish, he bit into the savory brisket, sliced thinly and piled an inch and a half between a toasted hamburger bun. He somehow managed a pleasured "mmmmmmmm" while he chewed the sauce-drenched beef.

"Lord! Now this is eatin' high on the hog!" The rancher gave his head a little twist to the side and winked his approval at the black man working the pit. "Harley, I swear each one of these sandwiches I eat is better than the last one. I don't know how you do it, but you turn a hunk of tough ol' beef into a meal fit for royalty!"

"Glad you find it proper." The barbecue's proprietor glanced around as though assuring himself that no one listened, then leaned toward Wayford to whisper, "Tell you the God's truth. I can't eat no brisket myself. After standin' in this smoke nigh on half of my life, the smell of barbecue turns my stomach."

Wayford barely stopped his mouth from dropping open and losing a bite of sandwich. He gave a couple of hasty chews and swallowed hard before the laughter that worked up from deep in his chest burst forth.

"You're pullin' my leg?" The rancher held out the half-eaten sandwich and pointed at it. "Harley, there isn't a man on God's green earth that could complain about the miracle you perform with beef."

The would-be miracle worker shrugged. "A lot of folks pay me a pile of compliments about my cookin'. That don't change the way it is. I haven't been able to eat brisket in no form whatsoever for ten years now. Worse, I'm gettin' that way about any cut that comes from a cow. Pork and chicken are about all my stomach can tolerate. That is, as long as they ain't even thought about gettin' near barbecue smoke."

Wayford chuckled and offered, "I reckon there's a bright side to your predicament. You got no worry about goin' and eatin' up your own profits."

"You can say that again." Harley grinned widely and winked at the rancher. "You can sure enough say that again."

Lifting the soft drink bottle to his lips, Wayford tilted it upward and let the cold root beer trickle into his mouth. Over a lifetime, the rancher had experimented with about every drink possible to complement the peppery heat of good barbecue sauce and smoked beef. He had found nothing better than root beer.

"What's the weather going to do tonight?" His eyes scanned a blue sky dotted with an occasional puff of fleecy white.

"If you're believin' the weatherman today—"

Harley's reply drowned in the screech of tire rubber biting concrete pavement. A sickening thud, the stomach churning sound of metal impacting flesh, filled Wayford's ears. At the same instant a pitiful, surprise-filled yelp rent the air.

"Damn!" Harley's head jerked toward the sounds.

Wayford turned. A wave of spine-numbing horror and nausea washed through him. Soft drink and sandwich fell from his hands. Vanberg lay in a shallow drainage ditch beside the road, his body twitching spasmodically. The rancher's mouth opened to form a silent "No!" as he ran toward the spotted dog.

"You killed it, Daddy!" A blond-tressed girl no more than seven years old, tears streaming down her face, poked her head from the window of a station wagon stopped in the middle of the traffic-clogged road. "You killed the dog."

Two more girls, younger than the first, had heads out of windows by the time Wayford reached the ditch and knelt beside Vanberg. He reached down and tenderly stroked the animal's head.

"What in hell have you gone and done to yourself?" The rancher's voice quavered and moisture welled in his eyes. There was no need for his knowing fingertips and palms to explore the hound's body for injury. A grotesque, twisted angle to Vanberg's back revealed the awful extent of the damage. The spine was broken, snapped by the impact. "What have you done?"

The dog's dark brown eyes rolled up to the man beside him. His tongue licked at the hand that slid beneath his head to gently cradle it.

"James, get out and see how it is," a woman in the station wagon's passenger seat demanded. She twisted around to the girls. "And you three stop your bawling. Your daddy will take care of it. Don't go on so. It's only a dog."

Wayford glanced away to escape the plea in Vanberg's eyes for his master to ease the pain as the rancher had done throughout the dog's life whether it be by removing cactus needles from a paw or doctoring a cut received while running through brush after a wayward calf. Wayford could do nothing except hold the dog's head in one palm while lovingly stroking it with the other hand, and softly reassure the hound:

"Easy, boy. Just lay here and take it easy. It'll stop hurtin' in a little while."

"Is that your dog?" The man from the station wagon trotted toward the ditch.

Wayford nodded, gaze returning to Vanberg, who continued to lick his hand.

"I didn't see him. It was an accident." The man stood over the rancher. "My daughters were acting up in back, and I was trying to get them to settle down. Your dog and another one, a white one, came running out of those trees straight for the road. I hit the brakes, but there wasn't time to stop."

A weak whine came from the hound. Vanberg's chest heaved, then he lay still.

With thumb and forefinger, Wayford closed the animal's eyes.

"Kimberly, can't you keep the girls quiet? I'm trying to talk with this man," the station wagon's driver shouted over a shoulder to his wife and wailing daughters. He looked back at the rancher. "Look, I'm willing to pay you for the dog—whatever you think he was worth."

Wayford eased both arms beneath the hound's limp body and lifted Vanberg from the ground. He tried not to recall the last time he actually had held the dog, but memories of a frisky puppy curling in lap pushed into his mind. He heard Lizzie chiding him for giving the pup far too much attention, warning that he would spoil the dog if he was not careful.

"Mister, if this isn't the time to talk, let me give you my business card. You can call me later and we'll settle this," the man urged as the rancher turned and walked toward the pickup.

"Let him be, friend," Wayford heard Harley say behind him. "Can't you see he don't want your money?"

The rancher gently placed Vanberg's body on the truck's bed and wrapped him in a ragged piece of tarpaulin. Digging the keys from a pocket, Wayford unlocked the cab and sat behind the wheel. Tears overflowed his eyes and ran down his cheeks while he started the engine and shifted into gear. He had been in Canton too long. It was time he drove back home, where Vanberg and he belonged.

ELEVEN

THE PLIERS snipped the two wires binding the bale of hay. Miguel grasped the wires in a gloved hand and nudged the hay from the pickup's tailgate. The bale struck the ground, scattering in flakes. A low mooing from a white-faced cow announced the discovery of the fresh hay, and ten cows, four with calves, trotted toward the open bale.

Miguel tapped the roof of the truck. "That is the last of the hay."

"Come on back in the cab," Wayford called to the young man.

While Miguel vaulted from the pickup's bed to the ground and hastened inside, Wayford scanned the fifty cows in this portion of his herd. In spite of the long winter, they appeared to be in good shape and to have kept their weight. Best were the calves; they'd come early this year.

"I counted four more calves." Miguel closed the door and tilted his head back to the cows. "That is a hundred in all."

"My count exactly." The rancher turned the pickup's motor over, pumped the accelerator once, and shifted into gear. "From the looks of the other cows, we got at least two hundred more on the way. If we'd get some early rain to get the grass going, we'll have 'em fattened up by late spring and ready for market. That, my friend, will mean money in the bank."

Wayford tried not to count his chickens before they hatched, but it was damned difficult not to anticipate the future. The calves and the price they would bring were needed to keep the Wide W going another year.

"You'll get a cut of that money." The rancher glanced at Miguel and added, "I can't promise how much that'll be, but I'll be fair. You've done more than your share 'round here, 'specially while I was getting over that bum ankle. I mean that. Even if you decide to move on, I want to know where you'll be stayin'. I'll send you the money."

Miguel smiled when he looked at the older man. "Does that mean I work for you now?"

"I'm workin' on that." Wayford was not prepared to tell the young man about the half-formed plans to make him legal. The rancher had not come up with a legitimate reason to apply for a green card. "I'm workin' on that."

Paul Moody's red pickup was parked beside the barn. A white pickup with a gooseneck trailer designed for six horses maneuvered to back into the open barn. Wayford smiled and shook his head. He had built the barn with its two sliding doors so that a truck and trailer might be pulled in one end and out the other. Leave it to Paul to ignore the obvious and do it the hard way.

"What should I do?" Worry lined Miguel's face as he stared at the visitors. "I thought you said we would be back from feeding before they came for the geldings."

"So did I. Paul's early." Wayford's head turned to the young man. "Everything's all right, son. Paul's a friend. He might suspect everything ain't all on the up and up with you being here, but he won't say anything to anyone. Go about your business and don't pay any heed to Paul and his hands. Saddle Frank's Pal and take him out to the calf pen. I'll help load the geldings."

Miguel nodded, but the gesture lacked confidence.

"You forget I was comin'?" Paul hailed Wayford when he stopped and opened the door to the old Ford.

"What I forgot was the time you said you'd be here," Wayford answered. "I'd swear you said 'noon.' "

Paul tugged back the sleeve to his gray leather coat to glance at the gold Rolex on his wrist. "So I'm two hours early—close enough for government work."

Miguel stepped from the pickup and moved into the barn without chancing a glance at Paul or the two ranch hands in the white truck.

"I don't recognize the boy. Who does he belong to, Clint? One of Eugenio's sons?" Paul studied Miguel for a moment then looked at his friend.

Wayford shook his head. "He drifted in the other day lookin' for work. Reckon he'll drift on after a couple of days."

Paul's cheeks expanded and gusted a breath. "I'd be careful if I was you. The boy has the look of a wetback. Even I don't want Immigration on my neck."

"I don't expect he'll be here more'n a few days. There's no money to be made in workin' for me." Wayford waved an arm to catch the attention of the man behind the white pickup's wheel. "Why don't you turn that thing around and drive in head on like you knew what you were doin' in the first place?"

When the rancher turned back, Paul riffled inside his coat and came out with a checkbook, which he opened to tear out the top check and hand to Wayford. "That should put us even to date. You sure you don't want to keep the sorrel, too? I still think he's got the looks of a fine cuttin' horse."

"The looks maybe, but not the heart. The little bay's the best of the lot." Wayford noted the disappointment on Paul's face. "I'll keep the sorrel if you're a mind, but I'll only be stealin' your money. He's never going to be competition material."

Paul glanced at the ground to nudge a rock with the side of his boot. "You're not wrong often, Clint. But this time, I think you are. Keep the sorrel and train him. It's only money."

"Long as it's your money and not mine," Wayford answered. "But don't go sayin' I fed you a line on what a fine cuttin' horse he'd make."

"You know I'd never do that." Paul winked and grinned. "Unless I needed an excuse to explain why I pissed away good money on a worthless horse."

"That's what I'm tryin' to avoid." Wayford realized his friend only half joked.

"Look, I only dropped by to give you that check. I've got a meeting at the bank at eleven. You comin' into town later?" Paul asked as he opened the door to his red pickup.

"Sometime after noon, if I can get things done around here."

"I'll probably be at the drugstore. See you there. We'll talk then." Paul closed the door behind him and immediately rolled down the window. "Hell, I almost forgot. John Allen over in Henderson called last night. Said he tried to call, but got a recording that said your phone had been disconnected. He wanted to send you three fillies to train. I told him to send them on. He said for you to expect them about Wednesday next week."

Wayford smiled. "Now that's good news."

"John also said for you to stop trying to act like some old frontier fart and get a phone put back in your house." Laughing, Paul rolled up the window, gunned the pickup, and departed in his usual cloud of dust.

The prospect of fat calves for spring, a check in his pocket, and three more horses on their way for training kept the smile on Wayford's face when he turned to the barn to call out, "Boys, we only got three of them geldings to load. Paul decided the sorrel should stay a mite longer."

Wayford leaned both elbows on the top rail of the fence and watched Miguel put Frank's Pal through his paces. A month of seeing the young man and horse work together served to fortify the rancher's earlier speculations about letting Miguel ride the colt in competition. Miguel and Frank's Pal were a natural team. The boy's intuitive feel for the colt was uncanny. It was as though Miguel had a direct connection to the horse's brain that prepared him for every sudden stop, sideways lunge, and lightning bob the colt made. Miguel sat in the saddle without jostling so much as a strand of his black hair.

I've got to come up with a way of getting him a green card, Wayford's resolve doubled. Not to have Miguel riding Frank's Pal in Fort Worth would be akin to a mortal sin.

The crunch of tire rubber on the dirt road leading to the house lifted the rancher's head while he rolled himself a smoke. The blue and white pickup with horse trailer in tow that turned toward the barn left him puzzled. Surely John Allen could not have gotten his fillies on the road this soon. He only talked with Paul last night.

The pickup eased beside the house on a line for the barn before Wayford recognized Bryan Owens behind the wheel of the new Dodge truck. Bryan braked beside the rancher and stepped from the cab. "I didn't know what to do, except bring these horses over to you."

"Horses?" Wayford hiked a questioning eyebrow.

"Yeah. I decided if you wouldn't work for me on a permanent basis, I'd have to hire you to break these five horses I just went and bought. Don't know of anyone else to trust until I can get myself someone to come work for me," Bryan said.

"For racing?" Wayford moved behind the trailer and perused the two horses inside. Both looked young, no more than two years old.

"You know, quarter-horse racin' isn't my line. I can break 'em for you, but I wouldn't know how to go about trainin' them for a track."

"Just want 'em broke." Bryan's attention shifted from his own horses to Frank's Pal in the calf pen. "I'll drive the other three over Monday or Tuesday. That's assuming you want to take on the work?"

"You're assumin' correct." The day, despite an overcast of thin gray clouds, was developing into the brightest Wayford had seen in months. "These two are halter-broke, aren't they?"

"Had no trouble loading them," Bryan said while he walked toward the pen.

Retrieving a shank from the barn, Wayford unloaded a chestnut with three white-socked ankles and a black with a small white star in the center of his forehead. Then he filled the water buckets in the two horses' stalls and rejoined Bryan by the pen.

"That your own colt, or are you trainin' it for someone?" Bryan asked, never taking his eyes off Miguel and Frank's Pal.

"Mine."

"You don't happen to have an askin' price for him, do you?"

Wayford pursed his lips. "Never thought about selling him. Always planned to take him to Fort Worth this fall."

"Damn fine horse." Bryan continued to study the colt and rider. "You know, I've never had myself a top-quality cutter. I wouldn't mind takin' him off your hands. I'd like to have an animal that would take some of the wind out of Paul Moody's sails. Hell, for a year now all I've heard from him is about that sorrel gelding and what a cuttin' horse he'll be."

Wayford smiled and shook his head. "No need to worry yourself about the sorrel. He ain't much horse."

"Ten thousand," Bryan offered out of thin air. "I'll draw up a check for ten thousand right here and now."

The offer drew Wayford back. He had never considered the possibility of selling Frank's Pal. The offer was genuine, as was the reason. Ten years younger than Paul Moody, Bryan always viewed the older rancher's success as a pinnacle to be conquered and surpassed. Competition had made Paul and Bryan friends and kept them close. For Bryan, surpassing Paul's achievements was a lifelong ambition; for Paul, the younger man kept him on his toes.

"Make it twelve while you're mullin' it over," Bryan upped the offer.

Twelve thousand dollars was thousands under what Frank's Pal would be worth once he proved himself in Fort Worth. That was a might be. The twelve thousand lay on the table now; it could clear away a lot of bills and edge the Wide W back into the black. Wayford could not ignore the temptation that tugged at him.

"No. I reckon he ain't for sale." Frank's Pal was the future he built; a man could not sell away the future even for twelve thousand dollars. "I'm gonna go all the way with the colt. I've put too much work in him not to."

"I guess you haven't changed your mind about the Wide W?" Bryan asked.

"I stand where I stood last time you asked."

With a shrug, Bryan turned back to his pickup. "You know where to get in touch with me if you do change your mind about this ranch or that colt." Bryan took a checkbook off the dash board. He scribbled out a check and handed it to Wayford. "This should get you started on my horses."

The two thousand written on the amount line made the day doubly bright. "This'll be a good start."

"See you in town later?" Paul slid behind the wheel.

"Later," Wayford confirmed.

As Bryan pulled away, the rancher half ran to the calf pen, patting the two checks folded in the breast pocket of his coat. "Miguel, take the colt in and cool him off. Soon as we get him in the stall, we're heading into town to do a little celebrating!"

Cueva de leon translated from Spanish into English as "the cave of the lion." CUEVA DE LEON was the name on the sign standing outside a Fort Davis Mexican food restaurant that served the best, in Wayford's opinion, chiles rellenos in Texas. The rancher and Miguel sat within the Cueva de Leon working on plates heaped with three of the deep-fried peppers stuffed with cheese and beef. Wayford particularly enjoyed the way the restaurant fried the breaded crust the peppers were dipped in until they were slightly crunchy.

This evening meal of chili rellenos, refried beans, rice, buttered corn tortillas, and iced tea tasted especially good. For the first time since Lizzie's death, Wayford did not feel like a man mere moments from drowning. After depositing Paul's and Bryan's checks in the bank, he had spent the majority of the afternoon tending to bills. There were still a few small ones floating around unpaid, but the big ones at the feed store and the veterinarian were erased from the books. To top that off, five hundred remained in the checking account. The amount would see him over until the calves were marketed in late spring.

Might even consider buying a new radio, he thought, remembering the fillies that would be in next week. More importantly, he had a little surprise for Miguel, which he drew from a back pocket and placed on the table. He edged the white envelope toward the young man.

Miguel looked up from his food, eying the envelope and the old man.

"Go on and take it," the rancher urged. "It ain't near enough for all the work you've done, but it's all I could spare right now. After we sell the calves, there'll be more, I promise you that."

Miguel picked up the envelope and opened it to reveal two crisp hundred-dollar bills inside. His eyes widened, and his head snapped up. *"Señor* Clint, are you certain?"

"Certain that if I had more, it would be in there," Wayford replied.

"My mother and father will be happy to see this." Miguel replaced the bills and put the envelope in the breast pocket of his shirt, his fingers lingering on it for a moment.

"If I'd been thinking, I'd given it to you earlier. We could have gotten a money order at the post office, and you could have sent it to them."

"I would like to take this to them." Miguel picked up his fork and edged a bite of chili meat around on the plate. "That is, if there is time. I would take no more than a couple of days."

Panic tightened Wayford's chest. Maybe he'd misjudged the boy; maybe Miguel *was* just another wetback. Once he left, the rancher would never see him again.

No, Wayford calmed himself. A month together taught him Miguel could be trusted. "You haven't taken off a day since you came back to the Wide W. You should take a few days off. Seein' your family would be a good thing. Besides, you still don't work for me."

"I will come back." Miguel apparently detected a hint of doubt in the older man's voice. "I like working with the horses."

For a moment, the rancher hesitated, pondering whether to tell

the young man the rest of his news. He did not want it to appear
that he dangled a carrot under Miguel's nose to make sure he would
return north of the border. His original intention had been to find a
method to allow the boy to stay in the United States. He hoped
Miguel took it that way.

"Son, I think I've figured a way to make you legal, get you a
green card," Wayford offered while he cut another bite of the spicy
stuffed pepper. "That is, if you're interested in stayin' in Texas."

Miguel, mouth full of food, nodded eagerly. He swallowed hastily. "Will I then work for you?"

"At least part-time."

The rancher explained his plan. The park service needed experienced workers for their reconstruction of the adobe brick buildings
at old Fort Davis. They had difficulty keeping any one who knew
adobe because of funding restrictions. Mainly there was not enough
federal money to hire knowledgeable workers except on a part-time
basis. Men could not survive on part-time wages.

"The way I see it, you take that job, work for the government in
the afternoons," Wayford continued. "In the mornings, you help
me with the horses. That would give you two jobs. The government
won't care much about what I need. But you're what they need. I
think we can swing it."

"And I will finally work for you?" Miguel smiled as he asked the
question.

"Yep. Though I can't promise much more than what you're already getting from me. You've seen the shape I'm in." The rancher
shrugged.

"Then I think you should see about getting me this green card."
Miguel's smile widened. "If I have to work with adobe mud to ride
the horses, I will work in the mud."

"I thought that would be your answer, but I wanted to make
certain before I went and talked with Immigration." The rancher
scooped the last bite from his plate, then used a tortilla to sop up
the remaining mixture of cheese and sauce. He rolled a cigarette
and smoked it while Miguel cleaned his own plate. "If either one of
us can waddle our stuffed bellies to the door, we should be headin'
home. Still got stock to feed before the sun goes down."

Miguel and Wayford rose, paid their bill at the cash register, and
walked outside into the face of an icy north wind. The rancher

inhaled deeply. He tasted moisture in the air although the late-afternoon sky was cloudless.

"Clinton Wayford." A man stepped from a dust-covered white Ford parked at the side of the restaurant. "Mr. Wayford, could I speak to you a moment?"

The rancher recognized Francisco Cristobal, who worked at the county courthouse. "Right with you, Paco." Wayford handed Miguel the pickup's keys. "Go on and get yourself warm. I'll be there in a minute. I have no idea what Paco wants. I never see much of him except when I have to get my license tags each year."

While Miguel trotted to the truck, rubbing the cold from his arms, the rancher walked to Francisco Cristobal's car. The man cracked open a briefcase and dug a hand around inside it.

"I'm sorry to bother you, but I saw you inside when I was catching a late lunch." Francisco's hand came out of the briefcase with an envelope. He passed it to Wayford. "It was easier to give this to you here than drive all the way out to your place Monday morning."

The rancher used a finger to rip open the flap. Inside was a tax notice. He caught his breath when his gaze dipped to the total. He had not seen that much money in one lump for at least two years.

"Part of that is delinquent and fines for not paying last year," Francisco explained before Wayford found his voice. "There's a big push to collect all the overdue taxes, Mr. Wayford. You know, the times being what they are, and the legislature and courts keeping the school systems all topsy-turvy what with the Robin Hood plan they passed."

Wayford followed the news articles on Texas's school taxing plan that had been tied up in the courts for years. He did not see how it affected the total to which his eyes kept returning.

"The pressure the legislature is putting on the commissioners is like nothing the county has ever seen before. The state is threatening to cut off all its funding unless the county does everything it can to collect all the back taxes. You aren't the only one who's getting a personally delivered notice. This briefcase has at least a hundred envelopes in it."

Francisco paused as though expecting Wayford to comment, but the rancher still recovered from the shock of seeing the total owed.

"The commissioners gave me very specific instructions that I was supposed to make certain everyone understood that it's a must they pay their taxes—a double-barreled must," Francisco said. "They're giving everyone until March first to get their business straight. If you haven't, your land and property will be placed on the auction block."

It took another breath for Wayford to find his voice. "It doesn't make sense. The county's always been lenient in hard times. Back in the early seventies, they carried me five years. They knew I'd make good when I could."

The county employee shrugged helplessly. "Those were different times, Mr. Wayford. And you were a young . . ."

Francisco cast an embarrassed glance at the ground as his voice trailed off.

"I'll have the money at the courthouse by the due date." The rancher stuffed the notice into a coat pocket. "And you can tell whoever's worried, I ain't about to go and die owin' the county one red cent."

He pivoted sharply without giving the man a chance to reply. He held his back straight and forced a proud crispness in his stride as he crossed the parking lot to the pickup. His posture, however, was no more than that, a posture. Fear encircled his heart and tightened like a steel band. He was not prepared for this. The total on the notice was far beyond his means. His mind spun as he desperately tried to shuffle the debts he owed and allow the property taxes to take precedence. Even if all the bills were set aside, it did not help. He saw no way of getting the tax money by the first of March, or even March first next year.

TWELVE

PAUL MOODY stepped behind the desk set in the corner of an unpretentious office. The wood-paneled walls were decorated sparsely with two shelves of books and a velvet-mounted .44 caliber 1851 model Navy Colt revolver. The revolver was the genuine article, handed down from Paul's great-great-grandfather, who bore the pistol while serving as a Texas Ranger.

"Here he is." Paul stabbed a finger at his open address book, then found a piece of paper and pen and began writing. "Last year when Enrique brought his cousin up from Mexico City, he helped get him a green card. You might have to send Miguel back across the border a few days and let the parks folks go down and bring him up like he's never set foot on U.S. soil, but I don't think they'll be any trouble. Especially since you're offering work, room, and board for the boy."

Wayford glanced at the name and phone number of the immigration officer Paul had jotted down, folded the paper, and slipped it in his back pocket. "Thanks, I'll drive into town and call him Monday."

The rancher fell silent, staring down at the open hands in his lap. Miguel was only one of the reasons he visited his best friend tonight. The second matter did not come as easily. A man tried to keep his debts to himself.

"What else is it, Clint?" Paul's gaze met his friend's eyes. "You've been as quiet as a church mouse most of the evening. Rachel noticed it at supper. She gave me at least twenty what's-the-matter looks. It ain't like you to be so quiet, and you didn't drop in just to talk about the Mexican boy."

"I thought I was hidin' it better than that." Wayford smiled weakly. He visited his friend for this; there was no reason for shyness. He went straight to the heart of the matter. "Paul, I need your advice. I'm ass-deep in tax problems, and I can't figure a way out of them. Try as I may, my mind refuses to get on the track."

Paul stepped from behind the desk and took a chair beside his friend to listen while Wayford told of the envelope Francisco Cristobal had handed him that afternoon. When the rancher completed the recounting, Paul sat silent for several moments.

Finally he said, "The easiest solution is for me to walk over to the desk and write you a check for the whole amount. I've no worries about you being good for it. You can pay it back whenever you get it. We've been friends for a long time. I'd like to—"

"I came for advice, not a handout, Paul." Wayford shook his head with finality.

"I was afraid your stubborn streak would show itself." Paul stared at his friend. "You know five thousand dollars isn't much in today's financial world. A bank would give you the money without blinking."

"I won't take from Peter to pay Paul. I'd still owe five thousand, only with interest." Wayford had considered going to a bank, but discarded the idea hours before driving to Paul's home. He had shied clear of bank loans all his life. As much as he needed the five thousand, he would not go to them now.

"Afraid of that, too." Paul leaned back in his chair and glanced at the ceiling. "Saturday at the drugstore, you mentioned having at least a hundred calves already. Sell them."

"If I sell my calves now, they'll bring less than half—"

"If you don't sell them, they won't be yours to fatten for spring," Paul cut him short. "Depending on the market, you can get fifty to a hundred a head for young calves. A lot of folks are always looking for calves to fatten and sell this time of year."

"Not around here. Don't know of a man needin' young calves." Wayford stared at his friend; Paul talked nonsense.

"Agreed, so we have to sell to folks who don't live around here." Paul rose and stepped to his desk again. He picked up a small brochure. "Got this a few weeks back. A feller over in Alpine has started a new business. He comes to a man's place and video tapes the stock he's trying to sell. That tape then goes out on satellite and is broadcast to buyers across the country. The stock then goes on auction, only everything is done by telephone rather than in an auction ring."

"Let me take a look at that." Wayford read the pamphlet three times before asking, "Think this feller will bother himself with just a hundred calves?"

"If he's really in business, he will." Paul hiked his eyebrows.

"Then let's see if he's in business. Let's give him a call."

Wayford signed the bill of sale, folded it into an envelope, and handed it to Jerry Alton, a businessman who turned out to be a junior at Sul Ross. The twenty-year-young man, armed with camera, audio equipment, tape editor, and backing from his Waco father, had read an article on satellite cattle auctions and decided to go into business for himself. Wayford was his third client.

"There'll be a cattle truck down from New Mexico in ten days to pick up the calves," the young entrepreneur said. "I gave my assurance the calves would be penned and ready to load."

"I'll have 'em right over there, ready to ship out the minute the truck gets here." The rancher pointed to the calf pen with its wooden loading chute.

"Here's your check, minus my five percent." Jerry passed a check for five thousand eight hundred fifty dollars to the rancher. "It's been a pleasure doing business with you, Mr. Wayford. Give me a call this spring when you're ready to sell the rest of your calves and those steers."

The rancher nodded. "That was our agreement, and that's what I'll do."

"Then I'll be seeing you this spring." The young man shook Wayford's hand, turned, climbed into a black Corvette, and drove from the house.

The rancher watched the young man depart for several moments, then reread the check from a Los Cruces stockman. Exactly one week had passed from video tape to check. When Jerry Alton had first arrived at the Wide W, and Wayford had seen how young he was, the rancher never expected any results at all.

Not only did the college student get results, he also assured himself of a repeat customer. The young man had absorbed the five percent cost of transmitting the video tape with the agreement that he would handle the Wide W sales for the next year. Thanks to his father's backing, Jerry Alton could afford to take a small loss now to make a bigger profit in a few months. The boy, or his father, had a good business head on his shoulders.

He wished he had a mite more business sense himself. With it, he might not have found himself in this predicament. Spring would not be as good as he had anticipated; he would have a rough time making ends meet. *But,* he told himself, *I'll still have the Wide W.* That was a striding step in the right direction, and a shoulder-bending burden lifted from his back.

Wayford walked into the house to clean himself up for the drive into town and his visit to the courthouse. Afterward he would stop by Paul's to tell him all that had happened and thank him again for his help.

The drugstore on Wednesday afternoon appeared to be the same gathering place Wayford had come to for coffee and pie all of his adult life. It was not. An alien feel permeated the air. The rancher sensed it the moment he walked in the door. There was nothing physically different about the drugstore, he realized while he surveyed the tables' occupants. It was the people indulging themselves on hamburgers, milk shakes, and malts. They were all tourists. Not one familiar face glanced up to greet the rancher.

He took a stool at the soda fountain and ordered coffee and lemon pie from a young girl who informed him that even George Scheppler was absent today. Scheppler had driven to Midland for supplies that morning and was not expected back before closing time.

Refusing to allow the lack of company to dampen his relief at having put the owed taxes behind him, Wayford sliced into the pie the waitress placed on the counter in front of him. Perhaps it was his mood, but the tartness of the lemon pleased his taste buds more than it had in months. Nor did he taste the slightest trace of bitterness in the coffee.

He resisted the urge to pull out his checkbook and take another glance at the remaining balance. There was enough to make it until he sold the spring calves. Continuing through the coming year was another thing. Paul's friend John Allen had not sent the promised fillies. Wayward made a mental note to get the man's phone number from Paul later. A call when he came back to town on Saturday would assure him the horses were still coming.

"Hi! How's it going?"

The rancher glanced over a shoulder to see the waitress greet a deputy sheriff who walked inside. The young woman's beaming smile and eager tone bespoke an interest that went beyond selling the handsome law officer coffee and lemon pie.

"Pretty quiet day until about an hour ago." The deputy settled on a stool and pointed to the coffee. "I need it good and strong."

The waitress poured a cup and brought it to the counter. "What happened an hour ago?"

"Had to escort an ambulance out to the Moody ranch . . ."

Wayford swung around on his stool, listening.

"Paul Moody had a heart attack," the deputy continued. "We must have covered that road at a hundred and twenty getting there. It didn't do a damned bit of good. He was dead by the time the paramedics got to him."

Wayford did not wait to hear more. Coffee and pie forgotten, he ran from the drugstore to his pickup. Paul Moody was dead. It could not be; it just could not be!

THIRTEEN

CLINT WAYFORD DROVE. Vaguely he remembered climbing into the pickup after the funeral and starting the engine. He was not certain of anything after that. The service, the final laying to rest of Paul Moody, dominated his mind, repeating itself over and over like a loop of video tape until every detail was acid-etched into his brain.

The rancher's gaze darted from side to side. He drove through the mountains, but he found no landmark to orient himself. A glance at the speedometer sent a cold shiver racing up his spine. The needle edged seventy; a speed guaranteed to send car or truck careening from the twisting highway. He jerked his foot from the gas pedal and eased to a grassy shoulder as the pickup gradually halted. He leaned forward, forehead resting against the steering wheel. A quavering breath escaped his lips in a shaky gust.

"He looks just like he's asleep."

"My, my, don't he look natural."

The inane comments of those who passed by Paul's open casket refused to leave Wayford's mind. Paul had not looked natural or asleep. He appeared cold and lifeless—dead. The embalmed lump of flesh lowered into the hard winter ground while the preacher uttered set and pat standard funeral rite Number 103A was not Paul Moody. Paul Moody was gone. Where, the rancher was uncertain, but he was gone. The emptiness left where he had once walked transformed to a mass of solid, contorting pain.

Slinging open the cab's door, Wayford stepped outside. A frigid blast of wind slapped his face. His eyes widened from the unexpected shock. He sucked down a series of quieting breaths and felt the pain and confused frustration subside.

Paul was dead; for three days he had been gone. There was nothing he could do for him now. Rachel, however, was alive. He had promised her that he would come to the ranch after the funeral. If the torment she endured was but a fraction of what he felt when Lizzie died, then Rachel needed a friend. He had to put aside his own sense of loss, straighten his back, and be there for her as she and Paul had been there for him.

Inhaling the frost carried on the wind, he surveyed his surroundings. What had been alien landscape but moments ago now contained a comforting familiarity. Over a shoulder he saw the gleaming white domes of McDonald Observatory. In spite of a lead foot on the accelerator, he had driven only twenty miles from town. He recalled his decision to take the scenic loop through the mountains to clear his head before having to face all the well-wishers who would gather at the Moody Ranch to pay their condolences to Rachel and her daughters.

He wanted to stand in the cold and allow the mountain to absorb him, but Rachel needed a friend now more than she ever had in her life. As much as he dreaded facing those at the ranch, it was his duty to be there for Rachel. He climbed back into the pickup and turned the engine over.

"Dammit, Clint, I'm going to miss Paul." Tom Voss stood in the open door, staring over the plains. "I wasn't as close to him as you were, but I liked Paul, liked him a hell of a lot. He'd give a friend the shirt off his own back if a man needed it. I know that's said about a lot of folks, but with Paul it was true. He might have been the richest man in the county, but he never lorded it over anyone. He was just good folks. I'll miss him."

"We'll all miss him, Tom." The words sounded hollow to Wayford's own ears. After saying goodbyes to parting friends for an hour, he felt like a sponge that had been wrung out. Any phrase he spoke sounded trite and worn.

Tom glanced back at his friend. "Tell Rachel that for me, will you, Clint? Tell her how much we'll miss Paul. I've never been good at putting things into words."

"I'll tell her, Tom," Wayford assured his fellow rancher.

"Thank you." Tom turned and walked to his pickup parked beneath a barren mesquite.

Wayford closed the door. Except for the clink of dish and glass as two Mexican maids worked in the kitchen, the immense house lay silent. He moved into the living room. Glasses, plates, and flatware left by the fifty people who had crammed into the house were gone. Not even a dirty ashtray remained. The maids knew what was required tonight and worked quickly and efficiently to do it. The den was as clean as the living room.

The rancher stepped to the kitchen where the women worked as a team on the stacks of dishes piled by a sink brimming with soap suds. The two looked up when he entered.

"*¿Dónde está Señora Moody?*" Wayford asked.

One of the women pointed to the back of the house. "*Alcoba.*"

Thanking them, he walked down a long hallway to the master bedroom and lightly rapped his knuckles on the door. Rachel answered the knock.

"Come inside, Clint." She stepped back to let him enter. "Sorry, I had to slip away. It was rude, but I would have broken down if another person told me how sorry they were. I had to get away."

The rancher nodded. "I understand. I just wanted to tell you everyone has left and see if there was anything I could do for you before I headed back to the house."

Rachel looked at her two daughters. "Suellen, Mary Beth, you two go into the den and give Clint and me a few moments, will you?"

The two women left the bedroom silently. Rachel stared down at a silk handkerchief wadded in her hands. "I thought about this day, Clint. Ever since Elizabeth passed on, I had to face the possibility of Paul dying. I knew it would be hard. I didn't know how hard. It feels like something reached inside me and ripped out half of me."

"I know." Wayford rested a hand on her shoulder. "I know."

"Does it ever get easier?" Her eyes lifted up to him. "Does the hurt finally go away?"

"You learn to live with it. But when you love someone the way you loved Paul, the hurt never goes away." He could not lie to her as much as he wanted to provide comfort. "You just learn to live with it."

His gaze traveled around the room. Four half-packed suitcases lay open on the bed. The closets stood open, and clothes were folded on dresser and chairs. He felt Rachel staring at him and turned to her.

"I'm leaving, Clint," she said. "I don't think I could stay here alone in this house even if that was one of my options. I'm taking a few things with me. Movers will come for the rest."

The rancher's brow furrowed. "Leaving?"

"I'm going back to Houston with Suellen. The sooner I'm out of here, the sooner the lawyers can get their work done and straighten everything out."

"Lawyers?" Each word she spoke befuddled him.

A sad smile played at the corners of Rachel's mouth. "I have to leave, Clint. Paul left enough debt to give any ten normal men heart attacks. It's a wonder the pressure didn't kill him sooner. Sometimes, I actually think he thrived on it."

Rachel stared at the rancher for a moment, then shook her head. "You don't know what I'm talking about, do you? No, I guess you don't. Paul always glossed things over so that they looked bright and shiny, even with you, his best friend. Maybe especially with you, Clint, because you were like the brother he never had."

Wayford nodded. "I always thought if God had intended me to have a brother, it would have been Paul."

"You would have been the big brother and Paul the little brother." Rachel took his hand and squeezed it. "Little brothers have a way of wanting to impress their older siblings. They paint a smooth picture so that everything seems better than it is."

"The lawyers? Did Paul have trouble with lawyers?" The rancher still was not sure what she was saying.

"No," Rachel replied, shaking her head. "It's the lawyers that are going to save me. It's the banks, Clint. It always was the banks. Half the people in this state thought Paul was knee-deep in millions. I guess he was—on paper. Paul might have been the last of the Texas wheeler-dealers when it came to shuffling paper with bankers."

Wayford listened while his best friend's widow revealed a life-style that was a whirlwind of financial triple switchbacks amid banks stretching from El Paso to Texarkana. Paul managed to raise the funds to pay off one deal to find himself indebted to ten new lending establishments. He balanced on a taut wire strung between success and disaster.

"The older Paul got, the desire to expand his interests, like some cattle baron in the Old West, became an obsession with him." Rachel's gaze focused on Clint. "He didn't understand a man, a man by himself, couldn't do that today. It's corporations and accountants who make empires now. Corporations made up of men who care about profit margins and tax shelters and have never set eyes on this land or a steer. A man who cares, a man with a conscience, can't compete with the corporations. Paul never understood that."

Numbed by the revelation, Wayford stared at the relative opulence of the Moody mansion compared to his own adobe ranch house. "None of this, the ranch, the oil interests, none of this was yours and Paul's?"

"Was and is—on paper, at least for the next couple of weeks. The attorneys tell me that by the time they sell off everything to pay the debts, there'll be a little left over. I'll have enough so I won't be a burden on my daughters and their husbands, but . . ." Her voice trailed away as she turned to gaze out the open bedroom window. The distance held in her unfocused stare spoke of a lost dream, one shared with Paul, one that died with him.

"Rachel, I feel out of my league here, but if there's anything I can do, you know you can call on me," the rancher offered, though he knew the scope of her problems lay far beyond his abilities.

"I know that, Clint." She turned from the window. "I gave your name to the lawyers. I told them to come to you if they had any questions about the ranch and the stock."

Wayford nodded.

"There is one thing I won't sell. Paul mentioned on several occasions that if anything ever happened to him, I was to see that you got it. He said he wanted to make sure you remembered him every day of your life." A weak smile attempted to climb to her lips and was stillborn.

Rachel reached out and took his hand. "Come with me a moment, and we'll get it. After that I've got to get back to my packing. Suellen wants to get on the road for Houston."

Rachel led him from the house to the center barn of three that stood behind her home. Inside they moved to a wood-paneled tack room.

"There it is. He wanted you to have it." She pointed to a black saddle inlaid with silver. "He always said it should have been yours in the first place. It would have been, if you hadn't had an unlucky break."

Wayford stared at the rodeo prize won by an eighteen-year-old Paul Moody. A million things that needed to be said crowded the rancher's mind, but when he tried to give them voice, they lodged in his throat.

"Clint, I've got to get back to my packing." Rachel rose on her toes and lightly kissed his cheek. "Soon as I'm settled in Houston, I'll write you. We have to stay in touch. We're all that's left of the four of us."

The words he wanted to say still refused to come. All he could do was stand and stare at the saddle while she turned and left him alone in the tack room. Memories of a lifetime and a friend called Paul Moody flooded his mind. He crossed to the wooden stand on which the black saddle was prominently displayed. Reverently he lifted it with both arms and carried it to his pickup. Rather than tossing it unceremoniously into the back, the usual treatment for tack, he opened the passenger door and placed it on the bench seat.

Once behind the wheel, he started the engine to move down the long dirt road to the highway. Two miles later, he pulled to a shoulder and stopped. The tears that filled his eyes totally obscured his vision. With the abandon of a child he wept for a lost friend, for Rachel, for himself.

FOURTEEN

WAYFORD turned from the highway onto the washboard road leading to the Wide W. He steeled himself for the task at hand. For a week, Paul's death had haunted him, forcing him to face the fool's reality he lived. The moment of truth approached. He had reached a decision; he had to be man enough to see it through.

He didn't understand a man, a man by himself, couldn't do that today. It's corporations and accountants who make empires now. Rachel's words echoed in his head as they had since she had spoken them. If a man like Paul Moody could not make it, what possible hope did he have?

The desire to leave his grandchildren a legacy was only an old man's foolish dream. The harsh reality was that he shuffled his monthly bills the way Paul juggled bank notes. The amounts might not tally, but the total was the same. He was a man in debt whose legacy would be a mountain of bills left for Mary and Frank to pay. He could not do that to them. He would not leave his family as Paul had left Rachel.

Pride. He recognized what burned within him for what it was. Many would label it simplemindedness. If pride meant a man standing on his own two feet, accepting the consequences of his own actions, then he was simpleminded.

The time God allotted for his life was drawing close to its end; Paul's death cruelly drove that home. He refused to be a burden to his daughter and her family in those remaining short years. He must assure that his grandchildren remembered him as a man and not some dirt-poor fool who sucked their family dry with his debts.

Braking outside the barn, Wayford stepped into the cold and called, "Miguel! Miguel! Come on out here. I need to talk with you."

As the boy ducked out of the barn, the rancher took an envelope from his coat and held it out to Miguel. "There's five hundred dollars in here."

A grin split Miguel's face. "You've got more horses for us!"

"I've decided to sell out." The words came easier than Wayford had expected. "I took that from the bank to set things straight between us. It ain't what you deserve, but it should help your family. I expect you'll be wantin' to take it down to them."

Miguel stared at the older man, his face awash with disbelief. "You are going to sell the ranch and the horses?"

"I've thought about it for a long time. I can't keep my head above water. I'm going to sell out before I lose everything." Wayford held out a hand to stop the young man when his mouth opened. "Ain't nothing you can say that'll make me change my mind. I'm tired of being a stubborn jackass. It's time I did the right thing."

"But my green card?" Miguel blinked in confusion. "I start to work at the fort next week. I do this so that I can work with you and the horses."

The rancher looked away. He had made promises to the boy that he could not fulfill. It was better Miguel faced reality now rather than losing himself in an old man's foolish dreams. "I'll talk with Bryan Owens about hiring you tomorrow when I drive over to see him. He's looking for someone who can handle horses. There shouldn't be a problem. The fact is, it will work out better for you. Bryan can pay regular wages."

Miguel's lips parted as though to speak. He swallowed and nodded. "If that is the way you want it."

"It ain't the way I want it. It's the way it is," Wayford answered. "If you want to visit your family in Mexico, now's the time to do it. However, you're more than welcome to stay on here until I get things worked out with Bryan. I owe you that, more than that."

Miguel stared at the ground and shook his head. "No, I will go. I will get my things."

The young man started toward the ranch house, then abruptly swung around. "*Señor* Clint, it may not be my place to say, but what you do is wrong. If it is money, then you can have the money I will make at the fort. It will be like an investment. There is more money in the horses than in adobe bricks. We can work together as we have been. We can—"

Wayford cut him off. "No, Miguel. I won't even think of you pissing away hard-earned money on this place. You got yourself a chance of making a go of it. Don't go and blow it by thinkin' crazy, son. Bryan Owens is a good man. You work for him."

Miguel's chest heaved, but he offered no further protest. The boy turned and disappeared into the house.

Wayford fed and watered the horses at a leisurely pace. He purposely stretched out the morning routine, soaking in the feel and smell of the barn. His eyes caressed every inch of the structure while his mind tried to memorize each detail. He acted like a sentimental old man, but did not care. After he talked with Bryan Owens this morning, the Wide W would no longer be his. Although it would take a few days for the papers to be worked out and the signatures to be placed on the dotted line, these few hours were the last he could truly call the ranch his.

Coiling the watering hose, he hung it on the wall and sat down on the stoop to the feed room. While he rolled a cigarette and lit it, he went over what must be done.

First he would load Frank's Pal and half the tack in the trailer. Next, drive into Fort Davis to call Bryan and let him know he was on his way. The colt and tack would assure his fellow rancher he was dead serious about selling. The money Frank's Pal brought would erase everything Wayford owed.

While the title transfer and the other necessary papers were drawn up, he would call Jerry Alton in Alpine and arrange for the young man to sell the rest of his stock. He would also have time to make arrangements for returning the horses to their owners.

After that?

He was not certain. But he was damned if he would go to Lubbock to live with Mary. Like as not, he would buy a few acres in the Davis Mountains Resort and have a trailer house pulled in like the Harpe sisters had done. It would not be the Wide W, but he could remain in this county he so loved. Whether he liked to admit it or not, a legacy of five acres as a weekend getaway was more likely to be of use to Mary and Frank and their children than a ranch.

"Damn!" The curse burst from his lips as his head turned to the barn's open door.

Snow, small white flakes, fell from the low, gray clouds that overcast the sky.

Abruptly robbed of the luxury of leisure, he tossed down the cigarette and crushed it as he rose. Bryan Owens's place was over by Kent a good sixty miles away, if the rancher added the distance into Fort Davis for the phone call. He did not relish the thought of a drive with snow dusting the road.

Outside, he hitched trailer to pickup and drove into the barn. He forced himself to think about the burden that would be lifted from his shoulders once he was free and clear of debt as he loaded the colt. However, Fort Worth kept wiggling itself into the forefront of his thoughts. The possibility of taking one of the top prizes in the competition was hard to let slip away. Until this moment, he had not realized how much seeing the colt perform in the arena had kept him going.

"You'll still get your chance to show what you're made of." Wayford patted the colt's rump as he walked toward the pickup's cab. "I'll see that Bryan understands you're meant for Fort Worth."

He was not as sure about Miguel. When he left earlier, the boy had the look of someone who never wanted to see this part of Texas again. He had money enough to make it to a city now, if that is what he wanted.

"Hope the hell he's got sense to find a place to keep warm until this snow lets up." Wayford eyed the clouds overhead as he eased truck and trailer from the barn.

Clint Wayford gave a start behind the wheel. Actinic lightning flashed and thunder boomed a split second later. He blinked to clear his eyes and leaned forward in the seat, straining to see beyond the heavy rain and sleet that pelted the windshield.

His right hand reached out to slide the defroster up two notches. In spite of the truck's interior heat, ice built at the perimeter of the wipers' sweeping path. If he had not called Bryan Owens and told him to expect him, he would have found a roadside park, turned around, and headed back to the Wide W. Now he hoped he could make it to Kent before the roads glazed over with ice.

Squinting, he leaned closer to the glass. Through the river of icy rain that sheeted the windshield, he saw the distorted flash of red and blue lights. His foot left the gas pedal and tapped the brake. Two highway patrol squad cars barricaded Highway 166. As Wayford brought the pickup to a halt, he saw an officer in a yellow slicker step from one of the cars and run toward him.

"Sorry, but you'll have to turn around and head back." The patrolman pointed to the east while the rancher partially rolled down a window. "Lightning struck a cliff about a mile ahead. Brought down a sizable chunk of rock onto the highway. Nobody'll be passin' this way for a few days. Not until the highway department can get some heavy equipment in and get it moved. Watch my signals. I'll help you get your rig turned around."

"Thank you, officer." Wayford shivered as he rolled up the window. The temperature felt as though it had dropped twenty degrees since he had left Fort Davis.

Outside, the patrolman switched on a flashlight. The rancher followed his directions as the officer swung the light from side to side. For one of the first times in his life, Wayford was grateful that the region's soil was more rock than dirt. Had the shoulder been of normal consistency, the pickup would have sunk axle deep in mud when he swung wide to reverse directions.

Cussing the unexpected inconvenience, the lightning, rain, and sleet, he edged back on to the highway and retraced his route. If 166 was closed, his only option was to return to Fort Davis and head for Kent on 118.

Hindsight brought a fresh string of uttered curses as Wayford eased from 166 onto 17 and trundled north at ten miles per hour into Fort Davis. Common sense had told him to take the turnoff to the Wide W miles back. He ignored it, wanting to call Bryan Owens instead, and found himself driving a road glazed with a sheet of glass-slick ice.

The radio announcer forecasted sleet and snow atop the freezing rain that pelted the Big Bend. His pronouncement came fifteen minutes too late. Snowflakes the size of two-bit pieces, mixed with birdshot-sized sleet, fell outside.

The rancher used a glove to wipe the moist fog from the side window. The snow rapidly transformed the world into a vast wash of white. In another hour it would be impossible to discern the highway. The ten miles an hour he drove would seem like lightning speed compared to his return to the Wide W. Wayford realized at five miles an hour he might, just might, be able to keep pickup and trailer on the pavement.

He forgot making his usual U-turn to park in front of the drug-store. Instead he eased to the side of the highway across from the drugstore and gently braked until the pickup came to a halt. He killed the engine and sat there for half a cigarette to make certain the heat of the tires did not melt the ice beneath them and start the truck sliding.

The rancher's steps were equally cautious when he crossed the road in a shuffling gait to enter a drugstore half filled with tourists who nursed cups of coffee while watching the snow and sleet outside. Wayford returned George Scheppler's wave while he crossed to a phone booth and dialed Bryan's number. Static answered the buttons he pushed. He replaced the receiver and tried again. More static crackled from the receiver. Three attempts to contact an operator produced the same results.

"Is there phone trouble?" he asked when settled at the soda fountain's counter where George placed coffee and lemon pie before him.

"Not that I've noticed." The drugstore owner walked to the cash register and lifted a phone beneath the counter to place the receiver to an ear. He shook his head as he returned. "The ice must have the lines down. The phone's dead."

"Damn," Wayford muttered. "I drove all the way back here to call Bryan Owens. I knew I should've given up and headed home."

George started to answer, but four tourists seeking rooms for the night entered the door. Wayford sipped at the coffee. His stomach rumbled in a rude reminder that hours had passed since a breakfast of two sausage and biscuit sandwiches. He waved a waitress to him, ordered a cheeseburger and fries, then took a bite of the pie. At five miles an hour the drive to the Wide W would take hours; he had no intention of making the drive on an empty stomach.

"That's the last of my rooms. I never thought bad weather could be so good for business." George returned to the rancher. "Why in hell are you out on a day like this?"

"Trying to take a horse over to—"

The drugstore's door opened and two deputy sheriffs entered. As heads turned toward them, one of the officers lifted his arms and said, "Folks, folks, could I have your attention for a minute?"

When the din of background conversation died away, he continued, "I reckon y'all've noticed we got ourselves some unexpected bad weather outside. I'd like to tell you the situation will improve, but I'm afraid it's going to get worse before it gets better."

Wayford took another bite of pie while the deputy announced the old news of a rockslide blocking Highway 166. However, the officer held his full attention when he reported a wreck involving two gasoline tankers and five other vehicles on Highway 118 near Mount Locke.

"Nobody's been hurt, and there's been no gasoline spill, but things are a mess out there. The road's blocked. Two wreckers sent to the scene have skidded off the road and are sitting in Limpia Creek at this minute. The fact is, it doesn't look like the wreck will be cleared until after the storm passes and the temperature warms up enough to melt the half an inch of ice we've got on the roads."

The pop and hiss of a radio on his partner's belt interrupted him. He waited while the other deputy answered the signal. The second deputy continued where the first left off as he slipped the radio back on his waist.

"Folks, that was more bad news. Interstate 10 is closed all the way from El Paso to Sonora. The same goes for 20 up to Monahans. The Department of Public Safety just asked us to close Highway 17 leading north and south from town—also 118 goin' to Alpine. I'm afraid all you folks will have to remain here in Fort Davis until this weather takes a turn for the better."

Wayford's mumbled "son-of-a-bitch" joined the rumble of disapproval that ran through the drugstore's patrons. He was stranded in town, at least for the night. The rancher turned to George. "You said you just rented your last room?"

"Don't worry," the drugstore's owner replied. "I got a big, wide sofa in my office you can use."

"I got a colt out in the trailer," Wayford said. "Got any idea where I can put him up for the night?"

"My garage," George suggested. "You can back the trailer in there. If we keep the lights on, it should be warm enough. If not, I'll dig up a space heater."

Wayford forced a smile. "Then I guess you've got yourself some visitors for the evening."

He swiveled on the stool and looked out the half-fogged windows. The falling snow nearly obliterated the pickup and trailer across the street. "Hell, if this doesn't let up and improve by tomorrow, I might have to consider takin' myself a long walk. I've got stock back home that needs tendin'."

"No cow's going to starve to death in a day," George replied.

"Might as well relax and enjoy your cheeseburger. There's nothing else you can do."

The rancher turned around and lifted the burger George slid across the counter. "When you're right, you're right."

Miguel flashed into Wayford's mind. He prayed the young man had found a warm place to ride out the storm.

FIFTEEN

WAYFORD AWOKE. He blinked, his head jerking from side to side in confusion until he recalled where he was. Then he groaned. George's office sofa had tied a dozen minor knots in his back during the night.

Rising, he tugged on his boots and found a small bathroom off the right side of the office. After relieving himself and washing face and hands, he returned to the sofa to neatly fold the blankets and leave them stacked with the two pillows. A glance at the falling snow through a window told him the bedding might be needed for another night.

He left the office to maneuver down a series of short angular hallways to a swinging door that led into the drugstore proper. In spite of the early hour, stranded tourists clustered around ten of the store's tables talking softly while they cast gloomy glances at the snowstorm outside. George Scheppler sat at a round table with four officers. Two of the lawmen wore the insignia of highway patrolmen. A waitress brought the rancher a cup of coffee and took his breakfast order as he joined his friend, who introduced the officers.

"Clint Wayford? You run a spread called the Wide W?" one of the patrolmen asked. When Clint nodded, he continued, "Then I guess I've got some good news for you. One of our units picked up a Mexican boy named Miguel Ramos yesterday when all this weather was getting started. They drove him over to your place after he showed them his green card."

"Glad to hear that." Wayford felt a weight lift from his shoulders. "He left to visit his family yesterday morning. I was afraid he was stuck out in all of this."

"We're glad to hear he belonged on the Wide W," the patrolman replied. "The boys were worried about leaving him there when they didn't find anyone at home."

"Miguel's where he belongs," the rancher assured him. "It's me that's out of pocket. The roads as bad as I think they are?"

"Worse," one of the two deputies at the table answered with a shake of his head. "We had some more rain last night. If you brush away the snow, the ice looks at least an inch thick."

"Brush away the snow!" The second deputy laughed. "Hell, a man's got to shovel it away. We got two feet of snow out there."

The pop of portable radios hissed around the table. A patrolman pulled his unit from his waist. Wayford tried to discern a voice amid the static, but could not. Apparently the officer deciphered the garbled tones, because he ten-foured the message and shook his head as he glanced at the others seated at the table. "Try number six just went off the road. This time we've got two injuries. Nothing serious, but Tug Newman broke an arm. They splinted it until they can get him into Alpine."

A deputy pulled a map from a back pocket and spread it on the table. After studying it a few minutes he shrugged. "I don't see any other way of getting in there. The winds are too strong for the Air Force to send in a rescue helicopter and every damned road is too icy to get a ground team in."

"Rescue?" Wayford's brow knitted.

"A single-engine plane went down in the mountains about four this morning," a patrolman explained. "Best we can make on the plane is, it was a Piper Cherokee Archer on route from Tucson to San Antonio. The pilot was a San Antonio real estate broker. His wife and four-year-old daughter were the only passengers. He was trying to make it to the airport in Marfa when he realized this storm was a killer. A couple of custodians out at the observatory saw the plane's lights as it went down."

"After the crash, the pilot got on his radio," George picked up. "He reported that his wife was dead and that he was seriously injured. The little girl had a few bumps and scratches, but appeared to be all right."

"That's all he got off before the radio apparently went dead." The deputy pushed the map across the table. "From what the janitors saw, we think it crashed in this area."

The rancher followed the deputy's fingertip to a point near Limpia Spring on Mount Livermore, the Davis Mountains' highest peak, standing at close to eighty-four hundred feet. "There are jeep trails and pack trails back up in there."

"We know," the deputy answered. "We can't get a vehicle, even a four-wheel drive, close enough to get to them. The ice outside is treacherous. Command is trying to decide what to do next. I guess they'll send a team in on foot if they have to, but that'll take hours to get the personnel and equipment together. What with the telephone lines being down over most this part of the state, it's damned hard to contact anyone who knows what he's doing."

"Meanwhile, the pilot and his daughter are likely to freeze to death before we can get help to them." This from a patrolman. "It doesn't look good, not good at all."

Again a blast of static from the radios demanded attention. The patrolman who answered the call looked at his fellow officers. "Break's over. We're to spell the crew down on 17."

"I'll send a thermos of coffee down to you in an hour or so." George stood with the officers. "Tell the other boys to come on up. I'll have ham and eggs waiting for them."

As the officers left, George moved to the kitchen, leaving Wayford to study the map left on the table. He estimated twenty miles lay between town and the crash site. *Twenty miles.* He rolled the figure over in his mind. In an age of high-speed automobiles and supersonic jets, the distance should have been covered in a matter of minutes. *Even this rough terrain.* It took Mother Nature to remind men how fragile the technological world they built was. Something as ordinary as an ice storm left them as helpless as babies.

He glanced out the drugstore's front windows. He was overly harsh in his judgment. There was nothing ordinary about this storm. Snow and ice were common for the Bend during the winter, but this bordered on a blizzard. The most snow he had ever seen on the ground at one time was eight inches. Two feet now blanketed the area, and the snow showed no signs of letting up.

His attention returned to the map. As boys, he and Paul had ridden to Limpia Spring on several occasions. That was long before either jeep or pack trails existed. It was hard to visualize that beautiful spot being the death place for a four-year-old girl and her parents.

Wayford sat straight. He lowered the coffee cup he had lifted toward his lips. He had no doubt a ground team could make its way to the crash site. But that little girl and her father did not have the luxury of the time it would take to organize that team. Corpses could be collected at any time. The father and child needed help now. And he knew a route to get to them.

He glanced around for an officer to explain his plan. Immediately he recognized the futility of approaching any authority with the idea running through his head. The plan would be viewed as the demented blatherings of a senile old fool. Once young officers trained to place their faith in squad cars and police radios heard what he had in mind, they would probably lock him up to make certain he did not attempt to go it alone.

Alone is the way it has to be. Wayford trembled. He was certain it could be done, but was he the man to do it? A lot of water had flowed from Limpia Spring since the days Paul and he visited it. Was he still playing the old fool by even considering trying to find the father and daughter? He was sixty-five years old!

"Clint!" George stepped from the kitchen and placed a thermos of coffee on the counter. "We're short on eggs. Can I interest you in pancakes instead?"

"Flapjacks will be fine," the rancher answered, his gaze homing in on the coffee when George disappeared into the kitchen again.

Old man or not, he had to try. There was no younger man around he could trust. Nor had he ever knowingly placed his own burdens on another man's shoulders.

He shoved from the table, afraid if he sat still a moment longer, his courage would fail. Snatching the thermos from the counter, he hastened through the swinging door toward the office at the back of the building.

SIXTEEN

HE MOVED with alacrity, frightened that if he hesitated, the consequences of what he intended would leave him frozen in his tracks. Everything he mentally weighed tilted the scales until they fell lopsided and out of kilter, needle pointing toward the desperate actions of an old fool.

Everything except the lives of a four-year-old girl and her father. They swung the balance in the opposite direction. They meant more than all the doubts that surged in his mind and cried out for reason. They meant more than the life of a sixty-five-year-old man who had given up on his life.

In George Scheppler's office, he tucked the three blankets under an arm. He then shook two pillows from their cases and added them to the pile of bedding. A hasty glance revealed nothing else he needed in the room except his coat and hat. He grabbed them and moved to the garage.

Wayford's mind raced while he deposited blankets and pillowcases on a work bench to one side of an old two-car garage that could easily accommodate two extended-bed pickups or four modern sedans. He pulled on his coat and buttoned it. He needed time to think, to ponder details and consider alternatives.

No, he shook his head. Alternatives belonged to the Department of Public Safety and their rescue teams. In the hours required to assemble the men needed to go in on foot, he could be in and back —hopefully with a father and daughter.

He had focused on reality since Paul's death. Simple reality that a horse was stronger and faster than a man on foot, even a horse with a rider. The rancher knew Frank's Pal was horse enough for the task; he silently prayed to his God that the colt's rider equaled the animal's strength.

He thanked God for the size of George's garage when he dropped the trailer's gate and backed the colt into the open. While he bridled and saddled Frank's Pal, his gaze darted about the garage in search of anything that might be of use. He decided on a coil of nylon line and a crowbar hung on the wall and a package of yard-sized, draw-stringed plastic garbage bags on the work bench.

The nylon cord went around the saddlehorn and the crowbar into a trash bag with a hammer, screwdrivers, metal cutters, and a hacksaw, which he took from the toolbox in the back of the pickup. He was headed to an airplane crash; he might be an old fool, but he was not fool enough to ride twenty miles without tools to pry away the wreckage in case father and daughter were trapped inside.

Yanking the yellow plastic drawstrings tightly and knotting them, he slung the bag from the saddlehorn. The blankets, neatly rolled with the thermos of coffee at their center—and secured within another plastic bag, were tied behind the saddle. He pulled a half-dozen trash sacks from the box and stuffed them beside the blankets.

He slid the deer rifle from behind the pickup's seat, hefted it in a hand, then shoved it back. There was no need to load down Frank's Pal with extra weight. Instead Wayford took his skinning knife from beneath the seat and attached the sheath to his belt.

A quick perusal said horse and gear were ready. He was all that remained. The wind, snow, and cold were the three dangers he faced. There was nothing to do to raise the temperature, but he could conserve his own body heat. That meant stopping the snow's moisture from permeating his clothing and the wind from leeching warmth from exposed skin.

He lined his boots with bottoms cut from two trash sacks. Snow might soak the boot leather, but his doubly socked feet would remain dry. He sliced holes in the bottoms of two more bags, then drew the bags over each leg and tied them to his belt. The plastic would keep his pants dry, of that he was sure. He hoped an article he had once read in a hunting magazine proved true. The author proclaimed a simple plastic garbage bag would help hold body heat should a hunter find himself stranded in the wilds.

With the knife's tip he ripped open the pillowcases' seams. The first case wrapped about his neck like a muffler. He buttoned the fleece-lined coat beneath his chin and tugged the collar high. *Snug as a bug in a rug.* Now, if Mother Nature did not decide to stomp on that rug . . .

He tore the remaining case in two. The first half he tied around his head in the fashion of a bandaged sore tooth. His teeth were not the problem, but his exposed ears were now covered. The remaining piece of pillowcase went over nose and mouth so that he looked like a desperado out of an old Grade B Western movie.

Back at the pickup, he found and put on a long yellow raincoat. Wire cutters from the toolbox went into the raincoat's pocket. It was still a criminal offense to cut another man's fence in Texas. If he managed to bring back the father and daughter, though, he reckoned no one would hold a few strands of severed barbed wire against him.

Lastly he took a heavy pair of work gloves from the toolbox. He frowned at the feel of the gloves. Designed to protect a man's hands from splinters while handling wood, the gloves lacked a lining for warmth. The rancher's gaze once more shot around the garage. He smiled. Atop a box of insecticides and fertilizers was a pair of rubberized gardening gloves. He tugged them on over the leather pair. They were not as warm as wool-lined gloves, but they would keep his hands dry.

He stepped toward Frank's Pal then swung around and hastened back to the truck to retrieve a pair of sunglasses from the dashboard. The sun's glare did not concern him; the glasses would help cut the wind that howled outside.

Grateful for a roll-up-style garage door, Wayford found the door's handle and tugged upward. The door skidded back on its rollers, opening wide. Wind straight from the Arctic Circle blasted into the garage nearly costing the rancher his balance. Snow pelted his face, stinging as it found skin unprotected by cloth mask or sunglasses.

An avalanche of doubt assailed his mind anew. He shoved them away. A father and daughter were out there in the mountains. If they could endure the cold and hold on, he could do the same.

He stepped back to Frank's Pal, put a foot in the stirrup, and climbed into the saddle. The crinkle of raincoat and plastic bags drew his eyes to his outrageous attire. A smile lifted the corners of his lips as memories of Marty Robbins singing the song "The Streets of Laredo" popped into mind. One particular line hung in his thoughts: "I can see by your outfit that you are a cowboy."

With a cluck of tongue and tap of heels, Wayford urged the bay colt toward the open door. Frank's Pal hesitated an instant, then stepped into the snow. His legs pranced high like a Tennessee Walker as he picked his way down an alley blanketed two feet deep in white.

Wayford drew the colt to a halt when they reached the first street. He awkwardly brushed away the snow clinging to the sunglasses and peered toward Highway 17. He expected to see no one; that was what he saw. A large, round thermometer hanging on the side of a gas station caught his eye. The red needle pointed directly at 18 degrees.

That piece of information was something he would have preferred left unknown. He knew how cold he felt in spite of clothing and plastic. *Eighteen!* It now seemed twice as cold as it had but a moment before.

Nor did the wind offer hope of relief. He estimated it at a steady twenty to twenty-five miles an hour. The howling gusts blasted with twice that speed as though intent on ripping away the exposed flesh of his face. He was glad he had no idea how weathermen calculated what they designated wind chill. Knowing the temperature had sunk to a bitter eighteen was bad enough.

Another tap of the heels and a flick of the wrist directed Frank's Pal to the right, down the house-lined street, away from the highway. Both the sheriff's department and highway patrol had officers manning the highway. If they saw him, they would try and stop him. He felt enough like a fugitive as it was; there was no need to actually become one.

He reached the wide street that marked the old Butterfield route and swung the colt to the left. Well away from the highway, he followed the stagecoach trail southward through the town. If any one noticed his progress, he did not see them watching from windows of the houses. Even if they did, there was no chance of them telling anyone. The telephone lines remained down, and no one in their right mind was going to run out in the cold and snow to alert Fort Davis to the presence of an old fool riding horseback down their streets.

Near the water tanks at the western edge of the town, which was marked by steeply rising granite cliffs, Wayford dismounted to dig the wire cutters from the raincoat's pocket. Three hasty snips opened the barbed wire fence and a clear southern route onto open plains. He remounted and clucked the colt forward.

A glance to the left proved the highway too distant to be seen through the snowfall. He released a soft sigh of relief. He had not expected the law to be a problem, but knowing that any possibility of the officers attempting to stop him was passed eased his mind. Farther south he would follow Highway 166 around Blue Mountain. With the roads iced, no cars would be on it.

The cold was another problem altogether. It seeped through the layers of plastic and clothing. His toes were first to feel the bite, then his fingers. Even beneath the white pillowcase wrapped around his head, his ears felt as though someone grasped them between thumb and forefinger and twisted. An invisible fire ant sat on the tip of his nose, gnawing away.

Each gust of wind drove the cold deeper until it settled like ice cubes in the joints of his arms and legs. He shifted his weight in the saddle from leg to leg. He stretched first one arm then the other. There was no escape from the arthritic throb of pain.

By the time he reached Chihuahua Creek and reined Frank's Pal westward, hugging the base of Blue Mountain, the desire to pull the thermos from the blankets and drink down its warm contents became overwhelming. He locked his hands to the saddlehorn to keep them away from the plastic sack tied behind the saddle.

Lone Tree Hill appeared like a dark shadow ahead. The rancher's heels tapped the bay's flanks. The colt's strides quickened to a brisk walk. For some rootless reason Wayford felt once he was past the hill the urge to turn back to Fort Davis would subside.

He was wrong. As he dismounted to cut through another fence and gain the highway's shoulder, he realized there was no point of no return. Until he reached Limpia Spring, it was always closer to turn back than to ride onward.

His fingers were like brittle icicles wrapped around the wire cutter. Too much pressure, he was certain, would shatter them. It did not; it merely brought excruciating agony. He tried to convince himself that the pain was a good sign, that numbness meant frost bite. The rancher discovered how difficult a person he was to convince—a stubborn jackass.

Astride Frank's Pal, he reined toward the west. The hope that massive Blue Mountain would shelter him from the gusting winds proved futile. Mountains and wind like to play tricks together. A

wind blowing from one direction runs head-on to a range and by
the time it gets through dancing along canyon and draw it seems to
come at a man from one direction and then another in the beat of a
heart. This wind was no different. One instant it ripped at
Wayford's back; in the next it tore at his face. Even when the gusts
subsided, there was no relief from the steady twenty-five-mile-an-
hour wind.

Past Ninemile Hill to the Point of Rocks, the rancher rode. Here
at a roadside park that marked an old stage way station, the tricks of
wind were clearly evident. The park with its picnic benches was
virtually clear of snow. Here and there glistened patches of ice sprinkled with white frost, but an equal number of grassy patches appeared to have escaped the freezing rain.

Wayford stepped from the saddle and tied the colt's reins to one
of the benches. While Frank's Pal dipped his head to the dry winter
grass, his rider walked to an oil drum that served as the park's trash
container. He lifted its lid and peered at the paper bags and food
wrappers stuffed inside.

It took half a book of matches to light the trash even with cupped
hands to shield the flaring heads from the wind. But once the first
piece of paper caught, flames spread. The rancher tugged off the
two pairs of gloves and warmed his aching hands. A fire had never
felt so good.

When the throbbing of fingertips and joints subsided, he took a
step back and swung a boot upward to rest it on the mouth of the
oil drum. Gradually the heat radiated through the leather and
washed the cold from one foot and then the other. Coffee from the
thermos eased some of the chill from his bones. He wished for a pan
to reheat the brew. Without it, the best he could hope for was
lukewarm the next time he opened the container.

He gave himself ten minutes beside the fire, lying to himself that
the break was to allow Frank's Pal time for a breather. He then
replaced the oil drum's lid to smother the fire, slid thermos back
into blankets, and remounted. He had covered half the distance to
the crash site and he was getting no closer by extending his visit in
the roadside park.

SEVENTEEN

CLINT WAYFORD closed his eyes as a shudder ran through his pain-riddled body. When he opened them, the ridge remained. If his tears would not have transformed to burning icicles on his cheeks, he would have cried without shame. There was no way around the obstacle, nor was there a way to ride over the steep slope; it had to be climbed—on foot. The last hogback he had climbed left him sprawled facedown in the snow, praying for death to claim him.

He eased from saddle to snow and slipped the reins over Frank's Pal's head. He tried to resign himself to the formidable task that stood in his path. Limpia Spring lay on the other side—the young girl and her father were less than a mile away.

Resignation fled. That a four-year-old girl would die meant nothing. The bitter cold and the agony that throbbed within every inch of his body leeched away all meaning. He took a step forward with his right foot, followed by one with his left because that was all that remained. He could do nothing else.

Leading the colt, he worked up the slope at an easy angle then switched back to angle upward in the opposite direction. He estimated fifteen hundred feet separated the draw at the foot of the ridge to its crest. Halfway up the side his twisting route had tripled that distance. Only now he recalled that even in their boyhood Paul and he had dreaded facing this ridge. Each time they reached its top, they had collapsed to the ground, gasping for breath with faces beet red and sweaty.

Sweat was not something he had to worry about today. Rocks, however, were. One gave way beneath his weight. He went down, shin slamming into a sharp edge of granite hidden under the snow. Crying out in pain, he rolled to his back while he massaged the injury with both hands. Gradually the agony lessened enough for him to climb back to his feet and continue upward—for three strides! Another rock slipped underfoot, and he banged down hard on the opposite shin. This time he gritted his teeth and pushed through the pain as he stood.

For a hundred yards he marked his progress by his falls. For each few steps, the rocks hidden by the blanket of white dumped him in the snow. Only after a dozen spills did it penetrate that he was attempting to cross a portion of the ridge that was no more than loose gravel. Rather than standing again, he crawled forward on all fours until he felt solid ground beneath him.

A hundred yards from the rounded crest, he rested against the ice-coated trunk of a pine. The coffee in the thermos had lost its heat long ago, but he drank the five remaining swallows, hoping caffeine coursing through his veins would provide the energy required to cover those last hundred yards. Tossing the empty thermos aside, he climbed once more.

Atop the crest, he dropped to his knees and gulped for thin air that burned his lungs with its cold. Twice he tried to lift his head and survey the terrain below. The strength for this simple act was lost to him. All he could do was kneel in the snow and gasp. Had time retained any meaning for the rancher, it would have been lost while he waited for his strength to return.

"No." The word trembled from his lips when at last he stood and studied the forest that swept down the ridge to Limpia Spring.

The plane was not there. Twice, three times, and a fourth his gaze methodically inched over the land, searching for the telltale evidence of a plane crash. Nothing—there was nothing. The janitors at McDonald had misjudged the lights they had seen falling from the sky. There was no airplane here—no plane anywhere below his position. He had ridden all this way for nothing.

Old fool! Damned old fool! The twenty-mile ride left him half dead. He could only pray that the twenty miles back would not finish the job.

A prickling sensation crept up his neck while he eased the reins over the bay colt's head. He slowly turned, searching for the unseen eyes he felt staring at him. As with the airplane, there was nothing except stunted trees and snow.

Now you're imagining things that aren't there, you old fool! he chided himself while he stepped into a stirrup and swung to the saddle. He had chosen the more difficult route to reach the spring to avoid the police who manned the barricades at the northern edge of Fort Davis. With no reason to fear detection now, he would ride the ridge to its end, then climb down to follow Limpia Canyon back to town. The ride would be long and twisting, but at least there would be no more—

The thought lay stillborn. Two hundred yards along the hogback's crest lay the airplane. On its back with crumpled wings compressed like accordions under the fuselage, the plane had gone unnoticed below because of the dense snowdrifts that all but buried it.

"Hello!" Wayford called out behind a mask transformed to ice by the moisture of his own breath. He nudged Frank's Pal forward. "Hello there! Can anyone hear me?"

No one answered the cry, nor did a reply come when he repeated the greeting twice more.

He understood the reason for the silence when he used the crowbar to pry open one of the airplane's dented doors. A young woman, body frozen by the cold, hung upside down from a seat. Its belt, taut about her waist, held her in place. The twisted angle of her neck told of a quick death when the single-engine aircraft had plowed into the mountainside. The gruesome purple and white splotches of death could not hide the beauty she once possessed.

Wayford arrived too late to help her husband. The rancher doubted the young man had lived more than a few moments after his radio Mayday call. Half the plane's engine had torn into the cockpit when the aircraft struck the ground. The pilot's chest had stopped the engine from ripping through the whole plane. That he had managed a signal before death claimed him was nothing short of a miracle.

The girl? Wayford did not see her. Both the plane's doors had been jammed in the crash. She could not have gotten out through them. Maybe she had climbed out one of the shattered windows.

A pile of clothing stirred on the roof of the overturned aircraft. Wayford had mistaken the clothes for the spilled contents of suitcases. Now he saw the layers of clothing were carefully placed over two heavy coats belonging to a man and woman. He glanced at the dead pilot and realized whose hands had arranged the coats and clothes. "You did a good job. She's still alive. I'll get her back for you. You've got my word on that."

The rancher edged aside the clothing and lifted the coats. A smile moved across his lips. The girl, bundled in coat, mittens, earmuffs, and a bright red ski cap, slept beneath the pile. She drew into a tight ball as a gust of wind whipped through the wreck.

"Little one," the rancher said gently as he pulled down the frozen mask. "Little one, it's time to go."

The girl's blue eyes blinked open sleepily, and she stared up at Wayford as though uncertain where she was. She stretched, yawned, and closed her eyes again.

"Little one," he repeated, "I know you're sleepy, but I've got to get you into town."

The four-year-old's eyes opened again. She stared at him for a long moment with a blank expression, then her face lit with a heart-melting smile. "Are you the man my daddy said would come for me?"

"I'm the one he sent for," Wayford assured her. "I've come to take you for a horse ride into town."

"A pony?" She pushed to her elbows eagerly. "I rode a pony at Kiddie Town. I liked him. His name was Star. Like the stars at night."

Noticing her shiver, the rancher gathered the coats around her again. "My pony's name is Frank's Pal. I named him after my grandson. My name's Clint. I was wondering what they call a pretty little girl like you?"

"Terri," she answered. "I have a grandpa. Two grandpas and two grandmas."

"Grandparents are good things to have."

He saw a larger toboggan cap that had belonged to one of her parents among the clothing. With holes cut for eyes and mouth, the wool cap would make a perfect ski mask for the child. He picked it up and started digging beneath the raincoat for the skinning knife. He stopped before freeing the blade. The last thing he wanted to do was scare the girl with a knife.

"You lay back down and cover up, all right? I've got to go and tell Frank's Pal he's got a pretty little girl who wants to ride him. Okay?"

He saw her eyes dart to the colt outside. "Is he a boy or a girl horse?"

"He's a boy," Wayford answered, "but he told me he likes girls better than boys."

She giggled with obvious delight as she huddled down once more. "I think I like your pony."

The rancher covered her head with one of the coats to prevent her from noticing her dead parents as much as to keep her warm. At the moment she did not comprehend that death had robbed her of mother and father. He wanted her safe and warm in town when the full extent of the tragedy weighted her small shoulders.

Backing from the wreck on hands and knees, he stood and freed the hunting knife. Three quick cuts, and hat became mask. He untied the plastic bag from the saddle and opened it. Inside the plane again, he pulled the mask over Terri's head, making certain it was twisted askew to block the horrible vision of her dead parents hanging upside down in their seats. He then wrapped the child in a cocoon of three blankets. Four-year-old and blankets were slipped into the bag, and Wayford securely tied the draw strings beneath her chin.

"This should keep you warm and dry for our ride," he said while he carried her in his arms from the overturned plane.

"I can't see," she complained, squirming in the sack as though attempting to free her arms to adjust the makeshift mask.

"I'll fix that right now." He sat her on the saddle, rearranged the mask, and climbed atop the colt. "Now let's go for our ride."

"Are you a garbage man?" Her blue eyes rolled back at him from behind the mask as he nudged Frank's Pal forward.

"Garbage man? What makes you ask that?" He reined for a gentle slope that led to Limpia Canyon below.

"You wear garbage bags, silly." She laughed and twisted around in his arms. "I want to pet the pony."

"Soon as we get into town, you can pet him all you want." Wayford tightened his arm around her. The trash bag kept her dry, but it made it damned difficult to retain a secure hold when she wiggled.

"You have a grandboy, do you have a grandgirl?" she asked.

"I most certainly do," he answered. "Her name is Elizabeth."

"Does she have any dolls?"

The rancher did not recall the names of Elizabeth's toys, but remembered the array of dolls and menagerie of stuffed animals that once inhabited Mary's bedroom. He named and provided the pertinent details on each, such as eye and hair color, that Terri required. By the time the colt reached the canyon floor, Wayford knew the

names and habits peculiar to each of the child's own toys, as well as
the names of her friends in playschool and Sunday school. Also, one
of her grandfathers wore false teeth and a toupee, which she called a
rug because her father did.

Three miles down the twisting canyon, Terri announced the need
to "potty." Wayford, who recalled automobile trips with his two
children, was prepared. He unbundled the child, handed her a tissue
from a jacket pocket and sent her behind a bushy cedar. Business
completed, she managed to give Frank's Pal's nose several loving
strokes while the rancher wrapped her in the blankets and returned
her to the trash sack.

The hairs on his neck rose for a second time that day when he
settled back into the saddle. As at the top of the ridge, his searching
eyes found nothing to warrant caution. Yet, the sensation he was
watched by unseen eyes remained.

"I'm sleepy," Terri said when Wayford clucked the colt into a
steady walk.

"Then why don't you snuggle down against me and let the
sandman visit you awhile?" he suggested.

She did.

Limpia Canyon opened onto Highway 118. At least, where
Wayford knew the highway to be. The road was hidden by the
blanketing snow. He tapped Frank's Pal with his heels, heading the
colt down the empty road.

His original intention had been to ride directly into town. Although the only injuries he discerned on Terri were a bump on her
forehead and minor scratches on her hands, he would not feel safe
until a doctor examined her and pronounced her healthy. With less
than ten miles to Fort Davis, the numbness he felt creeping into his
toes and fingertips said that he would have to change plans. He had
to find a place to warm himself and the child sleeping in his arms.

Prude Ranch, he considered, *or Indian Lodge in the state park.*
He discarded the latter. The Prude Ranch with its tourist facilities
was closer. There would be warmth and food at the ranch. Although she had not mentioned food, he was certain Terri would be
hungry when she awoke. She had not eaten all day, nor had he.

He tapped heels to flank again when Frank's Pal's pace flagged.
Like his riders, the colt had gone the day without food. Wayford felt
weariness in the bay's strides. A horse's endurance was no greater

than that of a man. Forty miles was close to the limit; the colt had covered at least thirty miles through snow-covered terrain. The rancher was certain the animal could carry them into Fort Davis; he was young, strong, and in top condition, but it would be well after—

Wayford's thoughts faltered when the colt topped a low rolling hill. Below lay the wreck that originally closed 118. An overturned gasoline tanker lay jackknifed in the snow with another half off the road and half in Limpia Creek. The five other vehicles involved were scattered in similar disarray on and off the highway. The two wreckers that had come to the rescue kept them company in the creek.

Determination set the rancher's brow. The warmth the child and he needed stood but a quarter of a mile down the highway. Again his heels urged the colt onward.

Bypassing the wreck in fear of spilled gasoline, Wayford rode onto the creek's snow-covered ice and halted beside the first wrecker. The doors were open, but the keys were missing from the ignition. The second truck offered no better. The curse that rose in the rancher's throat died before it reached his tongue. His gaze alighted on a citizen's band radio hung beneath the truck's dashboard.

"Can anyone out there hear me?" He watched the lights on the CB's face dance as he spoke into the microphone. "This is Clinton Wayford. I'm out at the wreck on Highway 118 and need help."

The radio crackled; a voice came from the grille. "You're who, and you're where?"

The rancher repeated himself then quickly recounted his ride to the crash. "I've got me a little girl about to freeze to death laying here on the seat. I need to know how to hot-wire this truck and get the heater working."

A new voice, one he recognized, came from the radio. "Clint, this is Sid Stilwell. That's my truck you're in. How in hell did you get the girl? The roads are so damned bad the law hasn't even been able to get a ground team together yet. I've sent the boy to get a deputy. They'll want to talk with you."

"Sid, I'll explain it later. Right now I need to get the heater going," Wayford pressed the service station owner. "How do I jump the wires to start this truck?"

"No need. There's a spare key in one of those little magnetic boxes inside the glove compartment . . ."

While Sid's static-filled voice continued to blast from the speaker, the rancher leaned across the cab and punched the glove compartment open. The box and its keys were half hidden by a map. With numb fingers he slid the box's lid back and emptied the keys onto a palm. Inserting key into ignition was more difficult without feeling in his fingertips, but after three fumbled tries the key slipped into the slot. He pumped the gas pedal twice and twisted the key. The engine caught, and the heater's blower came alive.

A smile rose on Wayford's face as he settled back in the seat and looked down at Terri. The child's eyes blinked open.

"I'm hungry," she said.

"Me too." He smiled at her. "Soon as we warm up a bit, I'll see about getting us some food. Think you can wait until then?"

She gave a sleepy nod and rolled to a side.

"Mr. Wayford? Mr. Wayford?"

The rancher picked up the microphone and answered, "I'm still here, Deputy." He did not recognize the voice and assumed Sid had retrieved the law officer he had promised.

"Sir, I understand you've got the little girl from the plane crash with you? Is that correct? What condition is she in?"

"She'll be a lot better once she's warm. Right now, she's telling me she's hungry. I noticed a recreational vehicle up there in the wreck. I want somebody's authority to pry open a door to see if there's any food inside. This child hasn't eaten all day."

"The sheriff'll have to do that."

Wayford shook his head with disgust. "Then tell him he'd damn well better do it, or be prepared to toss me in a cell for breaking and entering, 'cause that's exactly what I'm going to do soon as I get some of the feeling back in my hands and feet."

"You wait right there, Mr. Wayford."

"I'm not going anywhere."

The rancher grimaced. The heater began to do its job. Hot needles of pain lanced into his fingertips as sensation returned. Those same needles jabbed at his feet and toes.

The deputy came on the radio again. "Just got a hold of the sheriff. He said go ahead and break into the RV."

The rancher depressed the button on the side of the microphone. "I didn't expect he'd say less. The sheriff's a man who's always used the common sense God gave him."

"The sheriff also has an idea about how we can come out and pick you up," the deputy continued. "The snow's too high for a car to make it. Snow'll start building up beneath a car, lift it off high center, and send it flying off the road."

"What's his idea, son?" Wayford bit back a groan when he tried to wiggle his toes. In spite of joints alive with fire, he opened and closed his hands. His fingers seemed to work.

"He's got a nephew with one of them pickups that's jacked up halfway to the sky. He's getting chains put on it now. He said for you to sit tight where you are, and he'll drive out to get you himself."

"Tell him he just assured himself of one solid vote come next election. Hell, you can tell him I'll campaign from one end of this county to—"

Frank's Pal snorted outside. Wayford heard the colt dancing around in the snow. He wiped away the fog that formed on the truck's windows as the bay gave a high-pitched neigh. In a heartbeat Wayford recognized the hidden eyes he had felt following him on the ridge. A cougar launched itself from the snow straight for the colt's back.

"No! By God, no!" He threw the door open and stumbled outside. "Get away! Dammit, get away from him!"

The colt spun about, bucking high to dislodge the mountain lion. The cougar's foreclaws dug into the horse's shoulders to secure its purchase. Frank's Pal's scream mingled with the cat's hissing growl.

"No, dammit, no!"

Wayford's head jerked from side to side in a search for anything to use as a weapon. A length of chain in the back of the wrecker caught his eye. He snatched it up with both hands and ran toward the colt.

"Get away, you sonofabitch!" He swung the chain in a wide circle above his head. "Get the hell away from my colt!"

The cougar's head arched downward. Its mouth opened wide to expose long, yellow incisors an instant before the teeth disappeared into the bay's shoulder.

Frank's Pal reared. His powerful neck thrashed in wild desperation as he fought to free himself from the predator that rent his flesh. Straight up on his hind legs he rose—straight up and over. The colt fell backwards. His full weight slammed down into the snow atop his attacker.

The cougar's scream was one of surprise and fear. Releasing its hold on the colt, the cat squirmed and wiggled to freedom. The mountain lion roared as he spun around ready for the kill.

At that instant, the chain struck the cougar across the eyes. The puma's anger ripped the wind wide. The cat rolled in the snow to escape his unnoticed attacker, then bounded to his legs and faced the rancher.

With his weight behind the blow, Wayford lashed out again. The chain found its target, once more striking the cougar's head and sending the animal reeling in the snow. The rancher did not wait for the cat to regain his feet. He whipped the chain high and snapped it downward. Steel slammed into the mountain lion's head.

As another man might wield a sledgehammer, Wayford worked the chain in a figure eight that rose and fell with deadly accuracy. The cat never regained its footing, but died in snow stained crimson with its own blood. Nor did the rancher stop there. Tossing aside the chain, he freed the skinning knife and fell atop the twitching cat, lifted its powerful head, and slit its throat.

Gasping for his breath, he lay atop the cougar, knife poised high, feeling the death spasms pass through the cat's body. He was prepared to remain there until the sheriff arrived if necessary to make certain the puma did not rise again.

The sounds of Frank's Pal floundering in the snow brought the rancher to his feet. The colt's legs kicked at air and snow as the horse tried to find his footing and failed.

"No!" Wayford raged. "No, damn you. You're not going to go and die on me. I've put too much work into you for you to decide to die. Get up! Damn you, get up!"

He hurled the knife aside and trudged through the snow. Grabbing the colt's reins, he yanked the horse's head around. With every ounce of strength he could muster, he pulled on the reins.

"Get up! Dammit, I said get up!" Tears of anger burned as they rolled down his cheeks while he tugged. "I won't let you die. I won't, dammit! I won't!"

The colt rolled with the reins. His forelegs stretched out, hooves finding purchase. He struggled a moment before getting his hindlegs beneath his body. The colt shuddered violently, but he stood.

"Good boy!" Wayford scooped up snow with his bare hands and slapped it on the horse's open wounds to stanch the flowing blood. "You're going to live whether you want to or not. I'll make you live!"

Shock rather than the wounds themselves was the greatest danger facing the colt. The rancher had to get him warm and keep him moving. If only he had one of the woolen blankets neatly folded in the tack room back at the Wide W.

The truck's purring engine snapped Wayford's head around. He had blankets! "Terri, wiggle free of that sack. You'll be warm enough now. I've got another use for those blankets."

Holding the colt close to the bit, he walked toward the wrecker.

EIGHTEEN

THE VETERINARIAN'S THUMB and forefinger lifted and pinched the flesh of Frank's Pal's neck several times before deftly slipping the hypodermic needle into the fold of skin to inject the antibiotic. He removed the needle and vigorously rubbed a palm over the spot the needle had entered.

"Can't think of anything else to do for him, Clint," Doc Stowers said. "Watch the stitches to make sure they don't rip out before the wounds close. Keep them clean and bandaged so flies won't bother him."

The veterinarian tossed the disposable needle into a trash can at one side of the garage while Wayford loaded the colt into the trailer and closed the gate. Stowers rubbed a hand over his face and studied the horse. "I don't know what else to tell you. The cougar caused muscle damage. Only time will tell how bad the damage is. Keep him in a stall until the wounds heal. After that, turn him out to pasture for six months or so and let him build up strength in those shoulders at his own pace. You'll be able to tell when and if he should have a saddle on him."

The rancher nodded. The veterinarian's tone sounded more optimistic than Wayford felt. Frank's Pal's shoulders had swelled during the night, and, although the colt still walked, his movements were stiff and obviously filled with pain.

"I didn't see any sign of infection. The antibiotic I gave him and these should make sure the wounds stay that way." Stowers took an envelope containing a handful of white pills from his case. "Put one in his morning and evening feed until they're gone."

"Thanks, Doc." The rancher placed the medicine in the pickup's cab. "I'm afraid you'll have to send me your bill."

The veterinarian nodded. "If I tended people, I'd prescribe about two days of straight sleep for you, Clint. You look like you could use it."

The rancher grinned. "I feel like I could use it. After I grab some breakfast, I'll stretch out on George's sofa and saw a few logs."

The din of voices and the scuffle of feet came from within the drugstore. Both men turned to the open side door that led from the garage into the store.

"Sounds like something's stirring," Stowers said. "Might as well take a look before I head back to the office."

George Scheppler saw the two men push through the swinging door. From the grill, he pointed a spatula toward the front windows. "The sanding crews have got the road to Alpine open. An ambulance just pulled in to take little Terri over to the hospital for a thorough examination. Everybody piled out of here like they'd never seen an ambulance before in their lives."

Wayford blinked his eyes to adjust to the painful glare of sunlight that streamed through the windows. Having spent the night in the garage with Frank's Pal, he had not realized the morning had brought clear skies. The sun that rode high in the cloudless blue turned ice and snow to slush as he moved outside and hastened toward the ambulance parked in front of the doctor's office where Terri had spent the night.

Two paramedics wheeled a gurney from the office. The rancher saw Terri wave at the gathered onlookers as the paramedics lifted girl and gurney and eased them into the back of the ambulance.

Blonde. Wayford smiled to himself, realizing he had never noticed the color of the child's hair yesterday. When he found her in the wreck, her hair had been hidden beneath the cap she wore.

Edging through the bystanders, the rancher approached a paramedic who opened the door on the driver side of the ambulance. "Excuse me. How's the girl doing?"

"Why don't you excuse me, old man?" The paramedic climbed behind the wheel. "I've got a job to do and don't have time to be answering the questions of some nosy busybody. So why don't you and all the others get out of the way and let me do that job?"

The man slammed the door and gunned the engine. He hit the siren for a second to move the onlookers back, then eased onto the highway. An ironic smile twisted a corner of Wayford's mouth while he watched the ambulance turn toward Alpine.

"Don't let him get to you, Mr. Wayford. He's got a bug up his ass because he had to make a long run on bad roads." The deputy who approached had accompanied the sheriff to the wreck site last night. "The girl's doing fine. The doc wanted her in the hospital where someone can keep an eye on her until her relatives are contacted."

"Good." Wayford felt an invisible weight lift from his chest. "Doc said she was all right last night, but I was still worried."

"Well, she's a tough little camper. She's going to be okay," the deputy assured him.

The rancher nodded and smiled. "Then I guess this nosy busybody will carry himself back to the drugstore and eat some breakfast."

George stood at the cash register with the telephone receiver to an ear when Wayford entered the drugstore. "Got a dial tone. The line crews must be working around the clock to have the phones up so soon."

Ordering a breakfast of eggs, bacon, and flapjacks, the rancher dug a quarter from a pocket and crossed to the pay phone when George headed back to the grill. Wayford dialed Bryan Owens's number and deposited the coin at the first ring. Five rings later Bryan answered the line.

"Bryan, I know the weather's got you up to your backside in busy, but I wanted to let you know that I won't be dropping by when the roads clear." Wayford paused to draw a breath. "I've changed my mind. I won't be selling the Wide W."

A dry laugh came from the line. "Hell, Clint, I thought you had gone and got yourself half drunk when you called the other day. Men like you and me don't sell out. We're too hardheaded ornery. We'd rather let this damned dry land kill us before selling out."

"Jackass stubborn!" Wayford's laughter joined his friend's. Every joint and muscle in his body throbbed and ached, but he felt good —damned good. "Jackass stubborn!"

Miguel stood in the stall's door watching Wayford unsnap the shank from Frank's Pal's halter. The rancher studied the moisture that rimmed the young man's eyes while he walked outside and placed the webbing across the stall's entrance.

"There's no need to go and get all long-faced on me, son. I feel bad enough for the both of us and ten other men." Wayford watched the colt stiffly walk to the hay rack and begin to eat. "There's nothing we can do about what's already happened."

"What about Fort Worth this fall?" Miguel's voice quavered.

"Shell peas with one hand, wish with the other, and see which one gets filled first." The rancher shrugged. "He ain't the first horse to get hurt on me, and he damned sure won't be the last. Besides, there's always next year."

For a man who supported the New York Yankees, Texas Rangers, and Houston Astros each baseball season, the rancher's last phrase came easily. Wayford repeated what Doc Stowers had told him that morning. "If Frank's Pal can take a saddle again, then we'll put him back into training around the end of summer. He'll be ready for Fort Worth next year."

"And if he cannot take a saddle?" Miguel pressed.

"Then he'll live out his life in a pasture right here on the Wide W. He gave too much yesterday for me to do anything else."

"I think he should have a lady friend," the young man said. "They would have strong sons who we could take to Fort Worth."

"Buy a mare?"

"Maybe more than one mare." Miguel nodded eagerly. "The more wives he has, the more sons to win in his name at Fort Worth."

Wayford scratched at the unshaven stubble that prickled his neck. Putting Frank's Pal to stud always had been part of his dream. If he had to start with a mare or two of his own, then that was the way to start. "We'll wait until the end of summer to see how he's doing. If it doesn't look good, we'll try and find us a mare or two and let him go about making those sons."

The rancher turned and let his gaze run up and down each side of the shedrow. "Right now, what we need is another horse for the arena." He walked to the stall holding Paul Moody's bay gelding. "I gave it a long thought on the way home. I think I can work a deal with Rachel to buy this bay. She might even want to go in with us for old time's sake. He won't be ready for Fort Worth, but we could have him ready for some of the smaller competitions when fall rolls around."

Wayford walked to the barn's door. His gaze traced over the land old Amos had left to the generations who followed him. Terri and the cougar yesterday had retaught the rancher a lesson he had learned a long time ago. Sometimes life reared before a man, spat in his face, and challenged him to fight for what he loved. To do anything less than tear into it with tooth and claw bared was to be less than a man. And life made no guarantees that the fight would end when the bell rang after fifteen rounds.

"*Señor* Clint?"

The rancher turned. Miguel stood behind him with an envelope in his hand. "Now that you have decided to stay, you will need this five hundred dollars."

Wayford hesitated, then reached out and accepted the envelope. "Son, I ain't sure you know what you're doing, but I thank you for buyin' into the dreams of a stubborn jackass."

"Does this mean I now work for you?"

"Hell, no. It means you work *with* me. Next time we're in town, we'll go talk to a lawyer and see about making you a percentage partner in the Wide W." It was a spur-of-the-moment decision, but it felt fair and right to the rancher. Other than himself, Miguel was the only one he knew who gave a damn about this chunk of land called a ranch.

Mary and Frank saw the Wide W as a millstone around his neck. And as much as he loved Frank Junior and Elizabeth, he doubted city kids would understand what this land meant. He looked at Miguel and chuckled to himself. *I just might have to adopt me a wetback to make sure the Wide W stays in the hands of a Wayford!*

"I think I will like working with you better than for you." Miguel grinned from ear to ear.

"I hope so, son, because there's enough work here to kill both of us." Wayford tilted his head toward the pickup and trailer outside. "We might as well start now. Let's get that trailer unhitched and some hay into the pickup. We've got cattle that haven't eaten anything but snow for two days."

Wayford's mind raced ahead while he walked to the trailer. He had to drive over to the Moody place and get John Allen's phone number from Paul's address book before the mover and lawyers cleared out the house. And the first thing tomorrow morning Miguel and he needed to take a drive out on Highway 118. He knew where there was a dead cougar whose skull, if it was still in one piece, was bound to bring twice the price of a ram's skull in Canton.

The honking of a horn came from the dirt road. The rancher looked up to see Sam Norwood's pickup turning toward the house.

"I was on my way out here when I ran into this doctor feller in town who was looking for you," Sam bellowed out a window as he drove toward Wayford.

When Sam braked, his passenger stepped from the truck, walked to Wayford, shook his hand, and introduced himself as Terri's physician in Alpine. "You're a hard man to find, Mr. Wayford. Everybody's heard about what you did, but nobody seems to know the name of the man who did it. We've got three television news teams down from Midland and Abilene over in Alpine trying to locate you for an interview."

"No need for reporters coming out here." The rancher shook his head. "It's old news now, and I've got work to do. Let 'em take their pictures of little Terri. She's the one who's gone through hell."

"If that's the way you want it." The doctor offered no protest. "But there's some other folks who'd like to meet you. Terri's grandparents are in Alpine. They'd like to say thank you for saving the child."

"There's no need for them to go to all that trouble," Wayford replied. "But I'd like to drive over and see the girl before they take off with her, if that wouldn't inconvenience anyone?"

The doctor grinned. "No inconvenience, Mr. Wayford. I'll tell them you're coming."

"And no reporters," the rancher added. He had not ridden to the wreck to get his face flashed on television.

"No reporters and no cameras," the doctor assured him.

"Then tell 'em I'll drop by around noon tomorrow," Wayford said. "Maybe we can all go out for coffee and a piece of pie."

Sam Norwood's gravelly voice called, "Clint, if you're through arranging your luncheon schedule, come back here and see what I drove halfway to nowhere to show you."

Wayford glanced around to find Sam lowering the tailgate of his camper-covered pickup. "The other night when the storm hit, that bitch of mine climbed up in here to keep out of the snow. She curled up on a pile of burlap bags I threw in back last week. Come see what I found when I went to lookin' for her yesterday."

Wayford ducked his head and stared inside the camper. A grin stretched across his face. "I'll be damned."

"Ain't that something?" Sam's voice filled with the pride of a new father. "Eight pups in all, and every one of them all spotted like their daddy. You'd think one would be black like my Daisy."

"Vanberg had a way of doing things up right." Wayford laughed as he reached a hand inside and gently stroked the puppies while they suckled their mother.

A pup released his hold on a teat, lifted his head, and licked at the rancher's fingers. Gently, Wayford's palm scooted beneath the newborn dog and brought him into the sunlight. The small pink tongue continued to lap the fingers that held him high while the rancher carefully examined him.

"Sam, this one's already got his eyes open!" Wayford double-checked the puppy to make certain he was not seeing things.

"I know. The damnest thing, isn't it? Never saw a dog born with his eyes open," Sam replied.

Wayford drew the puppy close to his face, feeling its warmth against a cheek. "I think our deal was that I'd get first pick. This one's mine."

"Son of a bitch, I should've known you'd go and take the pick of the litter." The gravel deepened in Sam's voice. "Sure you won't reconsider? I sort of thought I'd keep that one for myself."

"Nope." Wayford gently stroked two fingers over the pup's velvet soft back. "This one and me are already friends. As soon as he's weaned, Moody'll be living here on the Wide W."

"Moody?" Sam's eyebrow arched for a questioning moment, then the retired rancher nodded his approval. "Moody—it's a good name."

"Yeah." Wayford glanced at Sam and looked back at the puppy that fit snugly in the palm of his hand. "It's a damned good name."

ABOUT THE AUTHOR

GEO. W. PROCTOR, a prolific Western writer and lifelong Texas resident, is the author of the critically acclaimed Double D Westerns *Enemies, Walks Without a Soul,* and *Comes the Hunter.* He and his wife currently reside in Arlington, Texas.